PRAISE FOR ELIZABETH HAND

Saffron and Brimstone

"This collection consists of both the type of fine stories expected from Elizabeth Hand and stories showing a fascinating new direction. A 'typical' Hand story is novella length, written in rich language, and full of human details of daily life that allow an intimate knowledge of characters. These damaged beings are often over-taken by darkness, but that doesn't mean death, loss, and loneliness ultimately triumph. The fantastic provides the possibility that darkness can be illumined and reality realigned by magic ... ['The Lost Domain'] quartet is shorter, more sparsely written, less fantastic, than 'old' Hand; the stories also seem more personally relevant. The entire collection further confirms Hand as an author of extraordinary vision who is unafraid to dream in new directions."—*Fantasy* magazine

"Enthusiasts for Hand's sensuously descriptive brand of literary fantasy are in for a treat with her latest collection of short fiction. Aptly subtitled 'strange stories,' the eight superbly crafted tales share Hand's predilection for probing the translucent borderline between magic and reality... In a separate section entitled 'The Lost Domain,' Hand offers four contemplative tales about transient relation-ships [linked by] poignant, recurring themes: the fragility of intimacy, the insidious unraveling of civilization following 9/11, the influence of Greek myth on modern love. Her beautifully nuanced, often disquieting style should inspire poets as well as lay down the gauntlet to colleagues also reaching for expressive heights in contemporary fantasy."—*Booklist*

" 'Cleopatra Brimstone' ... seems on its way to becoming a kind of classic of the sort of seriously literary horror which has emerged increasingly in the last few years. Concerning a young student entomologist who is brutally raped and flees to London ... the story elegantly balances a kind of supernatural revenge fantasy with an acute awareness of the real horrors of women's lives. [And] representing an adventurous new direction in Hand's writing, [the stories in 'The Lost Domain'] range freely from fantasy to SF to postmodern narrative fragmentation ... Remarkable ... in Hand's beautifully orchestrated tales, a world whose gorgeous fragility, like the pistils of those tulips that are gathered for saffron, positively glows."—*Locus*

SAFFRON
and
BRIMSTONE

strange stories

a collection by

ELIZABETH HAND

PRESS™
Milwaukie

Book design by Heidi Fainza and Tony Ong
Cover design by Lia Ribacchi
Cover photograph by B. A. Bosaiya

Some of the material in this collection previously appeared in *Bibliomancy*, published by PS Publishing. Unless otherwise noted, the stories in this book appear here for the first time:

"Cleopatra Brimstone," first published in *Redshift*, Roc Books, edited by Al Sarrantonio, 2001

"Pavane for a Prince of the Air," first published in *Embrace the Mutation*, Subterranean Press, edited by William K. Schafer & Bill Sheehan, 2002

"The Least Trumps," first published in *Conjunctions 39: The New Wave Fabulists*, Fall 2002, edited by Peter Straub

"Wonderwall," first published in *Flights: Extreme Visions of Fantasy*, Roc Books, edited by Al Sarrantonio, 2004

"Kronia," first published in *Conjunctions 44: The Quest Issue*, Spring 2005, edited by Bradford Morrow

"Calypso in Berlin," first appeared on SciFi.com, July 2005

"Echo," first published in *Fantasy and Science Fiction Magazine*, October 2005

M Press
10956 SE Main Street
Milwaukie, OR 97222

mpressbooks.com

Library of Congress Cataloging-in-Publication Data

Hand, Elizabeth.
  Saffron and brimstone : strange stories / a collection by Elizabeth Hand. -- 1st M Press ed.
    p. cm.
  ISBN-13: 978-1-59582-096-9
  ISBN-10: 1-59582-096-5
  I. Title.
PS3558.A4619S24 2007
813'.54--dc22

                                        2006037134

  ISBN-10: 1-59582-096-5
  ISBN-13: 978-1-59582-096-9

First M Press Edition: November 2006

10 9 8 7 6 5 4 3 2 1

Printed in U.S.A.
Distributed by Publishers Group West

CONTENTS

FOR JOHN CLUTE
True North

SAFFRON
and
BRIMSTONE

strange stories

CLEOPATRA BRIMSTONE

Her earliest memory was of wings. Luminous red and blue, yellow and green and orange; a black so rich it appeared liquid, edible. They moved above her and the sunlight made them glow as though they were themselves made of light, fragments of another, brighter world falling to earth about her crib. Her tiny hands stretched upwards to grasp them but could not: they were too elusive, too radiant, too much of the air.

Could they ever have been real?

For years she thought she must have dreamed them. But one afternoon when she was ten she went into the attic, searching for old clothes to wear to a Halloween party. In a corner beneath a cobwebbed window she found a box of her baby things. Yellow-stained bibs and tiny fuzzy jumpers blued from bleaching, a much-nibbled stuffed dog that she had no memory of whatsoever.

And at the very bottom of the carton, something else. Wings flattened and twisted out of shape, wires bent and strings frayed: a mobile. Six plastic butterflies, colors faded and their wings giving off a musty smell, no longer eidolons of Eden but crude representations of monarch, zebra swallowtail, red admiral, sulphur, an unnaturally elongated hairskipper and *Agrias narcissus*. Except for the *narcissus*, all were common New World species that any child might see in a suburban garden. They hung limply from their wires, antennae long since broken off; when she touched one wing it felt cold and stiff as metal.

The afternoon had been overcast, tending to rain. But as she held the mobile to the window, a shaft of sun broke through the darkness to ignite the plastic wings, blood-red, ivy-green, the pure burning yellow of an August field. In that instant it was as though her entire being was burned away, skin hair lips fingers all ash; and nothing remained but the butterflies and her awareness of them, orange and black fluid filling her mouth, the edges of her eyes scored by wings.

—

As a girl she had always worn glasses. A mild childhood astigmatism worsened when she was thirteen: she started bumping into things, and found it increasingly difficult to concentrate on the entomological textbooks and journals that she read voraciously. Growing pains, her mother thought; but after two months, Jane's clumsiness and concomitant headaches became so severe that her mother admitted that this was perhaps something more serious, and took her to the family physician.

"Jane's fine," Dr. Gordon announced after peering into her ears and eyes. "She needs to see the ophthalmologist, that's all. Sometimes our eyes change when we hit puberty." He gave her mother the name of an eye doctor nearby.

Her mother was relieved, and so was Jane—she had overhead her parents talking the night before her appointment, and the words *CAT scan* and *brain tumor* figured in their hushed conversation. Actually, Jane had been more concerned about another odd physical manifestation, one which no one but herself seemed to have noticed. She had started menstruating several months earlier: nothing unusual in that. Everything she had read about it mentioned the usual things— mood swings, growth spurts, acne, pubic hair.

But nothing was said about eyebrows. Jane first noticed something strange about hers when she got her period for the second time. She had retreated to the bathtub, where she spent a good half-hour reading an article in *Nature* about Oriental Ladybug swarms. When she finished the article, she got out of the tub, dressed and brushed her teeth, then spent a minute frowning at the mirror.

Something was different about her face. She turned sideways, squinting. Had her chin broken out? No; but something had changed. Her hair color? Her teeth? She leaned over the sink until she was almost nose-to-nose with her reflection.

That was when she saw that her eyebrows had undergone a growth spurt of their own. At the inner edge of each eyebrow, above the bridge of her nose, three hairs had grown remarkably long. They furled back towards her temple, entwined in a sort of loose braid. She had not noticed them sooner because she seldom looked in a mirror, and also because the odd hairs did not arch above the eyebrows, but instead blended in with them, the way a bittersweet vine twines around a branch. Still, they seemed bizarre enough that she wanted no one, not even her parents, to notice. She found her mother's eyebrow tweezers, neatly plucked the six hairs and flushed them down the toilet. They did not grow back.

At the optometrist's, Jane opted for heavy tortoiseshell frames rather than contacts. The optometrist, and her mother, thought she was crazy, but it was a very deliberate choice. Jane was not one of those homely B movie adolescent girls, driven to Science as a last resort. She had always been a tomboy, skinny as a rail, with long slanted violet-blue eyes; a small rosy mouth; long, straight black hair that ran like oil between her fingers; skin so pale it had the periwinkle shimmer of skim milk.

When she hit puberty, all of these conspired to beauty. And Jane hated it. Hated the attention, hated being looked at, hated that other girls hated her. She was quiet, not shy but impatient to focus on her schoolwork, and this was mistaken for arrogance by her peers. All through high school she had few friends. She learned early the perils of befriending boys, even earnest boys who professed an interest in genetic mutations and intricate computer simulations of hive activity. Jane could trust them not to touch her, but she couldn't trust them not to fall in love. As a result of having none of the usual distractions of high school—sex, social life, mindless employment—she received an Intel/Westinghouse Science Scholarship for a computer-generated schematic of possible mutations in a small population of viceroy butterflies exposed to genetically engineered crops. She graduated in her junior year, took her scholarship money, and ran.

She had been accepted at Stanford and MIT, but chose to attend a small, highly prestigious women's college in a big city several hundred miles away. Her parents were apprehensive about her being on her own at the tender age of seventeen, but the college, with its elegant, cloister-like buildings and lushly wooded grounds, put them at ease. That and the dean's assurances that the neighborhood was completely safe, as long as students were sensible about not walking alone at night. Thus mollified, and at Jane's urging—she was desperate to move away from home—her father signed a very large check for the first semester's tuition. That September she started school.

She studied entomology, spending her first year examining the genitalia of male and female Scarce Wormwood Shark Moths, a species found on the Siberian steppes. Her hours in the zoology lab were rapturous, hunched over a microscope with a pair of tweezers so minute they were themselves like some delicate portion of her specimen's physiognomy. She would remove the butterflies' genitalia, tiny and geometrically precise as diatoms, and dip them first into glycerine, which acted as a preservative, and next into a mixture of water and alcohol. Then she observed them under the microscope. Her glasses interfered with this work—they bumped into the microscope's viewing lens—and so she switched to wearing contact lenses. In retrospect, she thought that this was probably a mistake.

At Argus College she still had no close friends, but neither was she the solitary creature she had been at home. She respected her fellow students, and grew to appreciate the company of women. She could go for days at a time seeing no men besides her professors or the commuters driving past the school's wrought-iron gates.

And she was not the school's only beauty. Argus College specialized in young women like Jane: elegant, diffident girls who studied the burial customs of Mongol women or the mating habits of rare antipodean birds; girls who composed concertos for violin and gamelan orchestra, or wrote computer programs that charted the progress of potentially dangerous celestial objects through the Oort Cloud. Within this educational greenhouse, Jane was not so much orchid as sturdy milkweed blossom. She thrived.

Her first three years at Argus passed in a bright-winged blur with her butterflies. Summers were given to museum internships, where she spent months cleaning and mounting specimens in solitary delight. In her senior year Jane received permission to design her own thesis project, involving her beloved Shark Moths. She was given a corner in a dusty anteroom off the Zoology Lab, and there she set up her microscope and laptop. There was no window in her corner, indeed there was no window in the anteroom at all, though the adjoining lab was pleasantly old-fashioned, with high arched windows set between Victorian cabinetry displaying lepidoptera, neon-carapaced beetles, unusual tree fungi and (she found these slightly tragic) numerous exotic finches, their brilliant plumage dimmed to dusty hues. Since she often worked late into the night, she requested and received her own set of keys. Most evenings she could be found beneath the glare of the small halogen lamp, entering data into her computer, scanning images of genetic mutations involving female Shark Moths exposed to dioxin, corresponding with other researchers in Melbourne and Kyoto, Siberia and London.

The rape occurred around ten o'clock one Friday night in early March. She had locked the door to her office, leaving her laptop behind, and started to walk to the subway station a few blocks away. It was a cold clear night, the yellow glow of the crime lights giving dead grass and leafless trees an eerie autumn shimmer. She hurried across the campus, seeing no one, then hesitated at Seventh Street. It was a longer walk, but safer, if she went down Seventh Street and then over to Michigan Avenue. The shortcut was much quicker, but Argus authorities and the local police discouraged students from taking it after dark. Jane stood for a moment, looking across the road to where the desolate park lay; then, staring resolutely straight ahead and walking briskly, she crossed Seventh and took the shortcut.

A crumbling sidewalk passed through a weedy expanse of vacant lot, strewn with broken bottles and the spindly forms of half a dozen dusty-limbed oak trees. Where the grass ended, a narrow road skirted a block of abandoned row houses, intermittently lit by crime lights. Most of the lights had been vandalized, and one had been knocked down in a car accident—the car's fender was still there, twisted around the lamppost. Jane picked her way carefully among shards of shattered glass, reached the sidewalk in front of the boarded-up houses and began to walk more quickly, towards the brightly lit Michigan Avenue intersection where the subway waited.

She never saw him. He was *there*, she knew that; knew he had a face, and clothing; but afterwards she could recall none of it. Not the feel of him, not his smell; only the knife he held—awkwardly, she realized later, she probably could have wrested it from him—and the few words he spoke to her. He said nothing at first, just grabbed her and pulled her into an alley between the row houses, his fingers covering her mouth, the heel of his hand pressing against her windpipe so that she gagged. He pushed her onto the dead leaves and wads of matted windblown newspaper, yanked her pants down, ripped open her jacket and then tore her shirt open. She heard one of the buttons strike brick and roll away. She thought desperately of what she had read once, in a Rape Awareness brochure: not to struggle, not to fight, not to do anything that might cause her attacker to kill her.

Jane did not fight. Instead, she divided into three parts. One part knelt nearby and prayed the way she had done as a child, not intently but automatically, trying to get through the strings of words as quickly as possible. The second part submitted blindly and silently to the man in the alley. And the third hovered above the other two, her hands wafting slowly up and down to keep her aloft as she watched.

"Try to get away," the man whispered. She could not see him or feel him though his hands were there. "Try to get away."

She remembered that she ought not to struggle, but from the noise she made and the way he tugged at her, she realized that was what aroused him. She did not want to anger him; she made a small sound deep in her throat and tried to push him from her chest. Almost immediately he groaned, and seconds later rolled off her. Only his hand lingered for a moment upon her cheek. Then he stumbled to his feet—she could hear him fumbling with his zipper—and fled.

The praying girl and the girl in the air also disappeared then. Only Jane was left, yanking her ruined clothes around her as she lurched from the alley and began to run, screaming and staggering back and forth across the road, towards the subway.

◆◆

The police came, an ambulance. She was taken first to the police station and then to the City General Hospital, a hellish place, starkly lit, with endless underground corridors that led into darkened rooms where solitary figures lay on narrow beds like gurneys. Her pubic hair was combed and stray hairs placed into sterile envelopes; semen samples were taken, and she was advised to be tested for HIV and other diseases. She spent the entire night in the hospital, waiting and undergoing various examinations. She refused to give the police or hospital staff her parents' phone number, or anyone else's. Just before dawn they finally released her, with an envelope full of brochures from the local rape crisis center, New Hope for Women, Planned Parenthood, and a business card from the police detective who was overseeing her case. The detective drove her to her apartment in his squad car; when he stopped in front of her building, she was suddenly terrified that he would know where she lived, that he would come back, that he had been her assailant.

But, of course, he had not been. He walked her to the door and waited for her to go inside. "Call your parents," he said right before he left.

"I will."

She pulled aside the bamboo window shade, watching until the squad car pulled away. Then she threw out the brochures she'd received, flung off her clothes, and stuffed them into the trash. She showered and changed, packed a bag full of clothes and another of books. Then she called a cab. When it arrived, she directed it to the Argus campus, where she retrieved her laptop and her research on Tiger Moths, then had the cab bring her to Union Station.

She bought a train ticket home. Only after she arrived and told her parents what had happened did she finally start to cry. Even then, she could not remember what the man had looked like.

—

She lived at home for three months. Her parents insisted that she get psychiatric counseling and join a therapy group for rape survivors. She did so, reluctantly, but stopped attending after three weeks. The rape was something that had happened to her, but it was over.

"It was fifteen minutes out of my life," she said once at group. "That's all. It's not the rest of my life."

This didn't go over very well. Other women thought she was in denial; the therapist thought Jane would suffer later if she did not confront her fears now.

"But I'm not afraid," said Jane.

"Why not?" demanded a woman whose eyebrows had fallen out.

Because lightning doesn't strike twice, Jane thought grimly, but she said nothing. That was the last time she attended group.

That night her father had a phone call. He took the phone and sat at the dining table, listening; after a moment stood and walked into his study, giving a quick backward glance at his daughter before closing the door behind him. Jane felt as though her chest had suddenly frozen: but after some minutes she heard her father's laugh: he was not, after all, talking to the police detective. When after half an hour he returned, he gave Jane another quick look, more thoughtful this time.

"That was Andrew." Andrew was a doctor friend of his, an Englishman. "He and Fred are going to Provence for three months. They were wondering if you might want to housesit for them."

"In *London*?" Jane's mother shook her head. "I don't think—"

"I said we'd think about it."

"*I'll* think about it," Jane corrected him. She stared at both her parents, absently ran a finger along one eyebrow. "Just let me think about it."

And she went to bed.

—

She went to London. She already had a passport, from visiting Andrew with her parents when she was in high school. Before she left, there were countless arguments with her mother and father, and phone calls back and forth to Andrew. He assured them that the flat was secure, there was a very nice reliable older woman who lived upstairs, that it would be a good idea for Jane to get out on her own again.

"So you don't get gun-shy," he said to her one night on the phone. He was a doctor, after all: a homeopath not an allopath, which Jane found reassuring. "It's important for you to get on with your life. You won't be able to get a real job here as a visitor, but I'll see what I can do."

It was on the plane to Heathrow that she made a discovery. She had splashed water onto her face, and was beginning to comb her hair when she blinked and stared into the mirror.

Above her eyebrows, the long hairs had grown back. They followed the contours of her brow, sweeping back towards her temples; still entwined, still difficult to make out unless she drew her face close to her reflection and tilted her head just so. Tentatively she touched one braided strand. It was stiff yet oddly pliant; but as she ran her finger along its length a sudden *surge* flowed through her. Not an electrical shock: more like the thrill of pain when a dentist's drill touches a nerve, or an elbow rams against a stone. She gasped; but immediately the pain was gone. Instead there was a thrumming behind her forehead, a spreading warmth that trickled into her throat like sweet syrup. She opened her mouth, her gasp turning into an uncontrollable yawn, the yawn into a spike of such profound physical ecstasy that she grabbed the edge of the sink and thrust forward, striking her head against the mirror. She was dimly aware of someone knocking at the lavatory door as she clutched the sink and, shuddering, climaxed.

"Hello?" someone called softly. "Hello, is this occupied?"

"Right out," Jane gasped. She caught her breath, still trembling; ran a hand across her face, her fingers halting before they could touch the hairs above her eyebrows. There was the faintest tingling, a temblor of sensation that faded as she grabbed her cosmetic bag, pulled the door open and stumbled back into the cabin.

↤↦

Andrew and Fred lived in an old Georgian row house just north of Camden Town, overlooking the Regent's Canal. Their flat occupied the first floor and basement; there was a hexagonal solarium out back, with glass walls and heated stone floor, and beyond that a stepped terrace leading down to the canal. The bedroom had an old wooden four-poster piled high with duvets and down pillows, and French doors that also opened onto the terrace. Andrew showed her how to operate the elaborate sliding security doors that unfolded from the walls, and gave her the keys to the barred window guards.

"You're completely safe here," he said, smiling. "Tomorrow we'll introduce you to Kendra upstairs, and show you how to get around. Camden market's just up that way, and *that* way—"

He stepped out onto the terrace, pointing to where the canal coiled and disappeared beneath an arched stone bridge, "—that way's the Regent's Park Zoo. I've given you a membership—"

"Oh! Thank you!" Jane looked around delighted. "This is *wonderful*."

"It is." Andrew put an arm around her and drew her close. "You're going to have a wonderful time, Jane. I thought you'd like the zoo—there's a new exhibit there, 'The World Within' or words to that effect—it's about insects. I thought perhaps you might want to volunteer there—they have an active docent program, and you're so knowledgeable about that sort of thing."

"Sure. It sounds great—really great." She grinned and smoothed her hair back from her face, the wind sending up the rank scent of stagnant water from the canal, the sweetly poisonous smell of hawthorn blossom. As she stood gazing down past the potted geraniums and Fred's rosemary trees, the hairs upon her brow trembled, and she laughed out loud, giddily, with anticipation.

<hr />

Fred and Andrew left two days later. It was enough time for Jane to get over her jet lag and begin to get barely acclimated to the city, and to its smell. London had an acrid scent: damp ashes, the softer underlying fetor of rot that oozed from ancient bricks and stone buildings, the thick vegetative smell of the canal, sharpened with urine and spilled beer. So many thousands of people descended on Camden Town on the weekend that the tube station was restricted to incoming passengers, and the canal path became almost impassable. Even late on a weeknight she could hear voices from the other side of the canal, harsh London voices echoing beneath the bridges or shouting to be heard above the din of the Northern Line trains passing overhead.

Those first days Jane did not venture far from the flat. She unpacked her clothes, which did not take much time, and then unpacked her collecting box, which did. The sturdy wooden case had come through the overseas flight and customs seemingly unscathed, but Jane found herself holding her breath as she undid the metal hinges, afraid of what she'd find inside.

"*Oh!*" she exclaimed. Relief, not chagrin: nothing had been damaged. The small glass vials of ethyl alcohol and gel shellac were intact, as were the pillboxes where she kept the tiny #2 pins she used for mounting. Fighting her own eagerness she carefully removed packets of stiff archival paper, a block of styrofoam covered with pinholes; two bottles of clear Maybelline nail polish and a small container of Elmer's Glue; more pillboxes, empty, and empty gelatine capsules for very small specimens; and last of all a small glass-fronted display box, framed in mahogany and holding her most precious specimen: a hybrid *Celerio harmuthi Kordesch*, the male crossbreed of a Spurge and an Elephant Hawkmoth. As long as the first joint of her thumb, it had the hawkmoth's typically streamlined wings but exquisitely delicate coloring, fuchsia bands shading to a soft rich brown, its thorax thick and seemingly feathered. Only a handful of these hybrid moths had ever existed, bred by the Prague entomologist Jan Pokorny in 1961; a few years afterward, both the Spurge Hawkmoth and the Elephant Hawkmoth had become extinct.

Jane had found this one for sale on the Internet three months ago. It was a former museum specimen and cost a fortune; she had a few bad nights, worrying whether it had actually been a legal purchase. Now she held the display box in her cupped palms and gazed at it raptly. Behind her eyes she felt a prickle, like sleep or unshed tears; then a slow thrumming warmth crept from her brows, spreading to her temples, down her neck and through her breasts, spreading like a stain. She swallowed, leaned back against the sofa and let the display box rest back within the larger case; slid first one hand then the other beneath her sweater and began to stroke her nipples. When some time later she came, it was with stabbing force and a thunderous sensation above her eyes, as though she had struck her forehead against the floor.

She had not: gasping, she pushed the hair from her face, zipped her jeans and reflexively leaned forward, to make certain the hawkmoth in its glass box was safe.

--

Over the following days she made a few brief forays to the news-agent and greengrocer, trying to eke out the supplies Fred and Andrew had left in the kitchen. She sat in the solarium, her bare feet warm against the heated stone floor, and drank chamomile tea or claret, staring down to where the ceaseless stream of people passed along the canal path, and watching the narrow boats as they plied their way slowly between Camden Lock and Little Venice, two miles to the west in Paddington. By the following Wednesday she felt brave enough, and bored enough, to leave her refuge and visit the zoo.

It was a short walk along the canal, dodging bicyclists who jingled their bells impatiently when she forgot to stay on the proper side of the path. She passed beneath several arching bridges, their undersides pleated with slime and moss. Drunks sprawled against the stones and stared at her blearily or challengingly by turns; well-dressed couples walked dogs, and there were excited knots of children, tugging their parents on to the zoo.

Fred had walked here with Jane, to show her the way. But it all looked unfamiliar now. She kept a few strides behind a family, her head down, trying not to look as though she was following them, and felt a pulse of relief when they reached a twisting stair with an arrowed sign at its top.

REGENT'S PARK ZOO

There was an old old church across the street, its yellow stone walls overgrown with ivy; and down and around the corner a long stretch of hedges with high iron walls fronting them, and at last a huge set of gates, crammed with children and vendors selling balloons and banners and London guidebooks. Jane lifted her head and walked quickly past the family that had led her here, showed her membership card at the entrance, and went inside.

She wasted no time on the seals or tigers or monkeys, but went straight to the newly renovated structure where a multicolored banner flapped in the late-morning breeze.

AN ALTERNATE UNIVERSE:
SECRETS OF THE INSECT WORLD

Inside, crowds of schoolchildren and harassed-looking adults formed a ragged queue that trailed through a brightly lit corridor, its walls covered with huge glossy color photos and computer-enhanced images of hissing cockroaches, hellgrammites, morpho butterflies, death-watch beetles, polyphemous moths. Jane dutifully joined the queue, but when the corridor opened into a vast sun-lit atrium she strode off on her own, leaving the children and teachers to gape at monarchs in butterfly cages and an interactive display of honeybees dancing. Instead she found a relatively quiet display at the far end of the exhibition space, a floor-to-ceiling cylinder of transparent net, perhaps six feet in diameter. Inside, buckthorn bushes and blooming hawthorn vied for sunlight with a slender beech sapling, and dozens of butterflies flitted upwards through the new yellow leaves, or sat with wings outstretched upon the beech tree. They were a type of Pieridae, the butterflies known as whites; though these were not white at all. The females had creamy yellow-green wings, very pale, their wingspans perhaps an inch and a half. The males were the same size; when they were at rest their flattened wings were a dull, rather sulphurous color. But when the males lit into the air their wings revealed vivid, spectral yellow undersides. Jane caught her breath in delight, her neck prickling with that same atavistic joy she'd felt as a child in the attic.

"Wow," she breathed, and pressed up against the netting. It felt like wings against her face, soft, webbed; but as she stared at the insects inside her brow began to ache as with migraine. She shoved her glasses onto her nose, closed her eyes and drew a long breath; then took a step away from the cage. After a minute she opened her eyes. The headache had diminished to a dull throb; when she hesitantly touched one eyebrow, she could feel the entwined hairs there, stiff as wire. They were vibrating, but at her touch the vibrations like the headache dulled. She stared at the floor, the tiles sticky with contraband juice and gum; then looked up once again at the cage. There was a display sign off to one side; she walked over to it, slowly, and read.

CLEOPATRA BRIMSTONE

Gonepteryx rhamni cleopatra

This popular and subtly colored species has a range which extends throughout the Northern Hemisphere, with the exception of Arctic regions and several remote islands. In Europe, the brimstone is a harbinger of spring, often emerging from its winter hibernation under dead leaves to revel in the countryside while there is still snow upon the ground.

"I must ask you please not to touch the cages."

Jane turned to see a man, perhaps fifty, standing a few feet away. A net was jammed under his arm; in his hand he held a clear plastic jar with several butterflies at the bottom, apparently dead.

"Oh. Sorry," said Jane. The man edged past her. He set his jar on the floor, opened a small door at the base of the cylindrical cage, and deftly angled the net inside. Butterflies lifted in a yellow-green blur from leaves and branches; the man swept the net carefully across the bottom of the cage, then withdrew it. Three dead butterflies, like scraps of colored paper, drifted from the net into the open jar.

"Housecleaning," he said, and once more thrust his arm into the cage. He was slender and wiry, not much taller than she was, his face hawkish and burnt brown from the sun, his thick straight hair iron-streaked and pulled back into a long braid. He wore black jeans and a dark-blue hooded jersey, with an ID badge clipped to the collar.

"You work here," said Jane. The man glanced at her, his arm still in the cage; she could see him sizing her up. After a moment he glanced away again. A few minutes later he emptied the net for the last time, closed the cage and the jar, and stepped over to a waste bin, pulling bits of dead leaves from the net and dropping them into the container.

"I'm one of the curatorial staff. You American?"

Jane nodded. "Yeah. Actually, I—I wanted to see about volunteering here."

"Lifewatch desk at the main entrance." The man cocked his head towards the door. "They can get you signed up and registered, see what's available."

"No—I mean, I want to volunteer here. With the insects—"

"Butterfly collector, are you?" The man smiled, his tone mocking. He had hazel eyes, deep-set; his thin mouth made the smile seem perhaps more cruel than intended. "We get a lot of those."

Jane flushed. "No. I am not a *collector*," she said coldly, adjusting her glasses. "I'm doing a thesis on dioxin genital mutation in *Cucullia artemisia*." She didn't add that it was an undergraduate thesis. "I've been doing independent research for seven years now." She hesitated, thinking of her Intel scholarship, and added, "I've received several grants for my work."

The man regarded her appraisingly. "Are you studying here, then?"

"Yes," she lied again. "At Oxford. I'm on sabbatical right now. But I live near here, and so I thought I might—"

She shrugged, opening her hands, looked over at him and smiled tentatively. "Make myself useful?"

The man waited a moment, nodded. "Well. Do you have a few minutes now? I've got to do something with these, but if you want you can come with me and wait, and then we can see what we can do. Maybe circumvent some paperwork."

He turned and started across the room. He had a graceful, bouncing gait, like a gymnast or circus acrobat: impatient with the ground beneath him. "Shouldn't take long," he called over his shoulder as Jane hurried to catch up.

She followed him through a door marked AUTHORIZED PERSONS ONLY, into the exhibit laboratory, a reassuringly familiar place with its display cases and smells of shellac and camphor, acetone and ethyl alcohol. There were more cages here, but smaller ones, sheltering live specimens—pupating butterflies and moths, stick insects, leaf insects, dung beetles. The man dropped his net onto a desk, took the jar to a long table against one wall, blindingly lit by long fluorescent tubes. There were scores of bottles here, some empty, others filled with paper and tiny inert figures.

"Have a seat," said the man, gesturing at two folding chairs. He settled into one, grabbed an empty jar and a roll of absorbent paper.

"I'm David Bierce. So where're you staying? Camden Town?"

"Jane Kendall. Yes—"

"The High Street?"

Jane sat in the other chair, pulling it a few inches away from him. The questions made her uneasy, but she only nodded, lying again, and said, "Closer, actually. Off Gloucester Road. With friends."

"Mm." Bierce tore off a piece of absorbent paper, leaned across to a stainless steel sink and dampened the paper. Then he dropped it into the empty jar. He paused, turned to her and gestured at the table, smiling. "Care to join in?"

Jane shrugged. "Sure—"

She pulled her chair closer, found another empty jar and did as Bierce had, dampening a piece of paper towel and dropping it inside. Then she took the jar containing the dead brimstones and carefully shook one onto the counter. It was a female, its coloring more muted than the males'; she scooped it up very gently, careful not to disturb the scales like dull green glitter upon its wings, dropped it into the jar and replaced the top.

"Very nice." Bierce nodded, raising his eyebrows. "You seem to know what you're doing. Work with other insects? Soft-bodied ones?"

"Sometimes. Mostly moths, though. And butterflies."

"Right." He inclined his head to a recessed shelf. "How would you label that, then? Go ahead."

On the shelf she found a notepad and a case of Rapidograph pens. She began to write, conscious of Bierce staring at her. "We usually just put all this into the computer, of course, and print it out," he said. "I just want to see the benefits of an American education in the sciences."

Jane fought the urge to look at him. Instead she wrote out the information, making her printing as tiny as possible.

> *Gonepteryx rhamni cleopatra*
> *UNITED KINGDOM: LONDON*
> *Regent's Park Zoo*
> *Lat/Long unknown*
> *21.IV.2001*
> *D. Bierce*
> *Net/caged specimen*

She handed it to Bierce. "I don't know the proper coordinates for London."

Bierce scrutinized the paper. "It's actually the Royal Zoological Park," he said. He looked at her, then smiled. "But you'll do."

"Great!" She grinned, the first time she'd really felt happy since arriving here. "When do you want me to start?"

"How about Monday?"

Jane hesitated: this was only Friday. "I could come in tomorrow—"

"I don't work on the weekend, and you'll need to be trained. Also they have to process the paperwork. Right—"

He stood and went to a desk, pulling open drawers until he found a clipboard holding sheaves of triplicate forms. "Here. Fill all this out, leave it with me and I'll pass it on to Carolyn—she's the head volunteer coordinator. They usually want to interview you, but I'll tell them we've done all that already."

"What time should I come in Monday?"

"Come at nine. Everything opens at ten, that way you'll avoid the crowds. Use the staff entrance, someone there will have an ID waiting for you to pick up when you sign in—"

She nodded and began filling out the forms.

"All right then." David Bierce leaned against the desk and again fixed her with that sly, almost taunting gaze. "Know how to find your way home?"

Jane lifted her chin defiantly. "Yes."

"Enjoying London? Going to go out tonight and do Camden Town with all the yobs?"

"Maybe. I haven't been out much yet."

"Mm. Beautiful American girl, they'll eat you alive. Just kidding." He straightened, started across the room towards the door. "I'll see you Monday then."

He held the door for her. "You really should check out the clubs. You're too young not to see the city by night." He smiled, the fluorescent light slanting sideways into his hazel eyes and making them suddenly glow icy blue. "Bye then."

"Bye," said Jane, and hurried quickly from the lab towards home.

That night, for the first time, she went out. She told herself she would have gone anyway, no matter what Bierce had said. She had no idea where the clubs were; Andrew had pointed out the Electric Ballroom to her, right across from the tube station, but he'd also warned her that was where the tourists flocked on weekends.

"They do a disco thing on Saturday nights—Saturday Night Fever, everyone gets all done up in vintage clothes. Quite a fashion show," he'd said, smiling and shaking his head.

Jane had no interest in that. She ate a quick supper, vindaloo from the take-away down the street from the flat, then dressed. She hadn't brought a huge number of clothes—at home she'd never bothered much with clothes at all, making do with thrift-shop finds and whatever her mother gave her for Christmas. But now she found herself sitting on the edge of the four-poster, staring with pursed lips at the sparse contents of two bureau drawers. Finally she pulled out a pair of black corduroy jeans and a black turtleneck and pulled on her sneakers. She removed her glasses, for the first time in weeks inserted her contact lenses. Then she shrugged into her old, navy peacoat and left.

It was after ten o'clock. On the canal path, throngs of people stood, drinking from pints of canned lager. She made her way through them, ignoring catcalls and whispered invitations, stepping to avoid where kids lay making out against the brick wall that ran alongside the path, or pissing in the bushes. The bridge over the canal at Camden Lock was clogged with several dozen kids in mohawks or varicolored hair, shouting at each other above the din of a boom box and swigging from bottles of Spanish champagne.

A boy with a champagne bottle leered, lunging at her.

"'Ere, sweetheart, 'ep youseff—"

Jane ducked, and he careered against the ledge, his arm striking brick and the bottle shattering in a starburst of black and gold.

"Fucking cunt!" he shrieked after her. "Fucking bloody *cunt!*"

People glanced at her, but Jane kept her head down, making a quick turn into the vast cobbled courtyard of Camden Market. The place had a desolate air: the vendors would not arrive until early next morning, and now only stray cats and bits of windblown trash moved in the shadows. In the surrounding buildings people spilled out onto balconies, drinking and calling back and forth, their voices hollow and their long shadows twisting across the ill-lit central courtyard. Jane hurried to the far end, but there found only brick walls, closed-up shop doors, and a young woman huddled within the folds of a filthy sleeping bag.

"*Couldya—couldya—*" the woman murmured.

Jane turned and followed the wall until she found a door leading into a short passage. She entered it, hoping she was going in the direction of Camden High Street. She felt like Alice trying to find her way through the garden in Wonderland: arched doorways led not into the street but headshops and blindingly lit piercing parlors, open for business; other doors opened onto enclosed courtyards, dark, smelling of piss and marijuana. Finally from the corner of her eye she glimpsed what looked like the end of the passage, headlights piercing through the gloom like landing lights. Doggedly she made her way towards them.

"Ay watchowt watchowt," someone yelled as she emerged from the passage onto the sidewalk, and ran the last few steps to the curb.

She was on the High Street—rather, in that block or two of curving no-man's-land where it turned into Chalk Farm Road. The sidewalks were still crowded, but everyone was heading towards Camden Lock and not away from it. Jane waited for the light to change and raced across the street, to where a cobblestoned alley snaked off between a shop selling leather underwear and another advertising "Fine French Country Furniture."

For several minutes she stood there. She watched the crowds heading toward Camden Town, the steady stream of minicabs and taxis and buses heading up Chalk Farm Road toward Hampstead.

Overhead, dull orange clouds moved across a night sky the color of charred wood; there was the steady low thunder of jets circling after takeoff at Heathrow. At last she tugged her collar up around her neck, letting her hair fall in loose waves down her back, shoved her hands into her coat pockets and turned to walk purposefully down the alley.

Before her the cobblestone path turned sharply to the right. She couldn't see what was beyond, but she could hear voices: a girl laughing, a man's sibilant retort. A moment later the alley spilled out onto a cul-de-sac. A couple stood a few yards away, before a doorway with a small copper awning above it. The young woman glanced sideways at Jane, quickly looked away again. A silhouette filled the doorway; the young man pulled out a wallet. His hand disappeared within the silhouette, re-emerged, and the couple walked inside. Jane waited until the shadowy figure withdrew. She looked over her shoulder, then approached the building.

There was a heavy metal door, black, with graffiti scratched into it and pale blurred spots where painted graffiti had been effaced. The door was set back several feet into a brick recess; there was a grilled metal slot at the top that could be slid back, so that one could peer out into the courtyard. To the right of the door, on the brick wall within the recess, was a small brass plaque with a single word on it.

HIVE

There was no doorbell or any other way to signal that you wanted to enter. Jane stood, wondering what was inside; feeling a small tingling unease that was less fear than the knowledge that even if she were to confront the figure who'd let that other couple inside, she herself would certainly be turned away.

With a *skreek* of metal on stone the door suddenly shot open. Jane looked up, into the sharp, raggedly handsome face of a tall, still youngish man with very short blond hair, a line of gleaming gold beads like drops of sweat piercing the edge of his left jaw.

"Good evening," he said, glancing past her to the alley. He wore a black sleeveless T-shirt with a small golden bee embroidered upon the breast. His bare arms were muscular, striated with long sweeping scars: black, red, white. "Are you waiting for Hannah?"

"No." Quickly Jane pulled out a handful of five-pound notes. "Just me tonight."

"That'll be twenty then." The man held his hand out, still gazing at the alley; when Jane slipped the notes to him he looked down and flashed her a vulpine smile. "Enjoy yourself." She darted past him into the building.

Abruptly it was as though some darker night had fallen. Thunderously so, since the enfolding blackness was slashed with music so loud it was itself like light: Jane hesitated, closing her eyes, and white flashes streaked across her eyelids like sleet, pulsing in time to the music. She opened her eyes, giving them a chance to adjust to the darkness, and tried to get a sense of where she was. A few feet away a blurry greyish lozenge sharpened into the window of a coat-check room. Jane walked past it, towards the source of the music. Immediately the floor slanted steeply beneath her feet. She steadied herself with one hand against the wall, following the incline until it opened onto a cavernous dance floor.

She gazed inside, disappointed. It looked like any other club, crowded, strobe-lit, turquoise smoke and silver glitter coiling between hundreds of whirling bodies clad in candy pink, sky blue, neon red, rainslicker yellow. Baby colors, Jane thought. There was a boy who was almost naked, except for shorts, a transparent water bottle strapped to his chest and long tubes snaking into his mouth. Another boy had hair the color of lime Jell-O, his face corrugated with glitter and sweat; he swayed near the edge of the dance floor, turned to stare at Jane and then beamed, beckoning her to join him.

Jane gave him a quick smile, shaking her head; when the boy opened his arms to her in mock pleading she shouted "No!"

But she continued to smile, though she felt as though her head would crack like an egg from the throbbing music. Shoving her hands into her pockets she skirted the dance floor, pushed her way to the bar and bought a drink, something pink with no ice in a plastic cup. It smelled like Gatorade and lighter fluid. She gulped it down, then carried the cup held before her like a torch as she continued on her circuit of the room. There was nothing else of interest; just long queues for the lavatories and another bar, numerous doors and stairwells where kids clustered, drinking and smoking. Now and then beeps and whistles like birdsong or insect cries came through the stuttering electronic din, whoops and trilling laughter from the dancers. But mostly they moved in near-silence, eyes rolled ceiling-ward, bodies exploding into Catherine wheels of flesh and plastic and nylon, but all without a word.

It gave Jane a headache—a *real* headache, the back of her skull bruised, tender to the touch. She dropped her plastic cup and started looking for a way out. She could see past the dance floor to where she had entered, but it seemed as though another hundred people had arrived in the few minutes since then: kids were standing six-deep at both bars, and the action on the floor had spread, amoeba-like, towards the corridors angling back up towards the street.

"Sorry—"

A fat woman in an Arsenal jersey jostled her as she hurried by, leaving a smear of oily sweat on Jane's wrist. Jane grimaced and wiped her hand on the bottom of her coat. She gave one last look at the dance floor, but nothing had changed within the intricate lattice of dancers and smoke, braids of glow-lights and spotlit faces surging up and down, up and down, while more dancers fought their way to the center.

"Shit." She turned and strode off, heading to where the huge room curved off into relative emptiness. Here, scores of tables were

scattered, some overturned, others stacked against the wall. A few
people sat, talking; a girl lay curled on the floor, her head pillowed
on a Barbie knapsack. Jane crossed to the wall, and found first a
door that led to a bare brick wall, then a second door that held a
broom closet. The next was dark red, metal, official-looking: the
kind of door that Jane associated with school fire drills.

A fire door. It would lead outside, or into a hall that would lead
there. Without hesitating she pushed it open and entered. A short
corridor lit by EXIT signs stretched ahead of her, with another door
at the end. She hurried towards it, already reaching reflexively for the
keys to the flat, pushed the door-bar and stepped inside.

For an instant she thought she had somehow stumbled into a
hospital emergency room. There was the glitter of halogen light
on steel, distorted reflections thrown back at her from curved glass
surfaces; the abrasive odor of isopropyl alcohol and the fainter
tinny scent of blood, like metal in the mouth.

And bodies: everywhere, bodies, splayed on gurneys or suspended
from gleaming metal hooks, laced with black electrical cord and
pinned upright onto smooth rubber mats. She stared open-mouthed,
neither appalled nor frightened but fascinated by the conundrum
before her: how did *that* hand fit *there*, and whose leg was *that*? She
inched backward, pressing herself against the door and trying to stay
in the shadows—just inches ahead of her ribbons of luminous bluish
light streamed from lamps hung high overhead. The chiaroscuro of
pallid bodies and black furniture, shiny with sweat and here and there
red-streaked, or brown; the mere sight of so many bodies, real bodies—
flesh spilling over the edge of tabletops, too much hair or none at all,
eyes squeezed shut in ecstasy or terror and mouths open to reveal
stained teeth, pale gums—the sheer *fluidity* of it all enthralled her.
She felt as she had, once, pulling aside a rotted log to disclose the ant's
nest beneath, masses of minute fleeing bodies, soldiers carrying eggs
and larvae in their jaws, tunnels spiraling into the center of another
world. Her brow tingled, warmth flushed her from brow to breast . . .

Another world, that's what she had found then; and discovered again now.

"*Out.*"

Jane sucked her breath in sharply. Fingers dug into her shoulder, yanked her back through the metal door so roughly that she cut her wrist against it.

"No lurkers, what the fuck—"

A man flung her against the wall. She gasped, turned to run but he grabbed her shoulder again. "Christ, a fucking girl."

He sounded angry but relieved. She looked up: a huge man, more fat than muscle. He wore very tight leather briefs and the same black sleeveless shirt with a golden bee embroidered upon it. "How the hell'd you get in like *that*?" he demanded, cocking a thumb at her.

She shook her head, then realized he meant her clothes. "I was just trying to find my way out."

"Well you found your way in. In like fucking Flynn." He laughed: he had gold-capped teeth, and gold wires threading the tip of his tongue. "You want to join the party, you know the rules. No exceptions."

Before she could reply he turned and was gone, the door thudding softly behind him. She waited, heart pounding, then reached and pushed the bar on the door.

Locked. She was out, not in; she was nowhere at all. For a long time she stood there, trying to hear anything from the other side of the door, waiting to see if anyone would come back looking for her. At last she turned, and began to find her way home.

⊷

Next morning she woke early, to the sound of delivery trucks in the street and children on the canal path, laughing and squabbling on their way to the zoo. She sat up with a pang, remembering

David Bierce and her volunteer job; then recalled this was Saturday not Monday.

"Wow," she said aloud. The extra days seemed like a gift.

For a few minutes she lay in Fred and Andrew's great four-poster, staring abstractedly at where she had rested her mounted specimens atop the wainscoting—the hybrid hawkmoth; a beautiful Honduran owl butterfly, *Caligo atreus*; a mourning cloak she had caught and mounted herself years ago. She thought of the club last night, mentally retracing her steps to the hidden back room; thought of the man who had thrown her out, the interplay of light and shadow upon the bodies pinned to mats and tables. She had slept in her clothes; now she rolled out of bed and pulled her sneakers on, forgoing breakfast but stuffing her pocket with ten- and twenty-pound notes before she left.

It was a clear cool morning, with a high pale-blue sky and the young leaves of nettles and hawthorn still glistening with dew. Someone had thrown a shopping cart from the nearby Sainsbury's into the canal; it edged sideways up out of the shallow water, like a frozen shipwreck. A boy stood a few yards down from it, fishing, an absent, placid expression on his face.

She crossed over the bridge to the canal path and headed for the High Street. With every step she took the day grew older, noisier, trains rattling on the bridge behind her and voices harsh as gulls rising from the other side of the brick wall that separated the canal path from the street.

At Camden Lock she had to fight her way through the market. There were tens of thousands of tourists, swarming from the maze of shops to pick their way between scores of vendors selling old and new clothes, bootleg CDs, cheap silver jewelry, kilims, feather boas, handcuffs, cellphones, mass-produced furniture and puppets from Indonesia, Morocco, Guyana, Wales. The fug of burning incense and cheap candles choked her; she hurried to where a young woman was turning samosas in a vat of sputtering oil, and dug into her pocket for a handful of change, standing so that the smells of hot

grease and scorched chickpea batter cancelled out patchouli and
Caribbean Nights.

"Two, please," Jane shouted.

She ate and almost immediately felt better, then walked a few
steps to where a spike-haired girl sat behind a table covered with
cheap clothes made of ripstock fabric in Jell-O shades.

"Everything five pounds," the girl announced. She stood, smiling
helpfully as Jane began to sort through pairs of hugely baggy pants.
They were cross-seamed with velcro and deep zippered pockets.
Jane held up a pair, frowning as the legs billowed, lavender and
green, in the wind.

"It's so you can make them into shorts," the girl explained.
She stepped around the table and took the pants from Jane, deftly tugging at the legs so that they detached. "See? Or a skirt." The girl replaced the pants, picked up another pair, screaming orange with
black trim, and a matching windbreaker. "This color would look
nice on you."

"Okay." Jane paid for them, waited for the girl to put the clothes
in a plastic bag. "Thanks."

"Bye now."

She went out into High Street. Shopkeepers stood guard over the
tables spilling out from their storefronts, heaped with leather clothes
and souvenir T-shirts: MIND THE GAP, LONDON UNDER-
GROUND, shirts emblazoned with the Cat in the Hat toking on a
cheroot. THE CAT IN THE HAT SMOKES BLACK. Every three or
four feet someone had set up a boom box, deafening sound-bites of
salsa, techno, "The Hustle," Bob Marley, "Anarchy in the UK,"
Radiohead. On the corner of Inverness and High Street a few punks
squatted in a doorway, looking over the postcards they'd bought. A
sign in the smoked-glass window said ALL HAIRCUTS TEN
POUNDS, MEN WOMEN CHILDREN.

"Sorry," one of the punks said, as Jane stepped over them and
into the shop.

The barber was sitting in an old-fashioned chair, his back to her, reading the *Sun*. At the sound of her footsteps he turned, smiling automatically. "Can I help you?"

"Yes please. I'd like my hair cut. All of it."

He nodded, gesturing to the chair. "Please."

Jane had thought she might have to convince him that she was serious. She had beautiful hair, well below her shoulders—the kind of hair people would kill for, she'd been hearing that her whole life. But the barber just hummed and chopped it off, the *snick snick* of his shears interspersed with kindly questions about whether she was enjoying her visit and his account of a vacation to Disney World ten years earlier.

"Dear, do we want it shaved or buzz-cut?"

In the mirror a huge-eyed creature gazed at Jane, like a tarsier or one of the owlish caligo moths. She stared at it, entranced, then nodded.

"Shaved. Please."

When he was finished she got out of the chair, dazed, and ran her hand across her scalp. It was smooth and cool as an apple. There were a few tiny nicks that stung beneath her fingers. She paid the barber, tipping him two pounds. He smiled and held the door open for her.

"Now when you want a touchup, you come see us, dear. Only five pounds for a touchup."

She went next to find new shoes. There were more shoe shops in Camden Town than she had ever seen anywhere in her life; she checked out four of them on one block before deciding on a discounted pair of twenty-hole black Doc Martens. They were no longer fashionable, but they had blunted steel caps on the toes. She bought them, giving the salesgirl her old sneakers to toss into the waste bin. When she went back onto the street it was like walking in wet cement—the shoes were so heavy, the leather so stiff that she ducked back into the shoe shop and bought a pair of heavy wool socks and put them on. She returned outside, hesitating on the front step before crossing the street and heading in the direction of Chalk Farm Road. There was a shop here that Fred had shown her before he left.

"Now, that's where you get your fetish gear, Jane," he said, pointing to a shop window painted matte black. THE PLACE, it said in red letters, with two linked circles beneath. Fred had grinned and rapped his knuckles against the glass as they walked by. "I've never been in, you'll have to tell me what it's like." They'd both laughed at the thought.

Now Jane walked slowly, the wind chill against her bare skull. When she could make out the shop, sun glinting off the crimson letters and a sad-eyed dog tied to a post out front, she began to hurry, her new boots making a hollow thump as she pushed through the door.

There was a security gate inside, a thin, sallow young man with dreadlocks nodding at her silently as she approached.

"You'll have to check that." He pointed at the bag with her new clothes in it. She handed it to him, reading the warning posted behind the counter.

SHOPLIFTERS WILL BE BEATEN,
FLAYED, SPANKED, BIRCHED, BLED
AND THEN PROSECUTED
TO THE FULL EXTENT OF THE LAW

The shop was well lit. It smelled strongly of new leather and coconut oil and pine-scented disinfectant. She seemed to be the only customer this early in the day, although she counted seven employees, manning cash registers, unpacking cartons, watching to make sure she didn't try to nick anything. A CD of dance music played, and the phone rang constantly.

She spent a good half hour just walking through the place, impressed by the range of merchandise. Electrified wands to deliver shocks, things like meat cleavers made of stainless steel with rubber tips. Velcro dog collars, Velcro hoods, black rubber balls and balls in neon shades, a mat embedded with three-inch spikes that could be conveniently rolled up and came with its own lightweight carrying case. As she wandered about, more customers arrived, some of them greeting the clerks by name, others furtive, making a quick circuit of the shelves before darting outside again. At last Jane knew what she wanted. A set of wristcuffs and one of anklecuffs, both of very heavy black leather with stainless steel hardware; four adjustable nylon leashes, also black, with clips on either end that could be fastened to cuffs or looped around a post; a few spare S-clips.

"That it?"

Jane nodded, and the register clerk began scanning her purchases. She felt almost guilty, buying so few things, not taking advantage of the vast Meccano glory of all those shelves full of gleaming, somber contrivances.

"There you go." He handed her the receipt, then inclined his head at her. "Nice touch, that—"

He pointed at her eyebrows. Jane drew her hand up, felt the long pliant hairs uncoiling like baby ferns. "Thanks," she murmured. She retrieved her bag and went home to wait for evening.

·→←·

It was nearly midnight when she left the flat. She had slept for most of the afternoon, a deep but restless sleep, with anxious dreams of flight, falling, her hands encased in metal gloves, a shadowy figure crouching above her. She woke in the dark, heart pounding, terrified for a moment that she had slept all the way through till Sunday night.

But of course she had not. She showered, then dressed in a tight, low-cut black shirt and pulled on her new nylon pants and heavy boots. She seldom wore makeup, but tonight after putting in her contacts she carefully outlined her eyes with black, then chose a very pale lavender lipstick. She surveyed herself in the mirror critically. With her white skin, huge violet eyes and hairless skull, she resembled one of the Balinese puppets for sale in the market— beautiful but vacant, faintly ominous. She grabbed her keys and money, pulled on her windbreaker, and headed out.

When she reached the alley that led to the club, she entered it, walked about halfway, and stopped. After glancing back and forth to make sure no one was coming, she detached the legs from her nylon pants, stuffing them into a pocket, then adjusted the Velcro tabs so that the pants became a very short orange and black skirt. Her long legs were sheathed in black tights. She bent to tighten the laces on her metal-toed boots and hurried to the club entrance.

Tonight there was a line of people waiting to get in. Jane took her place, fastidiously avoiding looking at any of the others. They waited for thirty minutes, Jane shivering in her thin nylon windbreaker, before the door opened and the same gaunt blond man appeared to take their money. Jane felt her heart beat faster when it was her turn, wondering if he would recognize her. But he only scanned the courtyard, and, when the last of them darted inside, closed the door with a booming *clang*.

Inside all was as it had been, only far more crowded. Jane bought a drink, orange squash, no alcohol. It was horribly sweet, with a bitter, curdled aftertaste. Still, it had cost two pounds: she drank it all. She had just started on her way down to the dance floor when someone came up from behind to tap her shoulder, shouting into her ear.

"Wanna?"

It was a tall, broad-shouldered boy a few years older than she was, perhaps twenty-four, with a lean ruddy face, loose shoulder-length blond hair streaked green, and deep-set, very dark blue eyes. He swayed dreamily, gazing at the dance floor and hardly looking at her at all.

"Sure," Jane shouted back. He looped an arm around her shoulder, pulling her with him; his striped V-necked shirt smelled of talc and sweat.

They danced for a long time, Jane moving with calculated abandon, the boy heaving and leaping as though a dog was biting at his shins.

"You're beautiful," he shouted. There was an almost imperceptible instant of silence as the DJ changed tracks. "What's your name?"

"Cleopatra Brimstone."

The shattering music grew deafening once more. The boy grinned. "Well, Cleopatra. Want something to drink?"

Jane nodded in time with the beat, so fast her head spun. He took her hand and she raced to keep up with him, threading their way toward the bar.

"Actually," she yelled, pausing so that he stopped short and bumped up against her. "I think I'd rather go outside. Want to come?"

He stared at her, half-smiling, and shrugged. "Aw right. Let me get a drink first—"

They went outside. In the alley the wind sent eddies of dead leaves and newspaper flying up into their faces. Jane laughed, and pressed herself against the boy's side. He grinned down at her, finished his drink, and tossed the can aside, then put his arm around her. "Do you want to go get a drink, then?" he asked.

They stumbled out onto the sidewalk, turned and began walking. People filled the High Street, lines snaking out from the entrances of pubs and restaurants. A blue glow surrounded the streetlights, and clouds of small white moths beat themselves against the globes; vapor and banners of grey smoke hung above the punks blocking the sidewalk by Camden Lock. Jane and the boy dipped down into the street. He pointed to a pub occupying the corner a few blocks up, a large old green-painted building with baskets of flowers hanging beneath its windows and a large sign swinging back and forth in the wind: THE END OF THE WORLD. "In there, then?"

Jane shook her head. "I live right here, by the canal. We could go to my place if you want. We could have a few drinks there."

The boy glanced down at her. "Aw right," he said—very quickly, so she wouldn't change her mind. "That'd be aw right."

It was quieter on the back street leading to the flat. An old drunk huddled in a doorway, cadging change; Jane looked away from him and got out her keys while the boy stood restlessly, giving the drunk a belligerent look.

"Here we are," she announced, pushing the door open. "Home again, home again."

"Nice place." The boy followed her, gazing around admiringly. "You live here alone?"

"Yup." After she spoke Jane had a flash of unease, admitting that. But the boy only ambled into the kitchen, running a hand along the antique French farmhouse cupboard and nodding.

"You're American, right? Studying here?"

"Uh huh. What would you like to drink? Brandy?"

He made a face, then laughed. "Aw right! You got expensive taste. Goes with the name, I'd guess." Jane looked puzzled, and he went on, "Cleopatra—fancy name for a girl."

"Fancier for a boy," Jane retorted, and he laughed again.

She got the brandy, stood in the living room unlacing her boots. "Why don't we go in there?" she said, gesturing towards the bedroom. "It's kind of cold out here."

The boy ran a hand across his head, his blond hair streaming through his fingers. "Yeah, aw right." He looked around. "Um, that the toilet there?" Jane nodded. "Right back, then . . . "

She went into the bedroom, set the brandy and two glasses on a night table and took off her windbreaker. On another table, several tall candles, creamy white and thick as her wrist, were set into ornate brass holders. She lit these—the room filled with the sweet scent of beeswax—and sat on the floor, leaning against the bed. A few minutes later the toilet flushed and the boy reappeared. His hands and face were damp, redder than they had been. He smiled and sank onto the floor beside her. Jane handed him a glass of brandy.

"Cheers," he said, and drank it all in one gulp.

"Cheers," said Jane. She took a sip from hers, then refilled his glass. He drank again, more slowly this time. The candles threw a soft yellow haze over the four-poster bed with its green velvet duvet, the mounds of pillows, forest-green, crimson, saffron yellow. They sat without speaking for several minutes. Then the boy set his glass on the floor. He turned to face Jane, extending one arm around her shoulder and drawing his face near hers.

"Well then," he said.

His mouth tasted acrid, nicotine and cheap gin beneath the blunter taste of brandy. His hand sliding under her shirt was cold; Jane felt goose pimples rising across her breast, her nipple shrinking beneath his touch. He pressed against her, his cock already hard, and reached down to unzip his jeans.

"Wait," Jane murmured. "Let's get on the bed . . . "

She slid from his grasp and onto the bed, crawling to the heaps of pillows and feeling beneath one until she found what she had placed there earlier. "Let's have a little fun first."

"*This* is fun," the boy said, a bit plaintively. But he slung himself onto the bed beside her, pulling off his shoes and letting them fall to the floor with a thud. "What you got there?"

Smiling, Jane turned and held up the wrist cuffs. The boy looked at them, then at her, grinning. "Oh ho. Been in the back room, then—"

Jane arched her shoulders and unbuttoned her shirt. He reached for one of the cuffs, but she shook her head. "No. Not me, yet."

"Ladies first."

"Gentleman's pleasure."

The boy's grin widened. "Won't argue with that."

She took his hand and pulled him, gently, to the middle of the bed. "Lie on your back," she whispered.

He did, watching as she removed first his shirt and then his jeans and underwear. His cock lay nudged against his thigh, not quite hard; when she brushed her fingers against it he moaned softly, took her hand and tried to press it against him.

"No," she whispered. "Not yet. Give me your hand."

She placed the cuffs around each wrist, and his ankles, fastened the nylon leash to each one, and then began tying the bonds around each bedpost. It took longer than she had expected; it was difficult to get the bonds taut enough that the boy could not move. He lay there watchfully, his eyes glimmering in the candlelight as he craned his head to stare at her, his breath shallow, quickening.

"There." She sat back upon her haunches, staring at him. His cock was hard now, the hair on his chest and groin tawny in the half-light. He gazed back at her, his tongue pale as he licked his lips. "Try to get away," she whispered.

He moved slightly, his arms and legs a white X against a deep green field. "Can't," he said hoarsely.

She pulled her shirt off, then her nylon skirt. She had nothing on beneath. She leaned forward, letting her fingers trail from the cleft in his throat to his chest, cupping her palm atop his nipple and then sliding her hand down to his thigh. The flesh was warm, the little hairs soft and moist. Her own breath quickened; sudden heat flooded her, a honeyed liquid in her mouth. Above her brow the long hairs stiffened and furled straight out to either side: when she lifted her head to the candlelight she could see them from the corner of her eyes, twin barbs black and glistening like wire.

"You're so sexy." The boy's voice was hoarse. "God, you're—"

She placed her hand over his mouth. "Try to get away," she said, commandingly this time. "*Try to get away.*"

His torso writhed, the duvet bunching up around him in dark folds. She raked her fingernails down his chest and he cried out, moaning "Fuck me, God, fuck me . . . "

"Try to get away."

She stroked his cock, her fingers barely grazing its swollen head. With a moan he came, struggling helplessly to thrust his groin towards her. At the same moment Jane gasped, a fiery rush arrowing down from her brow to her breasts, her cunt. She rocked forward, crying out, her head brushing against the boy's side as she sprawled back across the bed. For a minute she lay there, the room around her seeming to pulse and swirl into myriad crystalline shapes, each bearing within it the same line of candles, the long curve of the boy's thigh swelling up into the hollow of his hip. She drew breath shakily, the flush of heat fading from her brow; then pushed herself up until she was sitting beside him. His eyes were shut. A thread of saliva traced the furrow between mouth and chin. Without thinking she drew her face down to his, and kissed his cheek.

Immediately he began to grow smaller. Jane reared back, smacking into one of the bedposts, and stared at the figure in front of her, shaking her head.

"No," she whispered. "No, no."

He was shrinking: so fast it was like watching water dissolve into dry sand. Man-size, child-size, large dog, small. His eyes flew open and for a fraction of a second stared horrified into her own. His hands and feet slipped like mercury from his bonds, wriggling until they met his torso and were absorbed into it. Jane's fingers kneaded the duvet; six inches away the boy was no larger than her hand, then smaller, smaller still. She blinked, for a heart-shredding instant thought he had disappeared completely.

Then she saw something crawling between folds of velvet. The length of her middle finger, its thorax black, yellow-striped, its lower wings elongated into frilled arabesques like those of a festoon, deep yellow, charcoal black, with indigo eye spots, its upper wings a chiaroscuro of black and white stripes.

Bhutanitis lidderdalii. A native of the eastern Himalayas, rarely glimpsed: it lived among the crowns of trees in mountain valleys, its caterpillars feeding on lianas. Jane held her breath, watching as its wings beat feebly. Without warning it lifted into the air. Jane cried out, falling onto her knees as she sprawled across the bed, cupping it quickly but carefully between her hands.

"Beautiful, beautiful," she crooned. She stepped from the bed, not daring to pause and examine it, and hurried into the kitchen. In the cupboard she found an empty jar, set it down and gingerly angled the lid from it, holding one hand with the butterfly against her breast. She swore, feeling its wings fluttering against her fingers, then quickly brought her hand to the jar's mouth, dropped the butterfly inside and screwed the lid back in place. It fluttered helplessly inside; she could see where the scales had already been scraped from its wing. Still swearing she ran back into the bedroom, putting the lights on and dragging her collection box from under the bed. She grabbed a vial of ethyl alcohol, went back into the kitchen and tore a bit of paper towel from the rack. She opened the vial, poured a few drops of ethyl alcohol onto the paper, opened the jar, and gently tilted it onto its side. She slipped the paper inside, very slowly tipping the jar upright once more, until the paper had settled on the bottom, the butterfly on top of it. Its wings beat frantically for a few moments, then stopped. Its proboscis uncoiled, finer than a hair. Slowly Jane drew her own hand to her brow and ran it along the length of the antennae there. She sat there staring at it until the sun leaked through the wooden shutters in the kitchen window. The butterfly did not move again.

•

The next day passed in a metallic gray haze, the only color the black and saturated yellow of the *lidderdalii's* wings, burned upon Jane's eyes as though she had looked into the sun. When she finally roused herself, she felt a spasm of panic at the sight of the boy's clothes on the bedroom floor.

"Shit." She ran her hand across her head, was momentarily startled to recall she had no hair. "Now what?"

She stood there for a few minutes, thinking, then gathered the clothes—striped V-neck sweater, jeans, socks, jockey shorts, Timberlake knockoff shoes—and dumped them into a plastic Sainsbury's bag. There was a wallet in the jeans pocket. She opened it, gazed impassively at a driver's license—KENNETH REED, WOLVER-HAMPTON—and a few five-pound notes. She pocketed the money, took the license into the bathroom and burned it, letting the ashes drop into the toilet. Then she went outside.

It was early Sunday morning, no one about except for a young mother pushing a baby in a stroller. In the neighboring doorway the same drunk old man sprawled, surrounded by empty bottles and rubbish. He stared blearily up at Jane as she approached.

"Here," she said. She bent and dropped the five-pound notes into his scabby hand.

"God bless you, darlin'." He coughed, his eyes focusing on neither Jane nor the notes. "God bless you."

She turned and walked briskly back toward the canal path. There were few waste bins in Camden Town, and so each day trash accumulated in rank heaps along the path, beneath streetlights, in vacant alleys. Street cleaners and sweeping machines then daily cleared it all away again: like elves, Jane thought. As she walked along the canal path she dropped the shoes in one pile of rubbish, tossed the sweater alongside a single high-heeled shoe in the market, stuffed the underwear and socks into a collapsing cardboard box filled with rotting lettuce, and left the jeans beside a stack of papers outside an unopened newsagent's shop. The wallet she tied into the Sainsbury's bag and dropped into an overflowing trash bag outside of Boots. Then she retraced her steps, stopping in front of a shop window filled with tatty polyester lingerie in large sizes and boldly artificial-looking wigs: pink afros, platinum blond falls, black-and-white Cruella DeVil tresses.

The door was propped open; Schubert lieder played softly on 32. Jane stuck her head in and looked around, saw a beefy man behind the register, cashing out. He had orange lipstick smeared around his mouth and delicate silver fish hanging from his ears.

"We're not open yet. Eleven on Sunday," he said without looking up.

"I'm just looking." Jane sidled over to a glass shelf where four wigs sat on styrofoam heads. One had very glossy black hair in a chin-length flapper bob. Jane tried it on, eyeing herself in a grimy mirror. "How much is this one?"

"Fifteen. But we're not—"

"Here. Thanks!" Jane stuck a twenty-pound note on the counter and ran from the shop. When she reached the corner she slowed, pirouetted to catch her reflection in a shop window. She stared at herself, grinning, then walked the rest of the way home, exhilarated and faintly dizzy.

⊶

Monday morning she went to the zoo to begin her volunteer work. She had mounted the *Bhutanitis lidderdalii* on a piece of styrofoam with a piece of paper on it, to keep the butterfly's legs from becoming embedded in the styrofoam. She'd softened it first, putting it into a jar with damp paper, removed it and placed it on the mounting platform, neatly spearing its thorax—a little to the right—with a #2 pin. She propped it carefully on the wainscoting beside the hawkmoth, and left.

She arrived and found her ID badge waiting for her at the staff entrance. It was a clear morning, warmer than it had been for a week; the long hairs on her brow vibrated as though they were wires that had been plucked. Beneath the wig her shaved head felt hot and moist, the first new hairs starting to prickle across her scalp. Her nose itched where her glasses pressed against it. Jane walked, smiling, past the gibbons howling in their habitat and the pygmy hippos floating calmly in their pool, their eyes shut, green bubbles breaking around them like little fish. In front of the Insect Zoo a uniformed woman was unloading sacks of meal from a golf cart.

"Morning," Jane called cheerfully, and went inside.

She found David Bierce standing in front of a temperature gauge beside a glass cage holding the hissing cockroaches.

"Something happened last night, the damn things got too cold." He glanced over, handed her a clipboard and began to remove the top of the gauge. "I called Operations but they're at their fucking morning meeting. Fucking computers—"

He stuck his hand inside the control box and flicked angrily at the gauge. "You know anything about computers?"

"Not this kind." Jane brought her face up to the cage's glass front. Inside were half a dozen glossy roaches, five inches long and the color of pale maple syrup. They lay, unmoving, near a glass petri dish filled with what looked like damp brown sugar. "Are they dead?"

"Those things? They're fucking immortal. You could stamp on one and it wouldn't die. Believe me, I've done it." He continued to fiddle with the gauge, finally sighed and replaced the lid. "Well, let's let the boys over in Ops handle it. Come on, I'll get you started."

He gave her a brief tour of the lab, opening drawers full of dissecting instruments, mounting platforms, pins; showed her where the food for the various insects was kept in a series of small refrigerators. Sugar syrup, cornstarch, plastic containers full of smaller insects, grubs and mealworms, tiny gray beetles. "Mostly we just keep on top of replacing the ones that die," David explained, "that and making sure the plants don't develop the wrong kind of fungus. Nature takes her course and we just goose her along when she needs it. School groups are here constantly, but the docents handle that. You're more than welcome to talk to them, if that's the sort of thing you want to do."

He turned from where he'd been washing empty jars at a small sink, dried his hands, and walked over to sit on top of a desk. "It's not terribly glamorous work here." He reached down for a styrofoam cup of coffee and sipped from it, gazing at her coolly. "We're none of us working on our PhDs anymore."

Jane shrugged. "That's all right."

"It's not even all that interesting. I mean, it can be very repetitive. Tedious."

"I don't mind." A sudden pang of anxiety made Jane's voice break. She could feel her face growing hot, and quickly looked away. "Really," she said sullenly.

"Suit yourself. Coffee's over there; you'll probably have to clean yourself a cup, though." He cocked his head, staring at her curiously, then said, "Did you do something different with your hair?"

She nodded once, brushing the edge of her bangs with a finger. "Yeah."

"Nice. Very Louise Brooks." He hopped from the desk and crossed to a computer set up in the corner. "You can use my computer if you need to, I'll give you the password later."

Jane nodded, her flush fading into relief. "How many people work here?"

"Actually, we're short-staffed here right now—no money for hiring and our grant's run out. It's pretty much just me, and whoever Carolyn sends over from the docents. Sweet little bluehairs mostly, they don't much like bugs. So it's providential you turned up, *Jane.*"

He said her name mockingly, gave her a crooked grin. "You said you have experience mounting? Well, I try to save as many of the dead specimens as I can, and when there's any slow days, which there never are, I mount them and use them for the workshops I do with the schools that come in. What would be nice would be if we had enough specimens that I could give some to the teachers, to take back to their classrooms. We have a nice website and we might be able to work up some interactive programs. No schools are scheduled today, Monday's usually slow here. So if you could work on some of *those*—" He gestured to where several dozen cardboard boxes and glass jars were strewn across a countertop. "—that would be really brilliant," he ended, and turned to his computer screen.

She spent the morning mounting insects. Few were interesting or unusual: a number of brown hairstreaks, some Camberwell Beauties, three hissing cockroaches, several brimstones. But there was a single *Acherontia atropos*, the Death's head hawkmoth, the pattern of gray and brown and pale yellow scales on the back of its thorax forming the image of a human skull. Its proboscis was unfurled, the twin points sharp enough to pierce a finger: Jane touched it gingerly, wincing delightedly as a pinprick of blood appeared on her fingertip.

"You bring lunch?"

She looked away from the bright magnifying light she'd been using and blinked in surprise. "Lunch?"

David Bierce laughed. "Enjoying yourself? Well, that's good, makes the day go faster. Yes, lunch!" He rubbed his hands together, the harsh light making him look gnomelike, his sharp features malevolent and leering. "They have some decent fish and chips at the stall over by the cats. Come on, I'll treat you. Your first day."

They sat at a picnic table beside the food booth and ate. David pulled a bottle of ale from his knapsack and shared it with Jane. Overhead scattered clouds like smoke moved swiftly southwards. An Indian woman with three small boys sat at another table, the boys tossing fries at seagulls that swept down, shrieking, and made the smallest boy wail.

"Rain later," David said, staring at the sky. "Too bad." He sprinkled vinegar on his fried haddock and looked at Jane. "So did you go out over the weekend?"

She stared at the table and smiled. "Yeah, I did. It was fun."

"Where'd you go? The Electric Ballroom?"

"God, no. This other place." She glanced at his hand resting on the table beside her. He had long fingers, the knuckles slightly enlarged; but the back of his hand was smooth, the same soft brown as the *Acherontia's* wingtips. Her brows prickled, warmth trickling from them like water. When she lifted her head she could smell him, some kind of musky soap, salt; the bittersweet ale on his breath.

"Yeah? Where? I haven't been out in months, I'd be lost in Camden Town these days."

"I dunno. The Hive?"

She couldn't imagine he would have heard of it—far too old. But he swiveled on the bench, his eyebrows arching with feigned shock. "You went to *Hive*? And they let you in?"

"Yes," Jane stammered. "I mean, I didn't know—it was just a dance club. I just—danced."

"Did you." David Bierce's gaze sharpened, his hazel eyes catching the sun and sending back an icy emerald glitter. "Did you."

She picked up the bottle of ale and began to peel the label from it. "Yes."

"Have a boyfriend, then?"

She shook her head, rolled a fragment of label into a tiny pill. "No."

"Stop that." His hand closed over hers. He drew it away from the bottle, letting it rest against the table edge. She swallowed: he kept his hand on top of hers, pressing it against the metal edge until she felt her scored palm begin to ache. Her eyes closed: she could feel herself floating, and see a dozen feet below her own form, slender, the wig beetle-black upon her skull, her wrist like a bent stalk. Abruptly his hand slid away and beneath the table, brushing her leg as he stooped to retrieve his knapsack.

"Time to get back to work," he said lightly, sliding from the bench and slinging his bag over his shoulder. The breeze lifted his long graying hair as he turned away. "I'll see you back there."

Overhead the gulls screamed and flapped, dropping bits of fried fish on the sidewalk. She stared at the table in front of her, the cardboard trays that held the remnants of lunch, and watched as a yellowjacket landed on a fleck of grease, its golden thorax swollen with moisture as it began to feed.

She did not return to Hive that night. Instead she wore a patchwork dress over her jeans and Doc Martens, stuffed the wig inside a drawer and headed to a small bar on Inverness Street. The fair day had turned to rain, black puddles like molten metal capturing the amber glow of traffic signals and streetlights.

There were only a handful of tables at Bar Ganza. Most of the customers stood on the sidewalk outside, drinking and shouting to be heard above the sound of wailing Spanish love songs. Jane fought her way inside, got a glass of red wine, and miraculously found an empty stool alongside the wall. She climbed onto it, wrapped her long legs around the pedestal, and sipped her wine.

"Hey. Nice hair." A man in his early thirties, his own head shaven, sidled up to Jane's stool. He held a cigarette, smoking it with quick, nervous gestures as he stared at her. He thrust his cigarette towards the ceiling, indicating a booming speaker. "You like the music?"

"Not particularly."

"Hey, you're American? Me too. Chicago. Good bud of mine, works for Citibank, he told me about this place. Food's not bad. Tapas. Baby octopus. You like octopus?"

Jane's eyes narrowed. The man wore expensive-looking corduroy trousers, a rumpled jacket of nubby charcoal-colored linen. "No," she said, but didn't turn away.

"Me neither. Like eating great big slimy bugs. Geoff Lanning—"

He stuck his hand out. She touched it, lightly, and smiled. "Nice to meet you, Geoff."

For the next half hour or so she pretended to listen to him, nodding and smiling brilliantly whenever he looked up at her. The bar grew louder and more crowded, and people began eyeing Jane's stool covetously.

"I think I'd better hand over this seat," she announced, hopping down and elbowing her way to the door. "Before they eat me."

Geoff Lanning hurried after her. "Hey, you want to get dinner? The Camden Brasserie's just up here—"

"No thanks." She hesitated on the curb, gazing demurely at her Doc Martens. "But would you like to come in for a drink?"

He was very impressed by her apartment. "Man, this place'd probably go for a half mil, easy! That's three quarters of a million American." He opened and closed cupboards, ran a hand lovingly across the slate sink. "Nice hardwood floors, high speed access—you never told me what you do."

Jane laughed. "As little as possible. Here—"

She handed him a brandy snifter, let her finger trace the top part of his wrist. "You look like kind of an adventurous sort of guy."

"Hey, big adventure, that's me." He lifted his glass to her. "What exactly did you have in mind? Big game hunting?"

"Mmm. Maybe."

It was more of a struggle this time, not for Geoff Lanning but for Jane. He lay complacently in his bonds, his stocky torso wriggling obediently when Jane commanded. Her head ached from the cheap wine at Bar Ganza; the long hairs above her eyes lay sleek against her skull, and did not move at all until she closed her eyes, and, unbidden, the image of David Bierce's hand covering hers appeared.

"Try to get away," she whispered.

"Whoa, Nellie," Geoff Lanning gasped.

"Try to get away," she repeated, her voice hoarser.

"Oh." The man whimpered softly. "Jesus Christ, what—oh my God, *what*—"

Quickly she bent and kissed his fingertips, saw where the leather cuff had bitten into his pudgy wrist. This time she was prepared when with a keening sound he began to twist upon the bed, his arms and legs shriveling and then coiling in upon themselves, his shaved head withdrawing into his tiny torso like a snail within its shell.

But she was not prepared for the creature that remained, its feathery antennae a trembling echo of her own, its extraordinarily elongated hind spurs nearly four inches long.

"*Oh*," she gasped.

She didn't dare touch it until it took to the air: the slender spurs fragile as icicles, scarlet, their saffron tips curling like Christmas ribbon, its large delicate wings saffron with slate-blue and scarlet eye-spots, and spanning nearly six inches. A Madagascan Moon Moth, one of the loveliest and rarest silk moths, and almost impossible to find as an intact specimen.

"What do I do with you, what do I do?" she crooned as it spread its wings and lifted from the bed. It flew in short sweeping arcs; she scrambled to blow out the candles before it could near them. She pulled on her kimono and left the lights off, closed the bedroom door and hurried into the kitchen, looking for a flashlight. She found nothing, but recalled Andrew telling her there was a large torch in the basement.

She hadn't been down there since her initial tour of the flat. It was brightly lit, with long neat cabinets against both walls, a floor-to-ceiling wine rack filled with bottles of claret and vintage burgundy, compact washer and dryer, small refrigerator, buckets and brooms waiting for the cleaning lady's weekly visit. She found the flashlight sitting on top of the refrigerator, a container of extra batteries beside it. She switched it on and off a few times, then glanced down at the refrigerator and absently opened it.

Seeing all that wine had made her think the little refrigerator might be filled with beer. Instead it held only a long plastic box, with a red lid and a red biohazard sticker on the side. Jane put the flashlight down and stooped, carefully removing the box and setting it on the floor. A label with Andrew's neat architectural handwriting was on the top.

DR. ANDREW FILDERMAN
ST. MARTIN'S HOSPICE

"Huh," she said, and opened it.

Inside there was a small red biohazard waste container, and scores of plastic bags filled with disposable hypodermics, ampules, and suppositories. All contained morphine at varying dosages. Jane stared, marveling, then opened one of the bags. She shook half a dozen morphine ampules into her palm, carefully reclosed the bag, put it back into the box, and returned the box to the refrigerator. Then she grabbed the flashlight and ran upstairs.

It took her a while to capture the moon moth. First she had to find a killing jar large enough, and then she had to very carefully lure it inside, so that its frail wing spurs wouldn't be damaged. She did this by positioning the jar on its side and placing a gooseneck lamp directly behind it, so that the bare bulb shone through the glass. After about fifteen minutes, the moth landed on top of the jar, its tiny legs slipping as it struggled on the smooth curved surface. Another few minutes and it had crawled inside, nestled on the wad of tissues Jane had set there, moist with ethyl alcohol. She screwed the lid on tightly, left the jar on its side, and waited for it to die.

❧

Over the next week she acquired three more specimens. *Papilio demetrius*, a Japanese swallowtail with elegant orange eyespots on a velvety black ground; a scarce copper, not scarce at all, really, but with lovely pumpkin-colored wings; and *Graphium agamemnon*, a Malaysian species with vivid green spots and chrome-yellow strips on its somber brown wings. She'd ventured away from Camden Town, capturing the swallowtail in a private room in an SM club in Islington and the *Graphium agamemnon* in a parked car behind a noisy pub in Crouch End. The scarce copper came from a vacant lot near the Tottenham Court Road tube station very late one night, where the wreckage of a chainlink fence stood in for her bedposts. She found the morphine to be useful, although she had to wait until immediately after the man ejaculated before pressing the ampule against his throat, aiming for the carotid artery. This way the butter-flies emerged already sedated, and in minutes died with no damage to their wings. Leftover clothing was easily disposed of, but she had to be more careful with wallets, stuffing them deep within rubbish bins, when she could, or burying them in her own trash bags and then watching as the waste trucks came by on their rounds.

In South Kensington she discovered an entomological supply store. There she bought more mounting supplies, and inquired casually as to whether the owner might be interested in purchasing some specimens.

He shrugged. "Depends. What you got?"

"Well, right now I have only one *Argema mittrei*." Jane adjusted her glasses and glanced around the shop. A lot of morphos, an Atlas moth: nothing too unusual. "But I might be getting another, in which case . . . "

"Moon moth, eh? How'd you come by that, I wonder?" The man raised his eyebrows, and Jane flushed. "Don't worry, I'm not going to turn you in. Christ, I'd go out of business. Well, obviously I can't display those in the shop, but if you want to part with one, let me know. I'm always scouting for my customers."

She began volunteering three days a week at the insect zoo. One Wednesday, the night after she'd gotten a gorgeous *Urania leilus*, its wings sadly damaged by rain, she arrived to see David Bierce reading that morning's *Camden New Journal*. He peered above the newspaper and frowned.

"You still going out alone at night?"

She froze, her mouth dry; turned and hurried over to the coffee-maker. "Why?" she said, fighting to keep her tone even.

"Because there's an article about some of the clubs around here. Apparently a few people have gone missing."

"Really?" Jane got her coffee, wiping up a spill with the side of her hand. "What happened?"

"Nobody knows. Two blokes reported gone, family frantic, sort of thing. Probably just runaways. Camden Town eats them alive, kids." He handed the paper to Jane. "Although one of them was last seen near Highbury Fields, some sex club there."

She scanned the article. There was no mention of any suspects. And no bodies had been found, although foul play was suspected. ("*Ken would never have gone away without notifying us or his employer. . . .*")

Anyone with any information was urged to contact the police.

"I don't go to sex clubs," Jane said flatly. "Plus those are both guys."

"Mmm." David leaned back in his chair, regarding her coolly. "You're the one hitting Hive your first weekend in London."

"It's a *dance* club!" Jane retorted. She laughed, rolled the newspaper into a tube, and batted him gently on the shoulder. "Don't worry. I'll be careful."

David continued to stare at her, hazel eyes glittering. "Who says it's you I'm worried about?"

She smiled, her mouth tight as she turned and began cleaning bottles in the sink.

It was a raw day, more late November than mid-May. Only two school groups were scheduled; otherwise the usual stream of visitors was reduced to a handful of elderly women who shook their heads over the cockroaches and gave barely a glance to the butterflies before shuffling on to another building. David Bierce paced restlessly through the lab on his way to clean the cages and make more complaints to the Operations Division. Jane cleaned and mounted two stag beetles, their spiny legs pricking her fingertips as she tried to force the pins through their glossy chestnut-colored shells. Afterwards she busied herself with straightening the clutter of cabinets and drawers stuffed with requisition forms and microscopes, computer parts and dissection kits.

It was well past two when David reappeared, his anorak slick with rain, his hair tucked beneath the hood. "Come on," he announced, standing impatiently by the open door. "Let's go to lunch."

Jane looked up from the computer where she'd been updating a specimen list. "I'm really not very hungry," she said, giving him an apologetic smile. "You go ahead."

"Oh, for Christ's sake." David let the door slam shut as he crossed to her, his sneakers leaving wet smears on the tiled floor. "That can wait till tomorrow. Come on, there's not a fucking thing here that needs doing."

"But—" She gazed up at him. The hood slid from his head; his gray-streaked hair hung loose to his shoulders, and the sheen of rain on his sharp cheekbones made him look carved from oiled wood. "What if somebody comes?"

"A very nice docent named Mrs. Eleanor Feltwell is out there, *even as we speak*, in the unlikely event that we have a single visitor."

He stooped so that his head was beside hers, scowling as he stared at the computer screen. A lock of his hair fell to brush against her neck. Beneath the wig her scalp burned, as though stung by tiny ants; she breathed in the warm acrid smell of his sweat and something else, a sharper scent, like crushed oak-mast or fresh-sawn wood. Above her brows the antennae suddenly quivered. Sweetness coated her tongue like burnt syrup. With a rush of panic she turned her head so he wouldn't see her face.

"I—I should finish this—"

"Oh, just *fuck* it, Jane! It's not like we're *paying* you. Come on, now, there's a good girl—"

He took her hand and pulled her to her feet, Jane still looking away. The bangs of her cheap wig scraped her forehead and she batted at them feebly. "Get your things. What, don't you ever take days off in the States?"

"All right, all right." She turned and gathered her black vinyl raincoat and knapsack, pulled on the coat and waited for him by the door. "Jeez, you must be hungry," she said crossly.

"No. Just fucking bored out of my skull. Have you been to Ruby in the Dust? No? I'll take you then, let's go—"

The restaurant was down the High Street, a small, cheerfully claptrap place, dim in the gray afternoon, its small wooden tables scattered with abandoned newspapers and overflowing ashtrays. David Bierce ordered a steak and a pint. Jane had a small salad, nasturtium blossoms strewn across pale green lettuce, and a glass of red wine. She lacked an appetite lately, living on vitamin-enhanced, fruity bottled drinks from the health food store and baklava from a Greek bakery near the tube station.

"So." David Bierce stabbed a piece of steak, peering at her sideways. "Don't tell me you really haven't been here before."

"I haven't!" Despite her unease at being with him, she laughed, and caught her reflection in the wall-length mirror. A thin plain young woman in shapeless Peruvian sweater and jeans, bad haircut and ugly glasses. Gazing at herself she felt suddenly stronger, invisible. She tilted her head and smiled at Bierce. "The food's good."

"So you don't have someone taking you out to dinner every night? Cooking for you? I thought you American girls all had adoring men at your feet. Adoring slaves," he added dryly. "Or slave girls, I suppose. If that's your thing."

"No." She stared at her salad, shook her head demurely and took a sip of wine. It made her feel even more invulnerable. "No, I—"

"Boyfriend back home, right?" He finished his pint, flagged the waiter to order another, and turned back to Jane. "Well, that's nice. That's very nice—for him," he added, and gave a short harsh laugh.

The waiter brought another pint, and more wine for Jane. "Oh really, I better—"

"Just drink it, Jane." Under the table, she felt a sharp pressure on her foot. She wasn't wearing her Doc Martens today but a pair of red plastic jellies. David Bierce had planted his heel firmly atop her toes; she sucked in her breath in shock and pain, the bones of her foot crackling as she tried to pull it from beneath him. Her antennae rippled, then stiffened, and heat burst like a seed inside her.

"Go ahead," he said softly, pushing the wineglass towards her. "Just a sip, that's right—"

She grabbed the glass, spilling wine on her sweater as she gulped at it. The vicious pressure on her foot subsided, but as the wine ran down her throat she could feel the heat thrusting her into the air, currents rushing beneath her as the girl at the table below set down her wineglass with trembling fingers.

"There." David Bierce smiled, leaning forward to gently cup her hand between his. "Now this is better than working. Right, Jane?"

——

He walked her home along the canal path. Jane tried to dissuade him, but he'd had a third pint by then; it didn't seem to make him drunk but coldly obdurate, and she finally gave in. The rain had turned to a fine drizzle, the canal's usually murky water silvered and softly gleaming in the twilight. They passed few other people, and Jane found herself wishing someone else would appear, so that she'd have an excuse to move closer to David Bierce. He kept close to the canal itself, several feet from Jane; when the breeze lifted she could catch his oaky scent again, rising above the dank reek of stagnant water and decaying hawthorn blossom.

They crossed over the bridge to approach her flat by the street. At the front sidewalk Jane stopped, smiled shyly, and said, "Thanks. That was nice."

David nodded. "Glad I finally got you out of your cage." He lifted his head to gaze appraisingly at the row house. "Christ, this where you're staying? You split the rent with someone?"

"No." She hesitated: she couldn't remember what she had told him about her living arrangements. But before she could blurt something out he stepped past her to the front door, peeking into the window and bobbing impatiently up and down.

"Mind if I have a look? Professional entomologists don't often get the chance to see how the quality live."

Jane hesitated, her stomach clenching; decided it would be safer to have him in, rather than continue to put him off.

"All right," she said reluctantly, and opened the door.

"Mmmm. Nice, nice, very nice." He swept around the living room, spinning on his heel and making a show of admiring the elaborate molding, the tribal rugs, the fireplace mantel with its thick ecclesiastical candles and ormolu mirror. "Goodness, all this for a wee thing like you? You're a clever cat, landing on your feet here, Lady Jane."

She blushed. He bounded past her on his way into the bedroom, touching her shoulder; she had to close her eyes as a fiery wave surged through her and her antennae trembled.

"*Wow*," he exclaimed.

Slowly she followed him into the bedroom. He stood in front of the wall where her specimens were balanced in a neat line across the wainscoting. His eyes were wide, his mouth open in genuine astonishment.

"Are these *yours*?" he marveled, his gaze fixed on the butterflies. "You didn't actually catch them—?"

She shrugged.

"These are incredible!" He picked up the *Graphium agamemnon* and tilted it to the pewter-colored light falling through the French doors. "Did you mount them, too?"

She nodded, crossing to stand beside him. "Yeah. You can tell, with that one—" She pointed at the *Urania leilus* in its oak-framed box. "It got rained on."

David Bierce replaced the *Graphium agamemnon* and began to read the labels on the others.

> Papilio demetrius
> UNITED KINGDOM: LONDON
> Highbury Fields, Islington

7.V.2001
J. Kendall

Loepa katinka
UNITED KINGDOM: LONDON
Finsbury Park
09.V.2001
J. Kendall

Argema mittrei
UNITED KINGDOM: LONDON
Camden Town
13.IV.2001
J. Kendall

He shook his head. "You screwed up, though—you wrote 'London' for all of them." He turned to her, grinning wryly. "Can't think of the last time I saw a moon moth in Camden Town."

She forced a laugh. "Oh—right."

"And, I mean, you can't have actually *caught* them—"

He held up the *Loepa katinka*, a butter-yellow Emperor moth, its peacock's-eyes russet and jet-black. "I haven't seen any of these around lately. Not even in Finsbury."

Jane made a little grimace of apology. "Yeah. I meant, that's where I found them—where I bought them."

"Mmmm." He set the moth back on its ledge. "You'll have to share your sources with me. I can never find things like these in North London."

He turned and headed out of the bedroom. Jane hurriedly straightened the specimens, her hands shaking now as well, and followed him.

"Well, Lady Jane." For the first time he looked at her without his usual mocking arrogance, his green-flecked eyes bemused, almost regretful. "I think we managed to salvage something from the day."

He turned, gazing one last time at the flat's glazed walls and highly waxed floors, the imported cabinetry and jewel-toned carpets.

"I was going to say, when I walked you home, that you needed someone to take care of you. But it looks like you've managed that on your own."

Jane stared at her feet. He took a step toward her, the fragrance of oak-mast and honey filling her nostrils, crushed acorns, new fern. She grew dizzy, her hand lifting to find him; but he only reached to graze her cheek with his finger.

"Night then, Jane," he said softly, and walked back out into the misty evening.

⸺

When he was gone she raced to the windows and pulled all the velvet curtains, then tore the wig from her head and threw it onto the couch along with her glasses. Her heart was pounding, her face slick with sweat—from fear or rage or disappointment, she didn't know. She yanked off her sweater and jeans, left them on the living room floor and stomped into the bathroom. She stood in the shower for twenty minutes, head upturned as the water sluiced the smells of bracken and leaf-mold from her skin.

Finally she got out. She dried herself, let the towel drop, and went into the kitchen. Abruptly she was famished. She tore open cupboards and drawers until she found a half-full jar of lavender honey from Provence. She opened it, the top spinning off into the sink, and frantically spooned honey into her mouth with her fingers. When she was finished she grabbed a jar of lemon curd and ate most of that, until she felt as though she might be sick. She stuck her head into the sink, letting water run from the faucet into her mouth, and at last walked, surfeited, into the bedroom.

She dressed, feeling warm and drowsy, almost dreamlike; pulling on red-and-yellow-striped stockings, her nylon skirt, a tight red T-shirt. No bra, no panties. She put in her contacts, then examined herself in the mirror. Her hair had begun to grow back, a scant velvety stubble, bluish in the dim light. She drew a sweeping black line across each eyelid, on a whim took the liner and extended the curve of each antenna until they touched her temples. She painted her lips black as well and went to find her black vinyl raincoat.

It was early when she went out, far too early for any of the clubs to be open. The rain had stopped, but a thick greasy fog covered everything, coating windshields and shop windows, making Jane's face feel as though it were encased in a clammy shell. For hours she wandered Camden Town, huge violet eyes turning to stare back at the men who watched her, dismissing each of them. Once she thought she saw David Bierce coming out of Ruby in the Dust, but when she stopped to watch him cross the street it was not David but someone else. Much younger, his long dark hair in a thick braid, his feet clad in knee-high boots. He crossed the High Street, heading towards the tube station. Jane hesitated, then darted after him.

He went to the Electric Ballroom. Fifteen or so people stood out front, talking quietly. The man she'd followed joined the line, standing by himself. Jane waited across the street, until the door opened and the little crowd began to shuffle inside. After the long-haired young man had entered, she counted to one hundred, crossed the street, paid her cover, and went inside.

The club had three levels; she finally tracked him down on the uppermost one. Even on a rainy Wednesday night it was crowded, the sound system blaring Idris Mohammed and Jimmie Cliff. He was standing alone near the bar, drinking bottled water.

"Hi!" she shouted, swaying up to him with her best First Day of School Smile. "Want to dance?"

He was older than she'd thought—thirtyish, still not as old as Bierce. He stared at her, puzzled, then shrugged. "Sure."

They danced, passing the water bottle between them. "What's your name?" he shouted.

"Cleopatra Brimstone."

"You're kidding!" he yelled back. The song ended in a bleat of feedback, and they walked, panting, back to the bar.

"What, you know another Cleopatra?" Jane asked teasingly.

"No. It's just a crazy name, that's all." He smiled. He was handsomer than David Bierce, his features softer, more rounded, his eyes dark brown, his manner a bit reticent. "I'm Thomas Raybourne. Tom."

He bought another bottle of Pellegrino and one for Jane. She drank it quickly, trying to get his measure. When she finished she set the empty bottle on the floor and fanned herself with her hand.

"It's hot in here." Her throat hurt from shouting over the music. "I think I'm going to take a walk. Feel like coming?"

He hesitated, glancing around the club. "I was supposed to meet a friend here . . . " he began, frowning. "But—"

"Oh." Disappointment filled her, spiking into desperation. "Well, that's okay. I guess."

"Oh, what the hell." He smiled: he had nice eyes, a more stolid, reassuring gaze than Bierce. "I can always come back."

Outside she turned right, in the direction of the canal. "I live pretty close by. Feel like coming in for a drink?"

He shrugged again. "I don't drink, actually."

"Something to eat then? It's not far—just along the canal path a few blocks past Camden Lock—"

"Yeah, sure."

They made desultory conversation. "You should be careful," he said as they crossed the bridge. "Did you read about those people who've gone missing in Camden Town?"

Jane nodded but said nothing. She felt anxious and clumsy—as though she'd drunk too much, although she'd had nothing since the two glasses of wine with David Bierce. Her companion also seemed ill at ease; he kept glancing back, as though looking for someone on the canal path behind them.

"I should have tried to call," he explained ruefully. "But I forgot to recharge my mobile."

"You could call from my place."

"No, that's all right."

She could tell from his tone that he was figuring how he could leave, gracefully, as soon as possible.

Inside the flat he settled on the couch, picked up a copy of *Time Out* and flipped through it, pretending to read. Jane went immediately into the kitchen and poured herself a glass of brandy. She downed it, poured a second one, and joined him on the couch.

"So." She kicked off her Doc Martens, drew her stockinged foot slowly up his leg, from calf to thigh. "Where you from?"

He was passive, so passive she wondered if he would get aroused at all. But after a while they were lying on the couch, both their shirts on the floor, his pants unzipped and his cock stiff, pressing against her bare belly.

"Let's go in there," Jane whispered hoarsely. She took his hand and led him into the bedroom.

She only bothered lighting a single candle, before lying beside him on the bed. His eyes were half-closed, his breathing shallow. When she ran a fingernail around one nipple he made a small surprised sound, then quickly turned and pinned her to the bed.

"Wait! Slow down," Jane said, and wriggled from beneath him. For the last week she'd left the bonds attached to the bedposts, hiding them beneath the covers when not in use. Now she grabbed one of the wristcuffs and pulled it free. Before he could see what she was doing it was around his wrist.

"Hey!"

She dove for the foot of the bed, his leg narrowly missing her as it thrashed against the covers. It was more difficult to get this in place, but she made a great show of giggling and stroking his thigh, which seemed to calm him. The other leg was next, and finally she leapt from the bed and darted to the headboard, slipping from his grasp when he tried to grab her shoulder.

"This is not consensual," he said. She couldn't tell if he was serious or not.

"What about this, then?" she murmured, sliding down between his legs and cupping his erect penis between her hands. "This seems to be enjoying itself."

He groaned softly, shutting his eyes. "Try to get away," she said. "Try to get away."

He tried to lunge upward, his body arcing so violently that she drew back in alarm. The bonds held; he arched again, and again, but now she remained beside him, her hands on his cock, his breath coming faster and faster and her own breath keeping pace with it, her heart pounding and the tingling above her eyes almost unbearable.

"Try to get away," she gasped. "Try to get away—"

When he came he cried out, his voice harsh, as though in pain, and Jane cried out as well, squeezing her eyes shut as spasms shook her from head to groin. Quickly her head dipped to kiss his chest; then she shuddered and drew back, watching.

His voice rose again, ended suddenly in a shrill wail, as his limbs knotted and shriveled like burning rope. She had a final glimpse of him, a homunculus sprouting too many legs. Then on the bed before her a perfectly formed *Papilio krishna* swallowtail crawled across the rumpled duvet, its wings twitching to display glittering green scales amidst spectral washes of violet and crimson and gold.

"Oh, you're beautiful, beautiful," she whispered.

From across the room echoed a sound: soft, the rustle of her kimono falling from its hook as the door swung open. She snatched her hand from the butterfly and stared, through the door to the living room.

In her haste to get Thomas Raybourne inside she had forgotten to latch the front door. She scrambled to her feet, naked, staring wildly at the shadow looming in front of her, its features taking shape as it approached the candle, brown and black, light glinting across his face.

It was David Bierce. The scent of oak and bracken swelled, suffocating, fragrant, cut by the bitter odor of ethyl alcohol. He forced her gently onto the bed, heat piercing her breast and thighs, her antennae bursting out like flame from her brow and wings exploding everywhere around her as she struggled fruitlessly.

"Now. Try to get away," he said.

PAVANE FOR A
PRINCE OF THE AIR

When I came back from visiting my family at Christmas, Tina's message was on the answering machine. I hadn't even taken my coat off, just dumped a suitcase on the floor as the kids ran past and I punched the play button. The voice was so faint I had to play it back three times to decipher parts of it, and then another two times to make sure it was Tina's voice at all; and finally one last time to convince myself that this was real, this was happening, this was how one part of my life was going to play out.

Carrie, it's Tina. Something really, really bad has happened. Cal's in the hospital, he got sick the day after Christmas. He has brain cancer. I'm taking him home tonight, I'll call you later.

I had seen them three days before. Everything was fine then.

Click.

➵

This was what was supposed to happen: me and Tina and Cal had been talking off and on for years about buying land, starting a commune, maybe here in Maine or up in Nova Scotia, someplace where we and a few of our friends could live together as we got older. The getting older part hadn't started yet, of course, not in earnest. Tina and I were the same age, forty-two, Cal had ten years on us, and most of our friends fell into the same demographic, skewing a few years older or younger but with the same dazed, weathered look of people whose party-barge ran aground while they were sleeping, and who now found themselves wandering about onshore, looking for fellow survivors, bits of sea-wrack to salvage, anyone got some smoke? Boisterously or apologetically middle-aged, their appetites—for sex, drugs, booze, music, magic, general larking about—tempered by time but not diminished, not extinguished, no not yet.

Yet.

I wrote a story about these people, I have written a lot of stories about them. In the stories things happen. People get sick but magic saves them, or else the world ends but then everyone dies anyway, which makes it easier, not so much to clean up. But no matter what happens in the stories, when they were finished, I could call them, Cal and Tina, on the phone and we could have dinner, they could smoke pot and I could drink red wine and we could watch a movie, something about King Arthur or pirates, something with Uma Thurman or Johnny Depp in it. Then we'd go home and the next day we'd talk on the phone and make plans for next time.

Then this happened.

→←

I never found out exactly what kind of brain cancer it was. Cal and Tina were not the sort of people who remembered and reported details from the oncology reports. I was going to find out what kind, only it all came down so fast, it was like a freak storm, spring snow, thunder in December; and pretty soon it was obvious that knowing what kind wouldn't make any difference.

It was lung cancer that metastasized to the brain. Cal had been having headaches for the last few weeks, but figured it was pressure from work—he was designing sets for an independent film, an adaptation of an early Stephen King story scheduled to begin shooting in Bangor right after New Year's. The day after Christmas, Cal felt so nauseated he could do nothing but lie down with a towel covering his eyes; it finally got so bad Tina took him to the ER, fearing it was food poisoning. The ER doctor thought it might be meningitis, and ordered a CAT scan. The CAT scan showed it wasn't meningitis but a constellation of small black stars, the largest slowly going nova, engulfing his optic nerve.

Tina didn't bring him home that night. They were at the hospital for two more days. I spent that time in bed, too stunned to do anything but down valerian capsules and Nyquil, trying to be anything but awake. Robert took care of the kids. As I slept I realized I had been dreaming this for the past year or more, recurring dreams with an urgency attached to my finding Cal, to seeing him as soon as I could. After waking from these dreams I called him and Tina, making arrangements to get together, dinners at their place where Cal made enchiladas with tomatillo sauce, dinners where Tina and my daughter sat in a corner whispering while Cal told me stories about his years with the Merry Pranksters in San Francisco, his stint as one of the first people to deal LSD, flying coast-to-coast with vials and blotters of Owsley acid, selling to rock bands and socialites and university professors. He told me about his years in Nepal, where he'd seen the corpse of a young man burning on a pyre on the rock-strewn road outside Katmandu. He and his first wife lived ten miles outside the city; they would walk back and forth every day, buying and trading rugs, temple bells, cakes of hashish, statues of demons and gods, prayer wheels. Later they moved back to Austin, where Cal sold antiquities and cocaine to private collectors and rock bands. That was where he'd met Tina. She was twenty-three and working at a radio station. He was thirty-three and called the station incessantly, to request "Tupelo Honey." Three months later they got married and moved to live on a wooden sailboat in Maine.

"I'm having a hard time adjusting to this," he whispered when I finally saw him, when Tina finally brought him home from the hospital in Bangor. There were tears in his eyes. He wore what he always wore, an extravagantly embroidered shirt and bell-bottoms, wool or denim depending on the time of year, wool now, a week after Christmas. His hands were on his knees, the skin asphalt-grey and stretched so that as I lay my hand on his I could feel bone and vein and muscle beneath, sharp as the tines of a rake. "Those doctors, they looked at me. Fifty-two, no kids, a man, cigarettes. They said all they could do was check me in. They said I should just check in and stay there till I die."

I grabbed his shoulders and hugged him. "I'm right here. We're all going to be here. We'll all help."

Tina told me later that she had already made the arrangements with the hospice in Ellsworth, for nurses to come check him daily. Cal would not go back to the hospital. They had no health insurance. There would be no chemo or radiation treatments, no second opinion. They would try other things. I told her about someone I knew, a nutritionist who worked with cancer patients. Tina had heard of an alternative treatment made from Venus Fly Trap. It was only available in Germany; when Cal felt better they were going to Germany to try it.

"He doesn't want to do anything," Tina whispered when Cal went to the bathroom. He was throwing up a lot, from the tumor's pressure on the optic nerve. It was like being seasick twenty-four hours a day. "I can't push him, it's not my decision." Her voice was breaking with anger. "It's his life and he has to make his own decision."

"What about some sort of operation?" I asked. "Wouldn't that relieve the pressure, at least?"

She shook her head. "A long time ago a shaman told Cal never to let anyone cut him. He won't have any surgery."

So that was that. In the meantime, the phone rang nonstop and the machine picked up the messages, hours worth of messages: from other pagans, massage therapists, nurses, acupuncturists, carpenters, boatbuilders, filmmakers, lapsed Episcopalians from the Unitarian Church where Cal and Tina performed solstice rituals.

"I can help," I said. I had cared for terminally ill people, and lived with my grandmothers when they were dying. "I know how to do this."

"We're going to need you, Carrie," she said. "All of you. Probably very soon."

It happened fast. For two weeks I helped out when I could, driving Cal to a dentist appointment, staying with him while Tina was at her job as an assistant to a documentary filmmaker. He couldn't drive anymore.

"He can't be left alone. He has seizures. Kenny and Lisa next door can come over if you have to leave."

Outside it was snowing. For the last few years we'd had little or no snow, only ice storms. This winter it snowed, it seemed to snow every day. Sometimes I had to leave Cal because school was canceled and I had to go meet my kids; I'd call Kenny and Lisa and they would come and sit with him, keep the woodstove going, roll him joints and cigarettes. He had a medical prescription for marijuana, something that he and Tina were gleefully triumphant about. Marijuana, laetrile, apricot kernels. I wondered what would happen if I got stopped by the police, driving around with Cal next to me smoking a joint.

"Do you carry your doctor's note with you?" I asked.

"Always." He laughed but very quietly, so he wouldn't start to cough. That was one of the things you had to get used to, laughing was like talking for Cal, he always laughed, stoned or not. Now he was so quiet.

During one snowstorm while he could still talk we sat and he saved my book. He always helped me, reading my books and telling me, usually too late, what I'd done wrong. He was an avid and acute reader, loved heroic fantasy and Arthurian epics. My own books were too dark for his taste but he read them because he loved me.

"The last one was really good, Carrie. But it's sort of the same, isn't it? You have the plucky heroine and her cynical best friend sidekick and the blood sacrifice."

"And sex," said Tina. "Don't forget the sex."

"And sex. But they're always so young. You should write about grownups now, Carrie."

I hadn't written much for months. I was depressed, battling the black dog for the hundredth time. It was only in the weeks before Christmas that I'd started to feel better.

Still, in the past I'd always managed to write, even through the worst parts. But since last summer this novel felt dead. The voices in my head had gone silent, and more terrible than any despair or fear was the discovery, day after day, that they would no longer speak to me.

"I need you to help me with my book, Cal." We were sitting in their living room, Tina putting on boots and parka and funny Laplander hat, getting ready to leave. "You too, Tina."

She smiled. "Cal will be better than I am."

All three of us knew this was something for Cal, something for him to look forward to: he loved talking about writing, about stories, about magicians and shamans and drugs.

I ran my hands through my hair. "I'm completely stalled. I'll tell you the story, okay, Cal? I'll tell you what I've done so far. All the elements are there but I don't know what to do with them, I can't see it anymore."

He could see it. While the snow fell outside and the wind hammered the windows and Tina drove to an appointment in Skowhegan, I sat and told Cal my story, and he fixed it. He blinked a lot because his eyes hurt, but he laughed too, and paced back and forth like he used to. For a few hours we talked, me spinning my story and Cal smoothing it out. By the time the call came that school had been canceled, again, we had finished.

"You're amazing." I hugged him and we both laughed. "You're a miracle worker. You saved my ass."

"I'm really glad, Carrie." He smiled, tired but happy. I helped him back into his chair.

"Robert's been trying to help me too, he's been trying but it's different, he has a different point of view."

Cal smiled again. "He doesn't believe in it."

"That's right." I hugged and kissed him goodbye. "Jesus, Cal, thank you. I'll be back tomorrow—"

I could never say, to him or Tina, that I didn't believe in it, either. But that night I dreamed I was in the city, in a vast apartment building that's a frequent site for my dreams; and there I met all the characters from my books, the characters and the people they were based on, coming by to say hello like guests at a party, a few of them introducing their real-life counterparts to me. When I woke the structure of my novel was as clear to me as if I had been given a map.

So I'm not sure what I believe in anymore.

—•—

Cal and Tina believed in everything. Fairies, elves, spirits of earth air water fire; Tibetan gods, Minoan sea goddesses, totemic animals, reincarnation, Iroquois spirits. Their names for each other were Fox and Wolf; when they were married, nineteen years before, it was a marriage by capture, with Tina and her attendants dressed as sprites and Cal and his men like Fafhrd and the Grey Mouser. Their house was a renovated barn filled with masks they'd made, columns and porticos and temples from sets Cal had built, Tina's galaxies of scarves and capes and hats, posters from Grateful Dead shows they'd attended over the course of decades. Cal's canvases covered the walls, and the gorgeous leather bags they made and sold, with Tina's elaborate beadwork and braiding and Cal's painting and leatherwork. There were papier-maché skeletons everywhere, crowned with paper roses; animal skulls on ribboned standards; grinning Day of the Dead figures holding chalices and hash pipes between bony fingers. The cats prowled among them, and slept beneath daturas drooping with waxy white blossoms, or alongside the marijuana plants growing in plastic pots by the big picture window, or in the tiny head-crunching loft above Cal and Tina's bed.

That was where I slept. After the first two weeks there was a small group of us who took turns staying over, two or even three at a time, so we could spell each other during the night. I was usually there for two nights a week; Robert took care of the children.

Cal and Tina's friend Loki often stayed over with me. Loki was unusually quiet, for a friend of theirs; wore chinos and polo shirts or, sometimes, a very old faded *Star Wars* T-shirt. He lived forty-five minutes away, in Rockland, where he worked as a paralegal. A few mornings a week before work he would drive over and take their laundry home with him, wash and dry it, and then return it that evening, sometimes staying overnight. I knew Loki from the elaborate solstice and equinoctial rituals Cal and Tina had staged over the years, where Loki wore an otter's mask he had made, and his usual beige pants and topsiders.

When Loki and I stayed over we didn't talk much. He was strong and serious but occasionally laughed unexpectedly; he was very fond of the cats. I wasn't as useful as I wanted to be. I wasn't a masseuse, like Luna, or strong, like Loki, although I had a strong stomach. I showed Loki how to give Cal morphine injections, after the hospice nurse taught me; then how to administer the morphine IV, morphine suppositories, morphine spikes, morphine pump.

"You know, I could get you a job down on Fifty-Second Street," another friend, Jerry, remarked one day. We laughed: Jerry and his wife, Pansy, laughed a lot. They stayed over together, and in the morning when I arrived they'd report on the previous night and show me the yellow legal pad where we kept track of Cal's injections, meds, liquid intake.

"Tina still hasn't slept," Pansy whispered hoarsely. She ran a greenhouse in Verona and looked like a flower herself, slender with huge violet-circled eyes, fine silvery hair, voice husky from sleeplessness and pot smoke. "See if you can get her to sleep."

"We can't," said Jerry. He was a boatbuilder who'd helped make the pagan standards that he and Pansy had put out on the porch, to billow in the winter wind. "She's getting kinda crazed."

"The nurse says if she doesn't sleep she'll have no strength left for when he goes." Pansy's eyes were bloodshot; she fingered a little leather bag around her neck, an amulet made by Cal with loons painted on it. "See if you can get her to sleep."

For five weeks that was my job: getting Cal and Tina to sleep. The morphine made Cal restless, struggling reflexively to rise from the futon, but he was too weak and dizzy to stand. If there was no one there to catch him he would fall, and did, lacerating his skull; or else he would have seizures. The medication to control these would knock him out for five or six hours, but Tina didn't like to give it to him. She was afraid he would die in his sleep; she was afraid to sleep herself, thinking he would die then. I would practically force her onto the futon beside him, tucking the two of them in, Cal unconscious, Tina wild-eyed and speaking slowly, purposefully, crazily, like a child with night terrors. Sometimes she would read to him, from Hans Christian Andersen. He would say, "I love you, Fox," she would say, "I love you, Little Wolf," and curl around him like a cat. He couldn't move by himself; she would lift her head every few minutes, checking that he was breathing and then looking around until she saw me, sitting in a chair and reading old issues of *Vogue*. A few times I got her to go up to the loft, where she finally would pass out for an hour, maybe two, before climbing back down the ladder again. Several times we had to contact the hospice nurse who was on call, to come help when an IV popped out, or to talk us through the process of administering a new type of pain-killer—opium suppositories, the morphine pump. The morphine continued to make Cal restless; he hadn't eaten for ten days, was taking in very little fluid, but he still tried to stand and walk to the bathroom. He couldn't walk, of course, and what water he did drink he would vomit up again within an hour, along with black bile.

One night while Tina was in the loft sleeping I read aloud to Cal, "The Seven Swans" from the Brothers Grimm. As I read his eyes flickered, so sunken in his white face they were like marbles buried in the snow.

"That's nice, Carrie," he whispered when I'd finished. "Thank you."

It was the last time he said my name. Afterwards, as he slept, I read "The Juniper Tree."

——

Meanwhile, Marlene gathered all the bones, tied them up in her silk kerchief and carried them outside. There she wept bitter tears and buried the bones beneath the juniper tree. But as she put them there, she suddenly felt relieved and stopped crying. That was when the juniper tree began to sway, its branches moving as though they were clapping. At the same time smoke came out of the tree, and a flame that seemed to be burning. Then a beautiful bird flew out of the fire and began to sing, the most beautiful song she had ever heard . . .

——

When I finished "The Juniper Tree" I started on the book of pagan death rituals that I found in the living room, alongside articles on cancer therapy and acupuncture left by Luna and Pansy. I prayed that up in the loft Tina was sleeping. But every time Cal stirred she would peer down, and I despaired of her ever resting at all. If Tina slept for two hours it was a triumph. I would always pass out before dawn and feel like Peter in Gethsemane, waking to the sound of Tina ringing a pair of piercingly clear Tibetan temple bells as she stood before the window facing the sun, reciting an incantation.

Spirits of the East, of water and sky and starlight, I welcome you.
Spirits of the West, land of fire and the dying sun, I welcome you.
Spirits of the North, hear us . . .

——

As the weeks passed, Cal grew frailer and weaker, though his hands when I helped him to stand were painfully strong, fingers like claws digging into my arm. There were always people around now, sometimes only two or three of us; at other times the house was full, like a party. Cal's ex-wife Yala came from Vermont and stayed for three weeks. Some cousins and an elderly aunt flew in from Texas and stayed for several days. That was the last time I saw Cal really happy, just beaming with delight, his eyes widening behind the morphine cloud when he saw them walking slowly towards him, like people on the moon.

"Hey Cal, you ol' peckerwood!" Cousin Bub shouted, and Cal laughed and fell into his arms, really fell, Bub yelping as he caught him. "Hooboy, too much of that reefer, huh!"

Before Cal got sick, their house had always seemed like backstage at Mardi Gras, masks and marijuana smoke, patchouli and the Neville Brothers or Joe Ely blasting from the speakers. But as the weeks passed it became more and more like a cave. The windows were covered with scarves and Tibetan hangings. Tiny blue Christmas lights blinked on the ceiling like phosphorescent insects; there were votive candles burning everywhere, in blue glasses and on plates, lined up in front of the corner altar where statues of goddesses and wolves and foxes peered out from thickets of ivy and datura blossoms. The smell of marijuana grew choking; sage and juniper burned in ashtrays and abalone shells, so that there was a constant sweet blue fume. When I smoothed out the bedclothes I found crystals the size of my fist beneath Cal's pillow, amethyst and rose quartz, and necklaces of red thread. The music was soft Japanese flute music, the shakuhachi flutes that Cal loved and played himself. We got in the habit of always whispering, of touching each other as we passed, not so much for solace but as though finding our way in the dark. On the futon Cal lay, eyes closed, breathing softly, and sometimes it seemed he did not breathe at all. He did not speak anymore, or wake. He smelled of marijuana and sweat, a harsh strong smell scarcely obviated by sponge baths and lavender oil and aloe ointment for his bedsores. His auburn hair lay in two long unraveling braids upon his breast, his hands and arms were curled like ferns. He had always worn gorgeous heathen jewelry, of bone and ivory and silver, Celtic torques and lunulas, wristbands wide and weighty as manacles, strings of turquoise and lapis lazuli, earrings and dragon pendants and bones threaded in his hair and beard. On his finger he wore a heavy gold ring with a dragon on it, from Nepal.

But little by little the jewelry had been removed, to make it easier to probe veins for the IV, to get him in and out of his clothes, to turn him so the bedsores would not get worse. He seemed to have only two modes of being now, anguish or unconsciousness. He was on eight different kinds of morphine, but when he was awake none of them really cut the pain. I became obsessed with giving him shots, and later with the morphine IV. I could not bear to see him, that beautiful face twisted in pain, the way he whispered *Oh, oh, oh fuck*, too weak to even turn his head, too weak, almost, to blink.

Someone asked me once, someone who didn't know Cal, "Have you thought of, you know?" Meaning, had I thought of killing him, of ending that interminable unendurable pain.

No, I said, never; and did not say what I *did* think, the impossible bargains I made at three o' clock in the morning with the pagan deities flitting about the room: what I would give up to save him, which digits, which hand, which leg; eyesight, the power of speech, an ear; two; my tongue.

⊷

One day when only Tina and I were home, a woman named Deirdre came. Deirdre was a friend of Luna's. Neither Tina nor I knew her.

"Are you a massage therapist?" I asked.

"No." Deirdre was my age, beautifully dressed in stark clothes, black soft trousers, white silk shirt, her dark hair sleek and expensively cut. She had strong patrician features and wore no makeup; her eyes were pale blue and sharply intelligent. "I'm a holistic advisor and a clairvoyant. I help people make transitions from one life-stage to the next. I can see their auras, and help them through the Seven Gates. I'm going to do some work with Cal. But I think Tina is the one who needs some help," she added softly. Her voice was calm, reassuring yet businesslike; she reminded me of the midwife who had delivered my children. "She looks exhausted."

"She is. She won't sleep. She hasn't slept for days." I didn't say that Tina seemed almost demented from sleeplessness and grief. She paced around the house, her long dark hair loose or hidden beneath one of her Laplander hats, a syringe in her hand or a mug of tea or a joint. Right now she was carrying an eagle feather and an abalone shell with juniper burning in it; she was fanning the smoke, moving quickly from corner to corner and returning again and again to Cal's motionless figure, wafting smoke over his face as she chanted.

"I'll work with her," said Deirdre. "But I'll see Cal first."

For over an hour she knelt on the floor behind Cal, cradling his head in her hands. Shakuhachi flute music played softly, incense burned, the cats crept across the beams overhead and light snow fell outside. I felt as though I had been here all my life; that life had shrunk and tightened like a telescoping lens to this pinpoint of being, Tina in the shower, myself doing the dishes and picking up newspapers and feeding the woodstove, a woman kneeling with a dying man's head in her hands, her eyes closed and her lips moving silently. When at last she finished, Deirdre stood, stretching, then came into the kitchen where Tina and I were drinking green tea.

"How is he?" asked Tina. Her eyes were huge and black, her wet hair neatly brushed and hanging down her back. "Is he still here? Is he still here?"

"He's here," said Deirdre. She smiled. She looked tired but peaceful, her face unlined, unmarked by her travels. When she looked at you, you felt as though she were shining a flashlight into your eyes. "He hasn't left. I've gone with him, we walked through all the gates but the last one. He's been there before—"

"He has!" Tina nodded urgently. "He has, lots of times—he's not afraid of dying, he's done it before and he's never been afraid! That's why I'm so confused—I think it's the morphine, he can't remember what he's supposed to do."

"That could be. He's worried about you. He doesn't want to leave you."

"I know!" Tina wailed. "I know, I know—but I don't want him to stay because of me, not if it's his time! But I don't want him to go, and he knows, and I'm afraid I'm confusing him, I'm keeping him when it's his time to go—"

She began to cry. Deirdre put her arms around her. She stared past Tina's shoulder into my eyes and I felt as though I had walked in on a mother nursing her child. "That's right, that's right, let it out, let it go. You're mad, aren't you? You're so angry at him—"

"I am, I am! It wasn't supposed to be like this! We did everything we could! We did everything! There's no time—it happened so fast, it wasn't supposed to be this fast—he's gone and I'll be alone, I don't know how to do anything, I just wanted to be able to make love to him again, I want to fight and have him make dinner for me, oh Little Wolf, Little Wolf—"

She began to sob, wrenchingly. I turned and tiptoed into the back room, where Cal and Tina's clothes hung on racks and were stacked in neatly folded piles; a hippie queen and king's ransom in brocade and velvet and hand-embroidered cowboy shirts. From the next room I could hear Tina's grief rushing out like water into a pool, Deirdre's soft voice comforting her and calling out loudly, encouragingly when Tina's sorrow choked into rage. Now and then I peeked through the India-print curtain, and these glimpses underscored the sense of watching someone give birth: the screaming, the agony, the constant strong presence of a woman who held you and talked you through it. The same knowledge of an inevitable outcome; the same exhaustion afterwards, when I finally came back out to hug both of them. There was even a sort of terrible joy, a radiance in Tina's face as she held me and the tears came again as I stared over her shoulder at Deirdre, so calm and strong. And I was helpless to do anything at all.

Tina went back to sit with Cal, kneeling to wipe his forehead with a washcloth. I walked Deirdre to the door, watching as she pulled on boots and coat and scarf.

"What can I do?" I asked. "For Tina? What can I do?"

"I know you want to make everything better, Carrie. I know you want to help her, and that's really good, she needs someone to take care of her. But you need to be open with your own grieving, and let Tina see that. Show her it's okay that she feels this way."

Deirdre's gaze met mine and I knew she saw right through me. I could only grieve like a teenager, alone in my room at night. At the benefit concert where famous and near-famous and formerly famous singers and musicians raised money for Cal's medical expenses, I sat in the front row and clenched my jaws so hard I had a headache. But I would not cry.

"And see if you can get her to sleep," Deirdre finished. She touched my hand and I nodded.

"Right," I said. I went back inside and watched Tina, curled up beside her husband with the cats sleeping at their feet, like Hansel and Gretel, Jorinda and Joringel, all those lost children. I stayed until Luna arrived for her night shift, and then drove home through the snow, not crying then either because I didn't want to go off the road; not crying until I woke up in the middle of the night from a dream where Cal was hugging me, strong and straight as ever. It was only a dream, but for a little while, at least, he had been there. And I was able to cry.

━━

Things started happening even faster then. Or rather, things stopped happening. Cal's periods of lucidity and consciousness became fewer and fewer. The hospice nurses told us it was only a matter of a day or two; but in fact it was nine days. Deirdre came again, and I listened as she and Tina discussed Cal's silent journeying.

"I know he'll come back, but will I know him?" One of the nurses had managed to get Tina to take some sleeping pills. She was sleeping as many as four hours a night now, and seemed less manic. "Do you think he might actually become a wolf? Or another person, do you think he might be a person? Maybe I could find him and we could do this all again? Will I recognize him? Will I *know* him?"

"No one knows." Deirdre leaned against the kitchen counter, sipping green tea. "I think it's partly a matter of luck and partly a matter of being in the right place at the right time. You just never know. But if you're mindful, if you're aware and consciously looking for him, you might find him sooner rather than later."

"I hope so," Tina said fervidly. "Oh god, I hope so."

There was a constant stream of people in and out of the house. Some stayed all day, talking quietly, taking turns to sit at Cal's side, stroking his head, chanting in low voices or kneeling with eyes closed and hands upturned. Praying, I guess, or looking for those seven gates, tapping into some secret stream of healing energy that evaded me. We stacked firewood, folded clothes, washed dishes, fed cats; unpacked groceries and heated the huge vats of chowder Lisa brought from next door.

I continued to drop by once and occasionally twice a day, if I wasn't staying over. Pansy was often there, and I'd kneel beside her and Tina, the three of us gently stroking Cal's face while Tina read from Lorca's poems. I could hardly bear to touch Cal, I was so afraid I might hurt or wake him; but he seemed very far away now. He lay curled upon his side, shrunken, his arms held close to his chest; he looked like a praying mantis, with his eyes so deep set and his limbs withered. It was two weeks since he had eaten anything at all, and then only a few bites of applesauce. Always wiry, he now seemed insubstantial as one of the delicate papier-maché figures in the room around him, skeletons wearing crowns of roses, a steer's skull ringed round with dried blossoms. I would close my eyes and try to find him, try to see the gates that Deirdre had described. I would picture Cal and Tina walking in a field of bluebonnets, their long hair streaming, or imagine mountains and Cal flying above them, not a wolf but an eagle.

Be there now, I thought, trying to make it real, to scale my own stony disbelief and somehow give him peace. *Be there.*

But still he would twitch and moan, so softly it was like a sigh. His skin was oily with sweat; Tina had washed and braided his hair, but reddish strands had come loose and stuck damply to his forehead. Each time I left I would kiss him, murmuring, *I love you, Cal, I love you.* It would be hours before the scent of his dying left my skin, the smell of candle wax and incense, marijuana, sweat, the heavy odor of farewell he exhaled.

We began to make plans for what happened next, what happened after. That was how we said it. Weeks before, Tina had asked me if I would make arrangements for cremation.

"Cal wants to be burned on a bonfire here in the woods," she told me. "Can you see if we can do that?"

"Sure," I said.

I went outside, huddled in my parka against heavy blowing snow, and in the middle of the dirt road hung out for a while with some of the other people caught between arriving and leaving.

"You're taking care of the cremation?" asked Jorge. He was one of Cal's oldest friends, lived just a few miles down Route 52. He stopped by every day, bringing carafes of coffee and fresh donuts from town, but he wouldn't stay inside. His inside expression was distant, almost bored, as though he were listening to radio reports of bad news far away. But once outside again he grew animated and could give way to worry and, sometimes, anger. "Tina said she asked you . . . ?"

"Yeah. But I'm pretty sure the whole Darth Vader trip is totally illegal."

Jorge laughed. "I figured. Larry and Paul want to build a coffin shaped like a boat, and then just push it into the harbor."

"I'm pretty sure that's illegal, too."

—▸—

Larry and Paul did end up making the coffin, a beautiful thing of dovetailed pine and maple and very old, hand-hammered nails. They painted it with runes and sacred symbols, Tibetan prayers and, on its sides, two enormous Argus eyes, like those on ancient Greek triremes. The coffin was immense, nearly seven feet long; but I'd made sure we'd gotten the correct dimensions from the crematorium, so that we'd be certain it would fit into the retort.

Previously, my only knowledge of cremation came from having watched *Jules and Jim* numerous times, taking especial note of those scenes at the end showing the lovers' coffins disappearing into the furnace. But that week I got to be on a first-name basis with the crematorium staff. Tina wanted to keep Cal's body at home for forty-eight hours after he died, and then arrange for our own transportation to the crematory facility in Lewiston, more than three hours away. To do this involved a draconian process of obtaining death certificates and medical examiner's reports, notarized forms from doctors, county clerks, the hospice. A Burial Transport Permit was needed, and a permit for the Disposition of Human Remains. Certain lines of the forms could only be handwritten in black ink. While being transported, the body could never be in public view. I spent hours and hours on the telephone sorting all this out and discussing the more salient aspects of cremation with Mr. Brusher, the crematorium director.

Mr. Brusher was polite, patient, and professionally dubious about the prospect of the bereaved, non-professionals all, performing the pagan duty of driving a corpse in an old red International pickup truck to his crematorium. He had a pleasantly oleaginous voice and seemed to enjoy discussing his work. After he had spent six or seven hours advising me on how best to obtain the proper papers, his tone became one of furtive and confiding amusement.

"The most *efficient* thing to do, Miss Waverley, would be to contact us as soon as possible, after the death has occurred. That way we can make certain we schedule you for the appropriate time.

"Between you and me," he added, giving a soft apologetic snort of laughter, "this has been a very *high volume* week. Mmm. You understand. And you see, we need time in between to thoroughly clean out the retort. *Some* people—"

He lowered his voice conspiratorially. "—*some* people, when they bring the casket in, can be quite distressed when they first see the interior of the retort. Because *occasionally* there is something left over, we do our best to clean it *thoroughly* but *sometimes* there might be a little piece of bone, or metal. Teeth. And this can be upsetting."

I knew he was trying to talk me out of doing any of this ourselves. I was not afraid of bones, although I was worried about Tina. Apart from any visceral shock or fear, there probably was some pagan proscription against somebody else's Judeo-Christian bones being included with your loved one's.

So I spared her the more graphic details provided by Mr. Brusher. I wished I could spare her all of them. Still, she would not be dissuaded; she had a kind of moral strength that was almost nunlike in its purity and the unwavering belief that she was doing the one true right thing.

Which, of course, she was. I could only watch, my chest aching as she braided and rebraided her husband's hair, dampened his cracked lips with a washcloth or her own mouth, kissed his forehead and hands and the staved-in curve of his shoulder blades. And I did what I could to prepare for Death, to lay down a paper trail, or at least provide a sort of map that would indicate where the paper trail would be. I was very, very organized.

But when I was in my own home, I would wake in the middle of the night and lie there for hours in a cold sweat. What terrified me was something so banal I was ashamed to even speak it aloud: I could not bear the thought of Cal's body being burned; of all that beauty, his long red hair and Viking jewelry, his gorgeous clothes and long slender fingers heavy with rings—of all that being consigned to the air.

And that was how I thought of it, not of smoke or ash or flame but of air and nothingness, an eternal blue sweep of sky and Cal nowhere to be seen. I had studied archaeology in college and always loved bones, fragments of stone and crushed beads, the patterns of livelihood and ritual that you could discern within a cubic yard of rich humus and potsherds, tibia and skulls and broken glass. I had no belief in resurrection beyond this.

But when I thought of that beautiful casket, painstakingly made and carved by men who loved their friend, and of my friend within it with all his treasure laid upon his breast—when I thought of that, I imagined Cal as a prince of the earth, one who might be found a thousand years hence, buried in a rocky northern graveyard. And when he was discovered, by archaeologists to whom he would be as remote as Scythian horselords were to me—why then he would live again! Cal would be a mystery, but he would be known.

He would be alive, and not forgotten, even if no one knew his name; even if no one understood the meaning of the tattoos upon his wrists or the runestones he carried in a leather bag at his side.

But if all of that were consigned to the air there would be nothing that remained of my friend; nothing at all.

＋＋

Cal died early on Thursday evening, during a snowstorm. I wasn't there; I would be snowed in with my children for the next forty-eight hours, and so I missed everything I had tried to plan for so diligently. Tina was there, of course, in the next room, talking to Leenamarie, the Wiccan priestess who would oversee the death rites. Later, Tina told me about everything.

"I walked back into the room and without even looking at him, I knew he was gone. I just knew. I walked over and looked at him. Then I went into the kitchen. I picked up a bowl, that heavy blue glass bowl? And I smashed it into the sink. I was screaming at the top of my lungs.

'You bastard, you sonofabitch, I spent the last two months never leaving you and now you go? Now you go?'

"I don't know what Leenamarie thought. Then I looked down at my hand. I hadn't felt anything when I smashed the bowl, but I was bleeding, like, a lot. And I thought, Hmmm. I better get a grip on this."

Within a few hours, the tribe had gathered around her. Tina and Leenamarie and Luna washed Cal's body and anointed it; Tina braided his hair, snipping a single long plait and putting it on the altar, to keep. They dressed him in his nineteenth-century naval captain's uniform, the one he had worn when he was Captain Ahab one Hallowe'en, and laid him out on a makeshift table made from planks and sawhorses, in the keeping room out back. It was so cold there that your fingers and nose grew numb within minutes, but everyone took turns keeping a vigil by his body. The men prepared a huge bonfire in the field behind the woods, and as the snow fell Leenamarie led a mooncircle out there, with dozens of friends chanting, singing, howling like wolves as the storm subsided and the full moon rose above the trees. Inside, Tina sat on a stool in the kitchen while her friend Doreen shaved her head. Doreen worked as a veterinary assistant; she used sheep shears on Tina, and then a series of disposable razors until her skull was smooth and yellow as a monk's. Afterward, Tina showed me a series of pictures, the women seeming never to change position, save their eyes and mouths, which were twisted between hysterical laughter and ravaged weeping. It was like some weird time-lapse film that recorded emotion and not movement.

"He looked so beautiful, Carrie." There were photographs of Cal, too; Tina made a little album of them. "He lost that old-man look and he looked the way he used to, the way he did when we first met. He was so beautiful, I couldn't stop touching him. I just kept going back into the back room and touching his face.

"But then, after about thirty-six hours, he changed. It happened really suddenly. And I went back into the house and said, 'Dead Body! Get him out of here!'"

↔

The night that Cal died, I had a dream about him. In my dream I was calling Tina on the phone, but Cal answered, his voice as strong and full of laughter as it had been once, three months gone by, oh so long ago. That was my only knowledge of his presence, his voice, and it filled me with an overwhelming mix of confusion and joy— had there, after all, been a mistake?

But no: even in my dream I couldn't let go of the facts.

"Cal," I said. "Aren't you—"

I stopped. I didn't want to embarrass him by pointing out he was a ghost.

"No, Carrie." He sounded amused, slightly annoyed, the way he'd sounded when we'd argued about politics during the Gulf War. "No, Carrie. I'm still here. I'm right here, Carrie. I'm here."

I woke, feeling not frightened but bemused and oddly exhilarated, which I guess was the closest I ever came to experiencing some kind of faith.

--

Early Friday morning I had called Mr. Brusher and informed him of the time of Cal's death, and told him when to expect the little procession of pickups and old four-wheel-drive Subarus and Saabs.

"The widow is aware that, after forty-eight hours, the body will start to—decay?

"Yes, she is." I had been warned about this by the hospice nurses, too; one of them advised me that we should all put Noxzema around and inside our nostrils. "They'll be there Saturday afternoon."

Saturday morning they put Cal into his coffin. They laid him upon a bed of marijuana, tucking it around his thin shoulders and wasted legs, and then filled his pockets with semi-precious stones, agates and Maine tourmaline, jade from Nepal and Indian cinnabar. Tina slipped coins into his pockets, and hand-rolled cigarettes, a six-ounce green glass bottle of Coca-Cola, a Defenders of Wildlife coffee mug with wolves on it. In one hand she put the last of the Owsley acid he'd hung onto since his days of dealing it thirty years before. His paints went into the casket, and his pastels; his shakuhachi flute and the new hand-beaded moccasins that were a Christmas present he'd never been able to wear. He wore most of his jewelry, save a few pieces that Tina had decided to keep; and so the casket was made that much heavier by golden rings and thick silver bracelets embossed with dragons and waves, his ivory torque, the yards and yards of Tibetan necklaces strung with little brass and bronze and copper and silver and jade dragons. Tina placed one of his painted and embroidered leather bags beside

him. Inside were his well-worn tarot deck and favorite books—
Howard Pyle's *King Arthur and the Knights of the Round Table*, the
Rockwell Kent *Moby Dick*, paperbacks of Dostoevsky and Tolstoy.
Another leather bag held his runestones. Last of all, on his breast there
was an exquisite wooden model of a Viking ship under full sail.

She had color photographs of all this, too, and when I saw them I
thought how Cal truly did look like a pagan prince, a shaman and not
a man who had been born in Dimebox, Texas, fifty-two years before.

—••—

And so I missed the cremation. They drove in a little caravan to
Lewiston, Cal's casket inside Jorge's old pickup truck, a big blue tarp
covering it and a Tibetan silk painting like a flag draped across the
tarp. During that weekend I continued to speak to Tina several
times a day. I finally saw her the day after the cremation.

"I missed you so much, Carrie," she said. She was dressed all in
black, black linen tunic and loose black trousers, a star-spangled
black scarf around her neck. "I wished you'd been there, it felt so
wrong you weren't there."

"I know," I said, and held her for a long time. She looked exhausted
but beautiful, her gaunt face even more striking now that her head
was shaved. "I'm sorry, I—"

"But I have something I'd like for you to do. I have Cal's ashes
and I'd like to sift through them with you."

"Sure," I said. I had wondered about this. Mr. Brusher had asked
me whether the widow would like the remains crushed.

"Most people do," he said. "But it takes a few extra hours, and
we need to schedule that time in. Can you let me know?"

This was one command decision I was not prepared to make. I
hadn't even mentioned it to Tina, but now I learned that she had
not opted to do what most people would have done.

"Sure," I told her. Of course. It would be an honor.

"Okay." She turned and picked up a little book from the coffee table. There was a largish cardboard carton there as well, sealed with tape and with Cal's name and address written on it in magic marker. Someone had drawn swirly moons and stars on the box in red and gold glitter ink. Tina ignored the box and opened the little book, flipping quickly through it. "Next Tuesday, nothing will be in retrograde, after—hmm, let's see, twelve forty-seven p.m. Can you come then?"

"Sure. I'll take you to lunch first, how's that?"

So our date was set, as though we were going to Belfast to have a manicure from the woman who used only non-toxic, vegetable-based nail products. That night, when I told Robert about what I was going to do, he frowned and shook his head.

"This sounds a bit dangerous to me. Psychologically risky, I mean."

"For Tina, you mean?"

"Well, yes. And you. There's no cultural safety net for this sort of thing, Carrie."

I nodded again but said nothing. But I thought, it was like everything else Cal and Tina and their friends did, part of their crazy-beautiful patchwork of belief. Magic mushrooms, shamans giving medical advice, moonrise and silver temple bells at dawn. Seat-of-the-pants religion: but who was I, a non-believer, to say it was wrong? I went into another room and put on the radio. Yet another DJ on the little local station was doing a tribute show for Cal, a scratchy vinyl recording of an old old song, a woman's husky vibrato and in the background noisy echoing feedback—

> *But Magic is no instrument*
> *Magic is the end.*

The following Tuesday I picked up Tina, and we went to have an early lunch in town. We both ordered the same thing, Japanese somen noodles with fresh ginger and garlic. We spoke about how she and Cal had first met, about all the e-mails she'd received from friends all over the world, all the letters. Afterwards we drove around for a little while, to give Tina a chance to talk more, I thought. But then I glanced at the clock on the dashboard of the old Saab and remembered that nothing would be in retrograde until close to one o'clock. At twelve forty-five we were driving back down the dirt road to Tina's house, dodging frost heaves and patches of black ice, listening to Cab Calloway on the radio.

"Well," she said when we finally pulled into the driveway. "Here we are."

Inside, I boiled water for tea, while Tina prepared a space in the living room. First she laid a white sheet on the floor atop the old kilim rug. Then she set down four candles in star-shaped glass holders, one at each corner of the sheet. In the middle she set the cardboard carton and a pair of scissors. At the edge of the sheet were dozens of containers—cookie tins, beautiful blown-glass decanters, tiny glass and metal vials, antique silver urns from Nepal, carved wooden boxes, terracotta pots with lids. There were also several boxes of Ziploc bags in varying sizes.

"I'm going to bury some of his ashes in the backyard," said Tina. "Along with whatever else we find."

The rest she was going to take with her on a months-long pilgrimage, first across the United States, then to Europe, India, and Nepal: all the places Cal had ever lived, all the places they had ever visited together, all the places they had planned to go. She would scatter his ashes everywhere, and bury some of whatever else we found in Dimebox, Chaco Canyon, on the road outside Katmandu.

"Well," Tina said at last. She seemed edgy, anxious to start but also uneasy: the first time in all the weeks of Cal's dying that I had seen her actually fearful about something. Outside the sun was shining; a sudden thaw had melted most of the snow over the last few days, and on the maple trees tiny red buds were swelling.

"I guess we should begin. Do you need to go to the bathroom or anything?"

I said no. We walked into the living room, set down our tea mugs. Tina went back and got the cardboard box from the coffee table and carried it to the white sheet laid out on the floor. She put the box in its center, then performed the ritual of charging the circle, lighting each of the four candles in turn and making a little recitation as she rang the silvery Tibetan temple bells.

"Spirits of the West, of Fire and—no, wait. I think East is Fire—"

She began again, while I knelt and listened. I knew that once the circle was charged we were not supposed to leave it; only children and cats could pass through a charged circle without disrupting the force, or something. When Tina was finished she knelt opposite me, her glasses glinting in the candlelight.

"Well," she said.

She took the scissors and slit open the heavy tape on the cardboard carton. Inside was a bag of heavy clear plastic, its sides opaque with grey dust. There was a twist tie at the top; Tina undid this and set it aside, then unfolded the plastic and smoothed it down over the sides of the box.

"*Oh, wow,*" she breathed. "*Oh, wow.*"

I gazed down and felt every hair on my body lift. I have never experienced anything like it. Tina's hands hovered above the bag's opening, then dipped down and into what the carton held. "Oh, oh, Little Wolf, my Little Wolf . . . "

"Jesus," I whispered; then slipped my hand inside.

It was not ashes, of course. Even ashes are not technically ashes, but a gritty substance more like kitty litter or medium-fine gravel.

What the box contained was not that at all, but bones. Most of them burned or broken up, but nearly all immediately recognizable. A forensic anthropologist would have been able to piece some of them together to form part of an arm, or hand; ribcage and spine and shoulder blade. Everything was covered with a fine layer of ash, pale-grey, almost white. I picked up a slender bone the length of my hand, hollow, like a bone flute, set it to one side and filled my palm with soft dust and shattered tibia, a lovely wing-shaped fragment of vertebra.

"Look," murmured Tina. Her eyes were huge, transfixed; she held up the tiny intact figure of a dragon, its ruby eyes winking as she rubbed the ash from them.

"That's amazing," I said, shaking my head. "Look—"

I let the fine ash trickle through my fingers, then plucked a curved smooth shard of green glass from my palm. "The Coke bottle!"

Tina nodded. She rubbed at her glasses, leaving a smear of ash; then said, "I'm going to get some bandannas, so we don't breathe this in—"

She stood, moving her hands back and forth above a candle as she recited the words that would let her leave the circle. She returned a few minutes later, closed the circle again and handed me a bright-red kerchief. I cleaned my glasses with it, then tied it over my mouth and bent back over the box. Very carefully, I began taking handfuls of what was inside and laying it on the sheet in front of me. Without discussing it, we began sorting everything in small heaps splayed in a long sweep across the white sheet. Larger bones here; glass there, melted blobs from the Coke bottle; here unidentifiable bits of charred and twisted metal.

What was extraordinary was not just how many things could be identified, but how many had not been destroyed by the incandescent heat of the furnace. We found Cal's gold-rimmed spectacles, the frames bent but the glass intact. We found dozens of tiny animal figurines of bronze and silvery metal, and the twin circlets of steel which were part of his leather bag. There were shards of semi-precious stone, and the wire that had formed the rigging of the Viking ship. There were the runestones, some of them split in two; only those that Cal had painted himself, with tiny V-shaped symbols and letters, still retained their color and whatever arcane meaning he had charged them with. As the hours passed the piles in front of us grew larger, and Tina began to make another series of orderly heaps, objects that she would keep, ultimately placing them on the little corner shrine where incense and candles burned round the clock.

"What do you think these are?" I asked, holding up a small, smooth cylinder. It was grey-white, the same color as the ashes. I had quite a little pile of them.

"Bones?"

"No. I think they're his pastels."

"That's it!" Tina picked one up and turned it to the light. "The color got all burned away . . . "

We found the metal ferrules from his paintbrushes, scores of beads and other remnants of jewelry. Tina was dismayed and surprised that none of his heavy bracelets or torques had survived, save for a tiny bit of silvery filigree, melted and charred like burned lace. Amazingly, we did find several small pieces of cloth that had somehow come through unscathed, dark wool soft and worn as felt, a shred of leather. And there was his wolf coffee mug, in three pieces, and a triangular piece of scorched paper, the corner of a page from one of the paperbacks.

He set out on his, it read.

Hours passed. I felt as though I had slipped through a crack in time, my back bent as I sifted and sorted and held fragments of bone before the candle-flame, enacting some nameless ritual that women had performed for a thousand thousand years, before ritual had a name; before women did. The world smelled of ash—it would take more than a faded red bandanna to keep that from me—of scorched metal and bone. My fingers felt as though they were gloved in something at once soft and slightly abrasive, the inside of an animal skin perhaps, or feathers. The sun had gone down, the room around us was growing almost too dark for us to see what we were doing; but we were almost done. In front of me was the pile of bones. Tina had a long line of smaller heaps beside her, jewelry and runestones and metal and tiny figurines. The only bones she had put aside were those of Cal's skull, which were larger than most of the others. There was a surprising number of these; I think you could probably have pieced his entire skull back together, like one of those ancient figures in a barrow, their skeletons dusted with ochre and pollen.

But at last, nothing remained in the box but very fine white ash. Tina looked around, dazed, at everything that surrounded us, bones and charred metal, a soft sifting of grey veiling her face.

"Carrie. You must want something. What would you like to have?"

I sat back on my heels, gazing at her and then at the orderly piles that surrounded us. "You choose for me," I said. "I will take this—"

I picked up the slender hollow bone I had first seen, cupped it in my hand. "And some of his pastels."

"Okay." Tina frowned studiously, then reached over and plucked the two metal rings that had come from Cal's leather bag. "And here—"

She placed them in my hand. They felt warm, as though they still held some of the retort's heat and flame. I put them, along with the bone and the pastels, into the leather bag Cal had made for me years before. "Thank you, Tina," I said, and leaned across the grey-streaked sheet to embrace her.

"I guess I better start putting this into the containers." She smiled weakly as she withdrew from me. She pushed at the kerchief covering her shaven skull, and I saw where dark ashy fingerprints covered her forehead. "God, I had no idea there would be so much. I hope I have enough to hold everything . . . "

As it turned out, she didn't. After she had filled as many containers as she could, sorting them out as to what would go to Texas, what would remain here in the woods behind the house, what would go to England, to India, to Nepal; after all that, enough remained that I filled several large Ziploc bags with the smallest fragments of bone, and several more with ashes.

"Well," Tina said at last. She looked exhausted, more in the grips of some intense hallucinogen than grief; and I imagined I must look exactly the same. "I guess we'd better stop."

I stood, my back aching, as she walked around the perimeter of the white sheet, reciting the words that would open the circle to us once more. Against one wall was the cardboard box, filled now with sealed Ziploc bags, and the dozens of containers that held Cal's remains. When Tina was finished, I picked up the white sheet and folded it, then walked out onto the back porch. The wind tugged at the sheet as I opened it and shook it out, and at that moment I felt how strange all this was, how I might have been shaking out a white tablecloth but instead was consigning the last of my friend to the cold night air.

Later, after I had kissed Tina goodbye and made plans to see her before she left on her pilgrimage, I went home. The taste of ash was in my mouth, not a bitter or horrible taste at all but warm, pleasantly acrid. When I got home I checked on the children and Robert, the three of them already asleep, then went into the bathroom and lit a series of votive candles in red glasses. I undressed, my clothes powdery with white dust, and took a bath and drank half a bottle of red wine as I soaked in the tub. When I slept that night I had no dreams that I could recall, no mystic voices or faces greeting me. But neither did I wake and lie for hours in the dark, haunted by the thought of empty blue air, of silence and the sound of the wind.

⚊

It is nearly two months now since Cal died. Just this morning I got another postcard from Tina, from Venice this time—a place Cal had never visited, but where the two of them had planned to go on their twenty-fifth wedding anniversary. She loved the city so much she was staying longer than she had planned, after having dropped some of his ashes into the Grand Canal; but she would be leaving within the week, with Tangiers her next stop. She couldn't wait to see me again, to tell me about all of her adventures: she had seen some amazing things, really unbelievable stuff, and of course she was always looking for Cal, always keeping her eyes and mind opened, so that she would recognize him when they met again.

Here in Maine spring has come earlier than usual, the snow melt deepening the lakes and rivers, the daffodils already starting to bloom even though it's only the second week of April, far too early for northern New England, the earliest spring I can remember. Outside the earth smells sweet, almost perfumed, bacteria thriving in the warm moist soil and the lake releasing its muddy hyacinth scent.

Last week, a bird appeared at the window where I work. I was hunched over my computer, writing, my back to the glass, when I heard a soft insistent tapping. When I turned I saw a tiny brown bird on the sill outside. As I stared it began to peck at the glass, gently but without stopping, like a thrush cracking a snail on a stone.

"Hello," I said. I sat and watched it for several minutes, expecting it to fly away, but it did not. I finally turned back to my computer, but the bird remained where it was, still tapping at the window.

"What're you doing?" I asked it. "Hmm? You want to see me?"

Moving slowly, I opened the window, letting in the cool April air, the faintest whiff of narcissus. To my surprise the bird did not fly away, but instead hopped onto the inside sill. It cocked its head and stared at me; I stared back, then laughed.

"Hey, what're you doing?" I held my hand out. The bird looked at my finger but would not step onto it. Neither did it fly away. Instead, it turned and began hopping along the sill, stopping to examine the things I have there: an old magic-lantern slide of Red Riding Hood and the Big Bad Wolf, a photograph of Robert and the children; Cal's bone, his pastels, the two steel rings from his leather bag, the small reddish curl of braid that Tina had given me the day I drove her to the airport. The bird looked at all of these, then turned and flew back outside.

It comes every day now and stays, watching me. I looked it up in my nature guides, going from one to another until I found the right description: the European wren, *troglodytes troglodytes*, a diminutive brown bird with white bars on its wings and breast, native to western Europe and the British Isles, but not North America. I called my friend Lucy, who writes the wildlife column for our local paper, and asked if she had ever heard of anyone seeing a European wren in Maine before. She had not, and when she posed the question to her readers, none of them had, either.

Still, the bird is here. I researched it online, and in some books of folklore I have, and learned that the European wren is the bird that was the subject of the annual wren hunt, an ancient pre-Christian ritual of death and resurrection, still practiced in obscure parts of Ireland and the Isle of Man. It is a creature known for its cheer and its valor, its bravery suiting a bird of far greater size; and also for its song, which is piercingly sweet and flutelike, carrying for miles on a clear day.

I can attest to this, writing as I do while the bird sits on the sill behind me and watches me work, as it plucks the last strands of Cal's hair from the braid and flies off to build its nest, somewhere in the rowan tree outside. There it sings, its voice rising and drowning out the songs of redwing blackbirds and chickadees, northern loons and kingfishers and the tapping of my fingers on the keyboard. It sings, day after day after day, and sometimes into the night as well. I never cease to marvel at the sound.

In the Lonely House there is a faded framed *Life* magazine article from almost half a century ago, featuring a color photograph of a beautiful woman with close-cropped blonde hair and rather sly grey eyes, wide crimson-lipsticked mouth, a red-and-white striped bateau-neck shirt. The woman is holding a large magnifying lens and examining a very large insect, a plastic scientific model of a common black ant, *Lasius niger*, posed atop a stack of children's picture books. Each book displays the familiar blocky letters and illustrated image that has been encoded into the dreamtime DNA of generations of children: that of a puzzled-looking, goggle-eyed ant, its antennae slightly askew as though trying, vainly, to tune into the signal from some oh-so-distant station.

Wise Aunt or Wise Ant? reads the caption beneath the photo. *Blake E. Tun Examines a Friend.*

The woman is the beloved children's book author and illustrator, Blake Eleanor Tun, known to her friends as Blakie. The books are the six classic *Wise Ant* books, in American and English editions and numerous translations—*Wise Ant, Brave Ant, Curious Ant, Formi Sage, Weise Ameise, Una Ormiga Visionaria*. In the room behind Blakie, you can just make out the figure of a toddler, out-of-focus as she runs past. You can see the child's short blonde hair cut in a pageboy, and a tiny hand that the camera records as a mothlike blur. The little girl with the Prince Valiant haircut, identified in the article as Miss Tun's adopted niece, is actually Blakie's illegitimate daughter, Ivy Tun. That's me.

Here in her remote island hidey-hole, the article begins, *Eleanor Blake Tun brings to life an imaginary world inhabited by millions.*

People used to ask Blakie why she lived on Aranbega. Actually, just living on an island wasn't enough for my mother. The Lonely House stood on an islet in Green Pond, so we lived on an island on an island.

"Why do I live here? Because enchantresses always live on islands," she'd say, and laugh. If she fancied the questioner she might add, "Oh, *you* know. Circe, Calypso, the Lady in the Lake—"

Then she'd give her, or very occasionally him, one of her mocking sideways smiles, lowering her head so that its fringe of yellow hair would fall across her face, hiding her eyes so that only the smile remained.

"The smile on the face of the tiger," Katherine told me once when I was a teenager. "Whenever you saw that smile of hers, you'd know it was only a matter of time."

"Time till what?" I asked.

But by then her attention had already turned back to my mother: the sun to Katherine's gnomon, the impossibly beautiful bright thing that we all circled, endlessly.

Anyway, I knew what Blakie's smile meant. Her affairs were notorious even on the island. For decades, however, they were carefully concealed from her readers, most of whom assumed (as they were meant to) that Blake E. Tun was a man—that *Life* magazine article caused quite a stir among those not already in the know. My mother was Blakie to me as to everyone else. When I was nine she announced that she was not my aunt but my mother, and produced a birth certificate from a Boston hospital to prove it.

"No point in lying. It would however be more *convenient* if you continued to call me Blakie." She stubbed out her cigarette on the sole of her tennis shoe and tossed it over the railing into Green Pond. "But it's no one's business who you are. Or who I am in relation to you, for that matter."

And that was that. My father was not a secret kept from me; he just didn't matter that much, not in Blakie's scheme of things. The only thing she ever told me about him was that he was very young.

"Just a boy. Not much older than you are now, Ivy," which at the time was nineteen. "Just a kid."

"Never knew what hit him," agreed my mother's partner Katherine, as Blakie glared at her from across the room.

It never crossed my mind to doubt my mother, just as it never crossed my mind to hold her accountable for any sort of duplicity she may have practiced, then or later. The simple mad fact was that I adored Blakie. Everyone did. She was lovely and smart and willful and rich, a woman who believed in seduction not argument; when seduction failed, which was rarely, she was not above abduction, of the genteel sort involving copious amounts of liquor and the assistance of one or two attractive friends.

The *Wise Ant* books she had written and illustrated when she was in her twenties. By her thirtieth birthday they had made her a fortune. Blakie had a wise agent named Letitia Thorne and a very wise financial adviser named William Dunlap, both of whom took care that my mother would never have to work again unless she wanted to.

Blakie did not want to work. She wanted to seduce Dunlap's daughter-in-law, a twenty-two-year-old Dallas socialite named Katherine Mae Moss. The two women eloped to Aranbega, a rocky spine of land some miles off the coast of Maine. There they built a fairytale cottage in the middle of a lake, on a tamarack-and-fern-covered bump of rock not much bigger than the Bambi Airstream trailer they'd driven up from Texas. The cottage had two small bedrooms, a living room and dining nook and wraparound porch overlooking the still, silvery surface of Green Pond. There was a beetle-black cast-iron Crawford woodstove for heat and cooking, kerosene lanterns, and a small red hand-pump in the slate kitchen sink. No electricity; no telephone. Drinking water was pumped up from the lake. Septic and grey water disposal was achieved through an ancient holding tank that was emptied once a year.

They named the cottage The Lonely House, after the tiny house where Wise Ant lived with her friends Grasshopper and Bee. Here they were visited by Blakie's friends, artistic sorts from New York and Boston, several other writers from Maine; and by Katherine's relatives, a noisy congeries of cattle heiresses, disaffected oil men and Ivy League dropouts, first-wave hippies and draft dodgers, all of whom took turns babysitting me when Blakie took off for Crete or London or Taos in pursuit of some new *amour*. Eventually of course Katherine would find her and bring her home: as a child I imagined my mother engaged in some world-spanning game of hide-and-seek, where Katherine was always It. When the two of them returned to the Lonely House, there would always be a prize for me as well. A rainbow map of California, tie-dyed on a white bedsheet; lizard-skin drums from Angola; a Meerschaum pipe carved in the likeness of Richard Nixon.

"You'll never have to leave here to see the world, Ivy," my mother said once, after presenting me with a Maori drawing, on bark, of a stylized honeybee. "It will all come to you, like it all came to me."

My mother was thirty-seven when I was born, old to be having a baby, and paired in what was then known as a Boston marriage. She and Katherine are still together, two old ladies now living in a posh assisted-living community near Rockland, no longer scandalizing anyone. They've had their relationship highlighted in an episode of *This American Life*, and my mother is active in local liberal causes, doing benefit readings of *The Vagina Monologues* and signings of *Wise Ant* for the Rockland Domestic Abuse Shelter. Katherine reconciled with her family and inherited a ranch near Goliad, where they still go sometimes in the winter. *The Wise Ant* books are now discussed within the context of mid-century American Lesbian Literature, a fact which annoys my mother no end.

"I wrote those books for *children*," she cries whenever the topic arises. "They are *children's books*," as though someone had confused the color of her mailbox, red rather than black. "For God's sake."

Of course Wise Ant will never be anything more than her antly self—wise, brave, curious, kind, noisy, helpful—just as Blakie at eighty-two remains beautiful, maddening, forgetful, curious, brave; though seldom, if ever, quiet. We had words when I converted the Lonely House to solar power—

"You're spoiling it. It was never *intended* to have electricity—"

Blakie and Katherine were by then well-established in their elegant cottage at Penobscot Fields. I looked at the room around me—Blakie's study, small but beautifully appointed, with a Gustav Stickley lamp that she'd had rewired by a curator at the Farnsworth, her laptop screen glowing atop a quartersawn oak desk, and Bose speakers and miniature CD console.

"You're right," I said. "I'll just move in here with you."

"That's not the—"

"Blakie. I need electricity to work. The generator's too noisy, my customers don't like it. And expensive. I have to work for a living—"

"You don't have to—"

"I *want* to work for a living." I paused, trying to calm myself. "Look, it'll be fun—doing the wiring and stuff. I got all these photovoltaic cells, when it's all set up you'll see. It'll be great."

And it was. The cottage is south-facing: two rows of cells on the roof, a few extra batteries boxed-in under the porch, a few days spent wiring and I was set. I left the bookshelves in the living room, mostly my books now, and a few valuable first editions that I'd talked Blakie into leaving. Eliot's *Four Quartets* and some Theodore Roethke; *Gormenghast*; a Leonard Baskin volume signed *For Blakie*. One bedroom I kept as my own, with a wide handcrafted oak cupboard bed, cleverly designed to hold clothes beneath and more books all around. At the head of the bed were those I loved best, a set of all six *Wise Ant* books and the five volumes of Walter Burden Fox's unfinished *Five Windows One Door* sequence.

The other bedroom became my studio. I set up a drafting table and autoclave and light box, a shelf with my ultrasonic cleaner and dri-clave. On the floor was an additional power unit just for my machine and equipment; a tool bench holding soldering guns, needle bars and jigs; a tall stainless steel medicine cabinet with enough disinfectant and bandages and gloves and hemostats to outfit a small clinic; an overhead cabinet with my inks and pencils and acetates. Empty plastic caps await the colored inks that fill the machine's reservoir. A small sink drains into a special tank that I bring to the Rockland dump once a month, when everyone else brings in their empty paint cans. A bookshelf holds albums filled with pictures of my own work and some art books—Tibetan stuff, pictures from Chauvet Cavern, Japanese woodblock prints.

But no flash sheets; no framed flash art; no fake books. If a customer wants flash, they can go to Rockland or Bangor. I do only my own designs. I'll work with a customer, if she has a particular image in mind, or come up with something original if she doesn't. But if somebody has her heart set on a prancing unicorn, or Harley flames, or Mister Natural, or a Grateful Dead logo, I send her elsewhere.

This doesn't happen much. I don't advertise. All my business is word of mouth, through friends or established customers, a few people here on Aranbega. But mostly, if someone wants me to do her body work, she *really* has to want me, enough to fork out sixty-five bucks for the round-trip ferry and at least a couple hundred for the tattoo, and three hundred more for the Aranbega Inn if she misses the last ferry, or if her work takes more than a single day. Not to mention the cost of a thick steak dinner afterwards, and getting someone else to drive her home. I don't let people stay at the Lonely House, unless it's someone I've known for a long time, which usually means someone I was involved with at some point, which usually means she wouldn't want to stay with me in any case. Sue is

an exception, but Sue is seeing someone else now, one of the other
occupational therapists from Penobscot Fields, so she doesn't come
over as much as she used to.

That suits me fine. My customers are all women. Most of them
are getting a tattoo to celebrate some milestone, usually something
like finally breaking with an abusive boyfriend, leaving a bad marriage,
coming to grips with the aftermath of a rape. Breast cancer survivors—
I do a lot of breast work—or tattoos to celebrate coming out, or giving
birth. Sometimes anniversaries. I get a lot of emotional baggage
dumped in my studio, for hours or days at a time; it always leaves
when the customers do, but it pretty much fulfills my need for any
kind of emotional connection, which is pretty minimal anyway.

And, truth to tell, it fulfills most of my sexual needs too; at least
any baseline desire I have for physical contact. My life is spent with
skin: cupping a breast in my hand, pulling the skin taut between my
fingers while the needle etches threadlike lines around the aureole,
tracing yellow above violet veins, turning zippered scars into coiled
serpents, an explosion of butterfly wings, flames or phoenixes rising
from a puckered blue-white mound of flesh; or drawing secret
maps, a hidden cartography of grottoes and ravines, rivulets and waves
lapping at beaches no bigger than the ball of my thumb; the ball of
my thumb pressed there, index finger there, tissue film of latex
between my flesh and hers, the hushed drone of the machine as it
chokes down when the needle first touches skin and the involuntary
flinch that comes, no matter how well she's prepared herself for this,
no matter how many times she's lain just like this, paper towels
blotting the film of blood that wells, nearly invisible, beneath the
moving needle bar's tip, music never loud enough to drown out
the hum of the machine. Hospital smells of disinfectant, blood,
antibacterial ointment, latex.

And sweat. A stink like scorched metal: fear. It wells up the way
blood does, her eyes dilate and I can smell it, even if she doesn't
move, even if she's done this enough times to be as controlled as I

am when I draw the needle across my own flesh: she's afraid, and I know it, needle-flick, soft white skin pulled taut, again, again, between my fingers.

I don't want a lot of company, after a day's work.

‑‑

I knew something was going to happen the night before I found the Trumps. Sue teases me, but it's true, I can tell when something is going to happen. A feeling starts to swell inside me, as though I'm being blown up like a balloon, my head feels light and somehow cold, there are glittering things at the edges of my eyes. And sure enough, within a day or two someone turns up out of the blue, or I get a letter or e-mail from someone I haven't thought of in ten years. Whenever I see something—a mink, a yearling moose, migrating elvers—I just know.

I shouldn't even tell Sue when it happens. She says it's just a manifestation of my disorder, like a migraine aura.

"Take your fucking medicine, Ivy. It's an early warning system: take your Xanax!"

Rationally I can understand that, rationally I know she's right. That's all it is, a chain of neurons going off inside my head, like a string of firecrackers with a too-short fuse. But I can never explain to her the way the world looks when it happens, that green glow in the sky not just at twilight but all day long, the way I can see the stars sometimes at noon, sparks in the sky.

I was outside the Lonely House, cutting some flowers to take to Blakie. Pink and white cosmos; early asters, powder-blue and mauve; white sweet-smelling phlox, their stems slightly sticky, green aphids like minute beads of dew beneath the flower-heads. From the other shore a chipmunk gave its warning *cheeet*. I looked up, and there on the bank a dozen yards away sat a red fox. It was grinning at me, I could see the thin black rind of its gums, its yellow eyes shining as though lit from within by candles. It sat bolt upright and watched me, its white-tipped brush twitching like a cat's.

I stared back, my arms full of asters. After a moment I said, "Hello there. Hello. What are you looking for?"

I thought it would lope off then, the way foxes do; but it just sat and continued to watch me. I went back to gathering flowers, putting them into a wooden trug and straightening to gaze back at the shore. The fox was still there, yellow eyes glinting in the late-summer light. Abruptly it jumped to its feet. It looked right at me, cocking its head like a dog waiting to be walked.

It barked—a shrill, bone-freezing sound, like a child screaming. I felt my back prickle; it was still watching me, but there was something distracted about its gaze, and I saw its ears flatten against its narrow skull. A minute passed. Then, from away across Cameron Mountain there came an answer, another sharp yelp, higher-pitched and ending in a sort of yodeling wail. The fox turned so quickly it seemed to somersault through the low grass, and arrowed up the hillside towards the birch grove. In a moment it was gone. There was only the frantic chatter of red squirrels in the woods and, when I drew the dory up on the far shore a quarter-hour later, a musky sharp smell like crushed grapes.

◆

I got the last ferry over to Port Symes, me and a handful of late-season people from away, sunburned and loud, waving their cellphones over the rail as they tried to pick up a signal from one of the towers on the mainland.

"We'll *never* get a reservation," a woman said accusingly to her husband. "I *told* you to have Marisa do it before she left—"

At Port Symes I hopped off before any of them, heading for where I'd left Katherine's car parked by an overgrown bank of dog roses. The roses were all crimson hips and thorns by now, the dark-green leaves already burning to yellow; there were yellow beech leaves across the car's windshield, and as I drove out onto the main road I saw acorns like thousands of green-and-bronze marbles scattered across the gravel road. Summer lingers for weeks on the islands, trapped by pockets of warmer air, soft currents and grey fog holding it fast till mid-October some years. Here on the mainland it was already autumn.

The air had a keen winey scent that reminded me of the fox. As I headed down the peninsula towards Rockland I caught the smell of burning leaves, the dank odor of smoke snaking through a chimney that had been cold since spring. The maples were starting to turn, pale gold and pinkish red. There had been a lot of rain in the last few weeks; one good frost would set the leaves ablaze. On the seat beside me Blakie's flowers sat in their mason jar, wrapped in a heavy towel; one good frost and they might be the last ones I'd pick this year.

I got all the way to the main road before the first temblors of panic hit. I deliberately hadn't taken my medication—it made me too sleepy, I couldn't drive and Sue would have had to meet me at the ferry, I would be asleep before we got to her place. The secondary road ended; there was a large green sign with arrows pointing east and west.

THOMASTON
OWLS HEAD
ROCKLAND

I turned right, towards Rockland. In the distance I could see the slate-colored reach of Penobscot Bay, a pine-pointed tip of land protruding into the waters, harsh white lights from Rockland Harbor; miles and miles off a tiny smudge like a thumbprint upon the darkening sky.

Aranbega. I was off island.

The horror comes down, no matter how I try to prepare myself for it, no matter how many times I've been through it: an incendiary blast of wind, the feeling that an iron helmet is tightening around my head. I began to gasp, my heart starting to pound and my entire upper body going cold. Outside was a cool September twilight, the lights of the strip malls around Rockland starting to prick through the gold-and-violet haze, but inside the car the air had grown black, my skin icy. There was a searing fire in my gut. My T-shirt was soaked through. I forced myself to breathe, to remember to exhale; to think *You're not dying, nobody dies of this, it will go, it will go* . . .

"*Fuck.*" I clutched the steering wheel and crept past the Puffin Stop convenience store, past the Michelin tire place, the Dairy Queen; through one set of traffic lights, a second. *You won't die, nobody dies of this; don't look at the harbor.*

I tried to focus on the trees—two huge red oaks, there, you could hardly see where the land had been cleared behind them to make way for a car wash. *It's just a symptom, you're reacting to the symptoms, nobody dies of this, nobody.* At a stop sign I grabbed my cell phone and called Sue.

"I'm by the Rite-Aid." *Don't look at the Rite-Aid.* "I'll be there, five minutes—"

An SUV pulled up behind me. I dropped the phone, feeling like I was going to vomit; turned sharply onto the side street. My legs shook so I couldn't feel the pedals under my feet. *How can I drive if my legs are numb?*

The SUV turned in behind me. My body trembled, I hit the gas too hard and my car shot forward, bumping over the curb then down again. The SUV veered past, a great grey blur, its lights momentarily blinding me. My eyes teared and I forced my breath out in long hoots, and drove the last few hundred feet to Sue's house.

She was in the driveway, still holding the phone in one hand.

"Don't," I said. I opened the car door and leaned out, head between my knees, waiting for the nausea to pass. When she came over I held my hand up and she stopped, but I heard her sigh. From the corner of my eye I could see the resigned set to her mouth, and that her other hand held a prescription bottle.

→←

Always before when I came over to visit my mother, I'd stay with Sue and we'd sleep together, comfortably, not so much for old time's sake as to sustain some connection at once deeper and less enduring than talk. Words I feel obliged to remember, skin I can afford to forget. A woman's body inevitably evokes my own small, wet mouth, my own breath, my own legs, breasts, arms, shoulders, back. Even after Sue started seeing someone else, we'd ease into her wide bed with its wicker headboard, cats sliding to the floor in a grey heap like discarded laundry, radio playing softly, *Tea and oranges, so much more.*

"I think you'd better stay on the couch," Sue said that night. "Lexie isn't comfortable with this arrangement, and . . . "

She sighed, glancing at my small leather bag, just big enough to hold a change of underwear, hairbrush, toothbrush, wallet, a battered paperback of *Lorca in New York.* "I guess I'm not either. Anymore."

I felt my mouth go tight, stared at the mason jar full of flowers on the coffee table.

"Yup," I said.

I refused to look at her. I wouldn't give her the satisfaction of seeing how I felt.

But of course Sue wouldn't be gleeful, or vindictive. She'd just be sad, maybe mildly annoyed. I was the one who froze and burned; I was the one who scarred people for a living.

"It's fine," I said after a minute, and looking at her smiled wryly. "I have to get up early anyway."

She looked at me, not smiling, dark-brown eyes creased with regret. *What a waste*, I could hear her thinking. *What a lonely wasted life*

I think the world is like this: beautiful, hard, cold, unmoving. Oh, it turns, things change—clouds, leaves, the ground beneath the beech trees grows thick with beechmast and slowly becomes black fragrant earth ripe with hellgrammites, millipedes, nematodes, deer mice. Small animals die, we die; a needle moves across honey-colored skin and the skin turns black, or red, or purple. A freckle or a mole becomes an eye; given enough time an eye becomes an earthworm.

But change, the kind of change Sue believes in—Positive Change, Emotional Change, Cultural Change—I don't believe in that. When I was young, I thought the world *was* changing: there was a time, years-long, when the varicolored parade of visitors through the Lonely House made me believe that the world Outside must have changed its wardrobe as well, from sere black suits and floral housedresses to velvet capes and scarlet morning coats, armies of children and teenagers girding themselves for skirmish in embroidered pants, feathered headdresses, bare feet, bare skin. I dressed myself as they did—actually, they dressed *me*, as Blakie smoked and sipped her whiskey sour, and Katherine made sure the bird feeders and wood box were full. And one day I went out to see the world.

It was only RISD—the Rhode Island School of Design—and it should have been a good place, it should have been a Great Place for me. David Byrne and a few other students were playing at someone's house, other students were taking off for Boston and New York, squatting in Alphabet City in burned-out tenements with a toilet in the kitchen, getting strung out, but they were doing things, they were having adventures, hocking bass guitars for Hasselblad cameras, learning how to hold a tattoo machine in a back room on St. Mark's Place, dressing up like housewives and shooting five hours of someone lying passed out in bed while a candle flickered down to a shiny red puddle and someone else laughed in the next room. It didn't look like it at the time, but you can see it now, when you look at their movies and their photographs and their vinyl 45s and their installations: it didn't seem so at the time, but they were having a life.

I couldn't do that. My problem, I know. I lasted a semester, went home for Christmas break and never went back. For a long time it didn't matter—maybe it never mattered—because I still had friends, people came to see me even when Blakie and Katherine were off at the ranch, or bopping around France. Everyone's happy to have a friend on an island in Maine. So in a way it was like Blakie had told me long ago: the world *did* come to me.

Only of course I knew better.

—

Saturday was Sue's day off. She'd been at Penobscot Fields for eleven years now and had earned this, a normal weekend; I wasn't going to spoil it for her. I got up early, before seven, fed the cats and made myself coffee, then went out.

I walked downtown. Rockland used to be one the worst-smelling places in the United States: there was a chicken processing plant, fish factories, the everyday reek and spoils of a working harbor. That's all changed, of course. Now there's a well-known museum, and tourist boutiques have filled up the empty storefronts left when the factories shut down. Only the sardine processing plant remains, down past the Coast Guard station on Tilson Avenue; when the wind is off the water you can smell it, a stale odor of fishbones and rotting bait that cuts through the scents of fresh-roasted coffee beans and car exhaust.

Downtown was nearly empty. A few people sat in front of Second Read, drinking coffee. I went inside and got coffee and a croissant, walked back onto the sidewalk, and wandered down to the waterfront. For some reason seeing the water when I'm on foot usually doesn't bother me. There's something about being in a car, or a bus, something about moving, the idea that there's *more* out there, somewhere; the idea that Aranbega is floating in the blue pearly haze and I'm here, away: disembodied somehow, like an astronaut untethered from a capsule, floating slowly beyond that safe closed place, unable to breathe and everything gone to black, knowing it's just a matter of time.

But that day, standing on the dock with the creosote-soaked wooden pilings beneath my sneakers, looking at orange peels bobbing in the black water and gulls wheeling overhead—that day I didn't feel bad at all. I drank my coffee and ate my croissant, tossed the last bit of crust into the air, and watched the gulls veer and squabble over it. I looked at my watch. A little before eight, still too early to head to Blakie's. She liked to sleep in, and Katherine enjoyed the peace and quiet of a morning.

I headed back towards Main Street. There was some early morning traffic now, people heading off to do their shopping at Shaw's and Wal-Mart. On the corner I waited for the light to change, glanced at a storefront and saw a sign taped to the window.

ST. BRUNO'S EPISCOPAL CHURCH
ANNUAL RUMMAGE SALE
SATURDAY SEPTEMBER 7
8:00 A.M.–3:00 P.M.
LUNCH SERVED FROM 11:30

Penobscot Fields had once been the lupine-strewn meadow behind St. Bruno's; proximity to the church was one of the reasons Blakie and Katherine had first signed on to the retirement community. I wasn't a churchgoer, but during the summer I was an avid haunter of yard sales in the Rockland area. You don't get many of them after Labor Day, but the rummage sale at St. Bruno's almost makes up for it. I made sure I had my wallet and checkbook in my bag, then hurried to get there before the doors opened.

There was already a line. I recognized a couple of dealers, a few regulars who smiled or nodded at me. St. Bruno's is a late-nineteenth century neo-gothic building, designed in the late Arts and Crafts style by Halbert Liston: half-timbered beams, local dove-grey fieldstone, slate shingles on the roof. The rummage sale was not in the church, of course, but the adjoining parish house. It had whitewashed walls rather than stone, the same half-timbered upper story, etched with arabesques of dying clematis and sere Virginia creeper. In the door was a diamond-shaped window through which a worried elderly woman peered out every few minutes.

"Eight o'clock!" someone called good-naturedly from the front of the line. Bobby Day, the greying hippie who owned a used bookstore in Camden. "Time to go!"

From inside, the elderly woman gave one last look at the crowd, then nodded. The door opened; there was a surge forward, laughter and excited murmurs, someone crying "Marge, look out! Here they come!" Then I was inside.

Long tables of linens and clothing were at the front of the hall, surrounded by women with hands already full of flannel sheets and crewel-work. I scanned these quickly, then glanced at the furniture. Nice stuff—a Morris chair and old oak settle, some wicker, a flax wheel. Episcopalians always have good rummage sales, better quality than Our Lady of the Harbor or those off-brand churches straggling down towards Warren.

But the Lonely House was already crammed with my own nice stuff, besides which it would be difficult to get anything back to the island. So I made my way to the rear of the hall, where Bobby Day was going through boxes of books on the floor. We exchanged hellos, Bobby smiling but not taking his eyes from the books; in deference to him I continued on to the back corner. An old man wearing a canvas apron with a faded silhouette of St. Bruno on it stood over a table covered with odds and ends.

"This is whatever didn't belong anywhere else," he said. He waved a hand at a hodgepodge of beer steins, Tupperware, mismatched silver, shoeboxes overflowing with candles, buttons, mason-jar lids. "Everything's a dollar."

I doubted there was anything there worth fifty cents, but I just nodded and moved slowly down the length of the table. A chipped Poppy Trails bowl and a bunch of ugly glass ashtrays. Worn Beanie Babies with the tags clipped off. A game of Twister. As I looked, a heavyset woman barreled up behind me. She had a rigidly unsmiling face and an overflowing canvas bag: I caught glints of brass and pewter, the telltale dull green glaze of a nice Teco pottery vase. A dealer. She avoided my gaze, her hand snaking out to grab something I'd missed, a tarnished silver flask hidden behind a stack of plastic Easter baskets.

I tried not to grimace. I hated dealers and their greedy bottom-feeder mentality. By this afternoon she'd have polished the flask and stuck a seventy-five-dollar price tag on it. I moved quickly to the end of the table. I could see her watching me whenever my hand hovered above something; once I moved on she'd grab whatever I'd been examining, give it a cursory glance before elbowing up beside me once more. After a few minutes I turned away, was just starting to leave when my gaze fell upon a swirl of violet and orange tucked within a Pyrex dish.

"Not sure what that is," the old man said as I pried it from the bowl. Beside me the dealer watched avidly. "Lady's scarf, I guess."

It was a lumpy packet a bit larger than my hand, made up of a paisley scarf that had been folded over several times to form a thick square, then wrapped and tightly knotted around a rectangular object. The cloth was frayed, but it felt like fine wool. There was probably enough of it to make a nice pillow cover. Whatever was inside felt compact but also slightly flexible; it had a familiar heft as I weighed it in my palm.

An oversized pack of cards. I glanced up to see the dealer watching me with undisguised impatience.

"I'll take this," I said, and handed the old man a dollar. "Thanks."

A flicker of disappointment across the dealer's face. I smiled at her, enjoying my mean little moment of triumph, and left.

Outside the parish hall a stream of people were headed for the parking lot, carrying lamps and pillows and overflowing plastic bags. The church bell tolled eight thirty. Blakie would just be getting up. I killed a few more minutes by wandering around the church grounds, past a well-kept herb garden and stands of yellow chrysanthemums. Behind a neatly trimmed hedge of boxwood I discovered a statue of St. Bruno himself, standing watch over a granite bench. Here I sat with my paisley-wrapped treasure, and set about trying to undo the knot.

For a while I thought I'd have to just rip the damn thing apart, or wait till I got to Blakie's to cut it open. The cloth was knotted so tightly I couldn't undo it, and the paisley had gotten wet at some point then shrunk—it was like trying to pick at dried plaster, or Sheetrock.

But gradually I managed to tease one corner of the scarf free, tugging it gently until, after a good ten minutes, I was able to undo the wrappings. A faint odor wafted up, the vanilla-tinged scent of pipe tobacco. There was a greasy feel to the frayed cloth, sweat, or maybe someone had dropped it on the damp grass. I opened it carefully, smoothing its folds till I could finally see what was tucked inside.

It was a large deck of cards, bound with a rubber band. The rubber band fell to bits when I tried to remove it, and something fluttered onto the bench. I picked it up: a scrap of paper with a few words scrawled in pencil.

The least trumps.

I frowned. The Greater Trumps, those were the picture cards that made up the Major Arcana in a tarot deck—the Chariot, the Magician, the Empress, the Hierophant. Eight or nine years ago I had a girlfriend with enough New Age tarots to channel the entire Order of the Golden Dawn. Marxist tarots, lesbian tarots, African, Zen, and Mormon tarots; Tarots of the Angels, of Wise Mammals, poisonous snakes and smiling madonni; Aleister Crowley's tarot, and Shirley MacLaine's; the dread Feminist Tarot of the Cats. There were twenty-two Major Arcana cards, and the lesser trumps were analogous to the fifty-two cards in an ordinary deck, with an additional four representing knights.

But the least trumps? The phrase stabbed at my memory, but I couldn't place it. I stared at the scrap of paper with its rushed scribble, put it aside and examined the deck.

The cards were thick, with the slightly furry feel of old pasteboard. Each was printed with an identical and intricate design of spoked wheels, like old-fashioned gears with interlocking teeth. The inks were primitive, too-bright primary colors, red and yellow and blue faded now to periwinkle and pale rose, a dusty gold like smudged pollen. I guessed they dated to the early or mid-nineteenth century. The images had the look of old children's picture books from that era, at once vivid and muted, slightly sinister, as though the illustrators were making a point of not revealing their true meaning to the casual viewer. I grinned, thinking of how I'd wrested them from the clutches of an antiques dealer, then turned them over.

The cards were all blank. I shook my head, fanning them out on the bench before me. A few of the cards had their corners neatly clipped, but others looked as though they had been bitten off in tiny crescent-shaped wedges. I squinted at one, trying to determine if someone had peeled off a printed image. The surface was rough, flecked with bits of darker grey and black, or white, but it didn't seem to have ever had anything affixed to it. There was no trace of glue or spirit gum that I could see, no jots of ink or colored paper.

A mistake, then. The deck had obviously been discarded by the printer. Not even a dealer would have been able to get more than a couple of bucks for it.

Too bad. I gathered the cards into a stack, and started wrapping the scarf around them when I noticed that one card was thicker than the rest. I pulled it out: not a single card after all but two that had become stuck together. I set the rest of the deck aside, safe within the paisley shroud; then gingerly slid my thumbnail between the stuck cards. It was like prising apart sheets of mica—I could feel where the pasteboard held fast towards the center, but if I pulled at it too hard or too quickly the cards would tear.

But very slowly, I felt the cards separate. Maybe the warmth of my touch helped, or the sudden exposure to air and moisture. For whatever reason, the cards suddenly slid apart so that I held one in each hand.

"*Oh.*"

I cried aloud, they were that wonderful. Two tiny, brilliantly inked tableaux like medieval tapestries, or paintings by Brueghel glimpsed through a rosace window. One card was awhirl with minute figures, men and women but also animals, dogs dancing on their hind legs, long-necked cranes, and crabs that lifted clacking claws to a sky filled with pennoned airships, exploding suns, a man being carried on a litter, and a lash-fringed eye like a greater sun gazing down upon them all. The other card showed only the figure of a naked man, kneeling so that he faced the viewer, but with head bowed so that you saw only his broad back, a curve of neck like a quarter-moon, a sheaf of dark hair spilling to the ground before him. The man's skin was painted in gold leaf; the ground he knelt upon was the dreamy green of old bottle-glass, the sky behind him crocus-yellow, with a tinge upon the horizon like the first flush of sun, or the protruding tip of a finger. As I stared at them I felt my heart begin to beat, too fast too hard but not with fear this time, not this time.

The Least Trumps. The term was used, just once, in the first chapter of the unfinished, final volume of *Five Windows One Door*. I remembered it suddenly, the way you recall something from early childhood, the smell of marigolds towering above your head, a blue plush dog with one glass eye, thin sunlight filtering through a crack in a frosted glass cold frame. My mouth filled with liquid and I tasted sour cherries, salt and musk, the first time my tongue probed a girl's cunt. A warm breeze stirred my hair. I heard distant laughter, a booming bass-note that resolved into the echo of a church clock tolling nine.

—❦—

Only when he was certain that Mabel had fallen fast asleep beside him would Tarquin remove the cards from their brocade pouch, her warm limbs tangled in the stained bedcovers where they emitted a smell of yeast and limewater, the surrounding room suffused with twilight so that when he held the cards before her mouth, one by one, he saw how her breath brought to life the figures painted upon each, as though she breathed upon a winter windowpane where frost-roses bloomed: Pavell Saved From Drowning, The Bangers, One Leaf Left, Hermalchio and Lachrymatory, Villainous Saltpetre, The Ground-Nut, The Widower: all the recusant figures of the Least Trumps quickening beneath Mabel's sleeping face.

—❦—

Even now the words came to me by heart. Sometimes, when I couldn't fall asleep, I would lie in bed and silently recite the books from memory, beginning with Volume One, *The First Window: Love Plucking Rowan Berries*, with its description of Mabel's deflowering that I found so tragic when I first read it. Only later in my twenties, when I read the books for the fifth or seventh time, did I realize the scene was a parody of the seduction scene in *Rigoletto*. In this way Walter Burden Fox's books eased my passage into the world, as they did in many others. Falling in love with fey little Clytie Winton then weeping over her death; making my first forays into sex when I masturbated to the memory of Tarquin's mad brother Elwell taking Mabel as she slept; realizing, as I read of Mabel's great love affair with the silent film actress Nola Flynn, that there were words to describe what I did sometimes with my own friends, even if those words had a lavender must of the attic to them: *tribadism, skylarking, sit Venus in the garden with Her Gate unlocked.*

My mother never explained any of this to me: sex, love, suffering, patience. Probably she assumed that her example alone was enough, and for another person it might well have been. But I never saw my mother unhappy, or frightened. My first attack came not long after Julia Sa'adah left me. Julia who inked my life Before and After; and while at the time I was contemptuous of anyone who suggested a link between the two events, breakup and crackup, I can see now that it was so. In Fox's novels, love affairs sometimes ended badly, but for all the lessons his books held, they never readied me for the shock of being left.

That was more than eleven years ago. I still felt the aftershocks, of course. I still dream about her: her black hair, so thick it was like oiled rope streaming through my fingers; her bronzey skin, its soft glaucous bloom like scuppernongs; the way her mouth tasted. Small mouth, smaller than my own, cigarettes and wintergreen, tea oil, coriander seed. The dream is different each time, though it always ends the same way, it ends the way it ended: Julia looking at me as she packs up her Rockland studio, arms bare so I can see my own apprentice work below her elbow, vine leaves, stylized knots. My name there, and hers, if you knew where to look. Her face sad but amused as she shakes her head. "You never happened, Ivy."

"How can you *say* that?" This part never changes either, though in my waking mind I say a thousand other things. "Six years, how can you fucking *say* that?"

She just shakes her head. Her voice begins to break up, swallowed by the harsh buzz of a tattoo machine choking down; her image fragments, hair face eyes breasts tattoos spattering into bits of light, jabs of black and red. The tube is running out of ink. "That's not what I mean. You just don't get it, Ivy. *You* never happened. *You*. Never. Happened."

Then I wake and the panic's full-blown, like waking into a room where a bomb's exploded. Only there's no bomb. What's exploded is all inside my head.

It was years before anyone figured out how it worked, this accretion of synaptic damage, neuronal misfirings, an overstimulated fight-or-flight response; the way one tiny event becomes trapped within a web of dendrites and interneurons and triggers a cascade of cortisol and epinephrine, which in turns wakes the immense black spider that rushes out and seizes me so that I see and feel only horror, only dread, the entire world poisoned by its bite. There is no antidote—the whole disorder is really just an accumulation of symptoms, accelerated pulse-rate, racing heartbeat, shallow breathing. There is no cure, only chemicals that lull the spider back to sleep. It may be that my repeated tattooing of my own skin has somehow oversensitized me, like bad acupuncture, caused an involuntary neurochemical reaction that only makes it worse.

No one knows. And it's not something Walter Burden Fox ever covered in his books.

I stared at the illustrated cards in my hands. Fox had lived not far from here, in Tenants Harbor. My mother knew him years before I was born. He was much older than she was, but in those days—this was long before e-mail and cheap long distance servers—writers and artists would travel a good distance for the company of their own kind, and certainly a lot further than from Tenants Harbor to Aranbega Island. It was the first time I can remember being really impressed by my mother, the way other people always assumed I must be. She had found me curled up in the hammock, reading *Love Plucking Rowan Berries*.

"You're reading Burdie's book." She stooped to pick up my empty lemonade glass.

I corrected her primly. "It's by Walter Burden Fox."

"Oh, I know. Burdie, that's what he liked to be called. His son was Walter too. Wally, they called him. I knew him."

Now, behind me, St. Bruno's bell rang the quarter-hour. Blakie would be up by now, waiting for my arrival. I carefully placed the two cards with their fellows inside the paisley scarf, put the bundle inside my bag, and headed for Penobscot Fields.

⊷

Blakie and Katherine were sitting at their dining nook when I let myself in. Yesterday's *New York Times* was spread across the table, and the remains of breakfast.

"Well," my mother asked, white brows raised above calm grey eyes as she looked at me. "Did you throw up?"

"Oh, hush, you," said Katherine.

"Not this time." I bent to kiss my mother, then turned to hug Katherine. "I went to the rummage sale at St. Bruno's, that's why I'm late."

"Oh, I meant to give them my clothes!" Katherine stood to get me coffee. "I brought over a few boxes of things, but I forgot the clothes. I have a whole bag, some nice Hermes scarves, too."

"You shouldn't give those away." Blakie patted the table, indicating where I should sit beside her. "That consignment shop in Camden gives us good credit for them. I got this sweater there." She touched her collar, dove-grey knit, three pearl buttons. "It's lamb's wool. Bergdorf Goodman. They closed ages ago. Someone must have died."

"Oh hush," said Katherine. She handed me a coffee mug. "Like we need credit for *clothes*."

"Look," I said. "Speaking of scarves—"

I pulled the paisley packet from the purse, clearing a space amidst the breakfast dishes. For a fraction of a second Blakie looked surprised; then she blinked, and along with Katherine leaned forward expectantly.

As I undid the wrappings the slip of paper fell onto the table beside my mother's hand. Her gnarled fingers scrabbled at the table, finally grabbed the scrap.

"I can't read this," she said, adjusting her glasses as she stared and scowled. I set the stack of cards on the scarf, then slid them all across the table. I had withheld the two cards that retained their color; now I slipped them into my back jeans pocket, carefully, so they wouldn't get damaged. The others lay in a neat pile before my mother.

"'The Least Trumps.'" I pointed at the slip of paper. "That's what it says."

She looked at me sharply, then at the cards. "What do you mean? It's a deck of cards."

"What's written on the paper. It says, 'The Least Trumps.' I don't know if you remember, but there's a scene in one of Fox's books, the first one? The Least Trumps is what he calls a set of tarot cards that one of the characters uses." I edged over beside her, and pointed at the bit of paper she held between thumb and forefinger. "I was curious if you could read that. Since you knew him? I was wondering if you recognized it. If it was his handwriting."

"Burdie's?" My mother shook her head, drew the paper to her face until it was just a few inches from her nose. It was the same pose she'd assumed when pretending to gaze at Wise Ant through a magnifying glass for *Life* magazine, only now it was my mother who looked puzzled, even disoriented. "Well, I don't know. I don't remember."

I felt a flash of dread, that now of all times would be when she started to lose it, to drift away from me and Katherine. But no. She turned to Katherine and said, "Where did we put those files? When I was going through the letters from after the war. Do you remember?"

"Your room, I think. Do you want me to get them?"

"No, no . . ." Blakie waved me off as she stood and walked, keeping her balance by touching chair, countertop, wall on the way to her study.

Katherine looked after her, then at the innocuous shred of paper, then at me. "What is it?" She touched one unraveling corner of the scarf. "Where did you get them?"

"At the rummage sale. They were wrapped up in that, I didn't know what they were till I got outside and opened it."

"Pig in a poke." Katherine winked at me. She still had her silvery hair done every Thursday, in the whipped-up spray-stiffened bouffant of her Dallas socialite days—not at the beauty parlor at the retirement center, either, but the most expensive salon in Camden. She had her nails done too, even though her hands were too twisted by arthritis to wear the bijoux rings she'd always favored, square-cut diamonds and aquamarines and the emerald my mother had given her when they first met. "I'm surprised you bought a pig in a poke, Ivy Bee."

"Yeah. I'm surprised too."

"Here we are." My mother listed back into the room, settling with a thump in her chair. "Now we can see."

She jabbed her finger at the table, where the scrap of paper fluttered like an injured moth, then handed me an envelope. "Open that, please, Ivy dear. My hands are so clumsy now."

It was a white, letter-sized envelope, unsealed, tipsy typed address.

Miss Blakie Tun,
The Lonely House,
Aranbega Island, Maine.

Before Zip Codes, even, one faded blue four-cent stamp in one corner. The other corner with the typed return address. W. B. Fox, Sand Hill Road, T. Harbor, Maine.

"Look at it!" commanded Blakie.

Obediently I withdrew the letter, unfolded it, and scanned the handwritten lines, front and back, until I reached the end. Blue ink, mouse-tail flourish on the final *e. Very Fondly Yours, Burdie.*

"I think it's the same writing." I scrutinized the penmanship, while trying not to actually absorb its content. Which seemed dull in any case, something about a dog, and snow, and someone's car getting stuck, and *Be glad when summer's here, at least we can visit again.*

Least. I picked up the scrap of paper to compare the two words.

"You know, they *are* the same," I said. There was something else, too. I brought the letter to my face and sniffed it. "And you know what else? I can smell it. It smells like pipe tobacco. The scarf smells like it, too."

"Borkum Riff." My mother made a face. "Awful sweet stuff, I couldn't stand it. So."

She looked at me, grey eyes narrowed, not sly but thoughtful. "We were good friends, you know. Burdie. Very loveable man."

Katherine nodded. "Fragile."

"Fragile. He would have made a frail old man, wouldn't he?" She glanced at Katherine—two strong old ladies—then at me. "I remember how much you liked his books. I'm sorry now we didn't write to each other more, I could have given you his letters, Ivy. He always came to visit us, once or twice a year. In the summer."

"But not after the boy died," said Katherine.

My mother shook her head. "No, not after Wally died. Poor Burdie."

"Poor Wally," suggested Katherine.

It was why Fox had never completed the last book of the quintet. His son had been killed in the Korean War. I knew that; it was one of the only really interesting, if tragic, facts about Walter Burden Fox. There had been one full-length biography, written in the 1970s, when his work achieved a minor cult status boosted by the success of Tolkien and Mervyn Peake, a brief vogue in those days for series books in uniform paperback editions. *The Alexandria Quartet, Children of Violence, A Dance to the Music of Time. Five Windows One Door* had never achieved that kind of popularity, of course, despite the affection for it held by figures like Anais Nin, Timothy

Leary, and Virgil Thomson, themselves eclipsed now by brighter, younger lights.

Fox died in 1956. I hadn't been born yet. I could never have met him.

Yet, in a funny way, he made me who I am—well, maybe not *me* exactly. But he certainly changed the way I thought about the world; made it seem at once unabashedly romantic and charged with a sense of imminence, as ripe with possibility as an autumn orchard is ripe with fruit. Julia and I were talking once about the 1960s—she was seven years older than me, and had lived through them as an adult, communes in Tennessee, drug dealing in Malibu, before she settled down in Rockland and opened her tattoo studio.

She said, "You want to know what the sixties were about, Ivy? The sixties were about *It could happen.*"

And that's what Fox's books were like. They gave me the sense that there was someone leaning over my shoulder, someone whispering *It could happen.*

So I suppose you could say that Walter Burden Fox ruined the real world for me, when I didn't find it as welcoming as the one inhabited by Mabel and Nola and the Sienno brothers. Could there ever have been a real city as marvelous as his imagined Newport? Who would ever choose to bear the weight of this world? Who would ever want to?

Still, that was my weakness, not his. The only thing I could really fault him for was his failure to finish that last volume. But, under the circumstances, who could blame him for that?

"So these are his cards? May I?" Katherine glanced at me. I nodded, and she picked up the deck tentatively, turned it over, and gave a little gasp. "Oh! They're blank—"

She looked embarrassed and I laughed. "Katherine! *Now* look what you've done!"

"But were they like this when you got them?" She began turning the cards over, one by one, setting them out on the table as though playing an elaborate game of solitaire. "Look at this! They're every single one of them blank. I've never seen such a thing."

"All used up," said Blakie. She folded the scarf and pushed it to one side. "You should wash that, Ivy. Who knows where it's been."

"Well, where *has* it been? Did he go to church there? St. Bruno's?"

"I don't remember." Blakie's face became a mask: as she had aged, Circe became the Sphinx. She was staring at the cards lying face-up on the table. Only of course there were no faces, just a grid of grey rectangles, some missing one or two corners or even three corners. My mother's expression was watchful but wary; she glanced at me, then quickly looked away again. I thought of the two cards in my back pocket but said nothing. "His wife died young, he raised the boy alone. He wanted to be a writer too, you know. Probably they just ended up in someone's barn."

"The cards, you mean," Katherine said mildly. Blakie looked annoyed. "There. That's all of them."

"How many are there?" I asked. Katherine began to count, but Blakie said, "Seventy-three."

"Seventy-three?" I shook my head. "What kind of deck uses seventy-three cards?"

"Some are missing, then. There's only seventy." Katherine looked at Blakie. "Seventy-three? How do you know?"

"I just remember, that's all," my mother said irritably. She pointed at me. "*You* should know. You read all his books."

"Well." I shrugged and stared at the bland pattern on the dining table, then reached for a card. The top right corner was missing; but how would you know it was the top? "They were only mentioned once. As far as I recall, anyway. Just in passing. Why do you think the corners are cut off?"

"To keep track of them." Katherine began to collect them back into a pile. "That's how card cheats work. Take off a little teeny bit, just enough so they can tell when they're dealing 'em out. Which one's an ace, which one's a trey."

"But these are all the same," I said. "There's no point to it."

Then I noticed Blakie was staring at me. Suddenly I began to feel paranoid, like when I was a teenager out getting high, walking back into the Lonely House and praying she wouldn't notice how stoned I was. I felt like I'd been lying, although what had I done, besides stick two cards in my back pocket?

But then maybe I was lying when I said there was no point; maybe I was wrong. Maybe there *was* a point. If two of the cards had a meaning, maybe they all did; even if I had no clue what their meaning was. Even if nobody had a clue: they still might mean something.

But what? It was like one of those horrible logic puzzles—you have one boat, three geese, one fox, an island: how do you get all the geese onto the island without the fox eating them? Seventy-three cards: seventy that Katherine had counted, the pair in my back pocket; where was the other one?

I fought an almost irresistible urge to reveal the two picture cards I'd hidden. Instead I looked away from my mother, and saw that now Katherine was staring at me, too. It was a moment before I realized she was waiting for the last card, the one that was still in my hand. "Oh. Thanks—"

I gave it to her, she put it on top of the stack, turned and gave the stack to Blakie, who gave it to me. I looked down at the cards and felt that cold pressure starting to build inside my head, helium leaking into my brain, something that was going to make me float away, talk funny.

"Well." I wrapped the cards in the paisley scarf. It still smelled faintly of pipe tobacco, but now there was another scent too, my mother's Chanel N°5. I stuck the cards in my bag, turned back to the dining table. "What should we do now?"

"I don't have a clue," said my mother, and gave me the smile of an octogenarian tiger. "Ivy? You decide."

Julia's father was Egyptian, a Coptic diplomat from Cairo. Her mother was an artist manqué from a wealthy Boston family that had a building at Harvard named for it. Her father, Narouz, had been married and divorced four times; Julia had a much younger half-brother and several half-sisters. The brother died in a terrorist attack in Egypt in the early nineties, a year or so before she left me. After her mother's death from cancer the same year, Julia refused to have anything else to do with Narouz or his extended family. A few months later, she refused to have anything to do with me as well.

Julia claimed that *Five Windows One Door* could be read as a secret text of ancient Coptic magic; that there were meanings encoded within the characters' ceaseless and often unrequited love affairs, that the titles of Nola Flynn's silent movies corresponded to oracular texts in the collections of the Hermitage and the Institut Francais d'Archeologie Orientale in Cairo; that the scene in which Tarquin sodomizes his twin is in fact a description of a ritual to leave a man impotent and protect a woman from sexual advances. I asked her how such a book could possibly be conceived and written by a middle-aged inhabitant of Maine, in the middle of the twentieth century.

Julia just shrugged. "That's why it works. Nobody knows. Look at Lorca."

"Lorca?" I shook my head, trying not to laugh. "What, was he in Maine, too?"

"No. But he worked in the twentieth century."

That was almost the last thing Julia Sa'adah ever said to me. This is another century. Nothing works anymore.

I caught an earlier ferry back than I'd planned. Katherine was tired; I had taken her and my mother to lunch at the small café they favored, but it was more crowded than usual, with a busload of blue-haired leaf-peepers from Newburyport who all ordered the specials so that the kitchen ran out and we had to eat BLTs.

"I just hate that." Blakie glowered at the table next to us, four women the same age as she was, scrying the bill as though it were tea-leaves. "Look at them, trying to figure out the tip! Fifteen percent, darling," she said loudly. "Double the tax and add one."

The women looked up. "Oh, thank you!" one said. "Isn't it pretty here?"

"I wouldn't know," said Blakie. "I'm blind."

The woman looked shocked. "Oh, hush, you," scolded Katherine. "She is not," but the women were already scurrying to leave.

I drove them back to their tidy modern retirement cottage, the made-for-TV version of the Lonely House.

"I'll see you next week," I said, after helping them inside. Katherine kissed me and made a beeline for the bathroom. My mother sat on the couch, waiting to catch her breath. She had congestive heart disease, payback for all those years of smoking Kents and eating heavily marbled steaks.

"You could stay here if you wanted," she said, and for almost the first time I heard a plaintive note in her voice. "The couch folds out."

I smiled and hugged her. "You know, I might do that. I think Sue wants a break from me. For a little while."

For a moment I thought she was going to say something. Her mouth pursed and her grey eyes once again had that watchful look. But she only nodded, patting my hand with her strong cold one, then kissed my cheek, a quick furtive gesture like she might be caught.

"Be careful, Ivy Bee," she said. "Goodbye."

On the ferry I sat on deck. There were only a few other passengers. I had the stern to myself, a bench sheltered by the engine house from spray and chill wind. The afternoon had turned cool and grey.

There was a bruised line of clouds upon the horizon, violet and slate-blue; it made the islands look stark as a Rockwell Kent woodblock, the pointed firs like arrowheads.

It was a time of day, a time of year, I loved; one of the only times when things still seemed possible to me. Something about the slant of the late year's light, the sharp line between shadows and stones, as though if you slid your hand in there you'd find something unexpected.

It made me want to work.

I had no customers lined up that week. Idly I ran my right hand along the top of my left leg, worn denim and beneath it muscle, skin. I hadn't worked on myself for a while. That was one of the first things I learned when I was apprenticed to Julia: a novice tattoo artist practices on herself. If you're right-handed, you do your left arm, your left leg; just like a good artist makes her own needles, steel flux and solder, jig and needles, the smell of hot tinning fluid on the tip of the solder gun. That way people can see your work. They know they can trust you.

The last thing I'd done was a scroll of oak leaves and eyes, fanning out above my left knee. My upper thigh was still taut white skin. I was thin and rangy like my mother had been, too fair to ever have tanned. I flexed my hand, imagining the weight of the machine, its pulse a throbbing heart. As I stared at the ferry's wake, I could see the lights of Rockland Harbor glimmer then disappear into the growing dusk. When I stuck my head out to peer towards the bow, I saw Aranbega rising from the Atlantic, black firs and granite cliffs buffed to pink by the failing sun.

I stood, keeping my balance as I gently pulled the two cards from my back pocket. I glanced at both, then put one into my wallet, behind my driver's license; sat and examined the other, turning so that the wall of the engine house kept it safe from spray. It was the card that showed only the figure of a kneeling man. A deceptively simple form, a few fluid lines indicating torso, shoulders, offertory stance—that crescent of bare neck, his hands half-hidden by his long hair.

Why did I know it was a man? I'm not sure. The breadth of his shoulders, maybe; maybe some underlying sense that any woman in such a position would be inviting disaster. This figure seemed neither resigned nor abdicating responsibility. He seemed to be waiting.

It was amazing, how the interplay of black and white and a few drops of gold leaf could conjure up an entire world. Like Pamela Colman Smith's designs for the Waite tarot—the High Priestess, the King of Wands—or a figure that Julia had shown me once. It was from a facsimile edition of a portfolio of Coptic texts on papyrus, now in the British Library. There were all kinds of spells—

For I am having a clash with a headless dog, seize him when he comes. Grasp this pebble with both your hands, flee eastward to your right, while you journey on up.

A stinging ant: In this way, while it is still fresh, burn it, grind it with vinegar, put it with incense. Put it on eyes that have discharge. They will get better.

The figure was part of a spell to obtain a good singing voice. Julia translated the text for me as she had the others:

Yea, yea, for I adjure you in the name of the seven letters that are tattooed on the chest of the father, namely AAAAAAAA, EEEEEEE, EEEEEEE, IIIIIII, OOOOOOO, UUUUUUU, OOOOOOO. Obey my mouth, before it passes and another one comes in its place! Offering: wild frankincense; wild mastic; cassia.

The Coptic figure that accompanied the text had a name: DAVITHEA RACHOCHI ADONIEL. It looked nothing like the figure on the card in front of me; it was like something you'd see scratched on the wall of a cave.

Yet it had a name. And I would never know the name of this card.

But I would use it, I decided. *The least trumps.* Beneath me the ferry's engine shifted down, its dull steady groan deepening as we drew near Aranbega's shore. I slid the card into the Lorca book I'd brought, stuffed it into my bag, and waited to dock.

→

I'd left my old GMC pickup where I always did, parked behind the Island General Store. I went inside and bought a sourdough baguette and a bottle of Toquai. I'd gotten a taste for the wine from Julia; now the store ordered it especially for me, though some of the well-heeled summer people bought it as well.

"Working tonight?" said Mary, the store's owner.

"Yup."

Outside it was full dusk. I drove across the island on the rugged gravel road that bisected it into north and south, village and wild places. To get to Green Pond you drive off the main road, following a rutted lane that soon devolves into what resembles a washed-out streambed. Soon this rudimentary road ends, at the entrance to a large grove of hundred-and-fifty-year-old pines. I parked here and walked the rest of the way, a quarter-mile beneath high branches that stir restlessly, making a sound like the sea even on windless days. The pines give way to birches, ferns growing knee-high in a spinney of trees like bones. Another hundred feet and you reach the edge of Green Pond, before you the Lonely House rising on its grey islet, a dream of safety. Usually this was when the last vestiges of fear would leave me, blown away by the cool wind off the lake and the sight of my childhood home, my wooden dory pulled up onto the shore a few feet from where I stood.

But tonight the unease remained. Or no, not unease exactly; more a sense of apprehension that, very slowly, resolved into a kind of anticipation. But anticipation of what? I stared at the Lonely House with its clumps of asters and yellow coneflowers, the ragged garden I deliberately didn't weed or train. Because I wanted the illusion of wilderness, I wanted to pretend I'd left something to chance. And suddenly I wanted to see something else.

If you walk to the other side of the small lake—I hardly ever do—you find that you're on the downward slope of a long boulder-strewn rise, a glacial moraine that eventually plummets into the Atlantic Ocean. Scattered white pines and birches grow here, and ancient white oaks, some of the very few white oaks left in the entire state, in fact, the rest having been harvested well over a century before, as masts for the great schooners. The lesser trees—red oaks, mostly, a few sugar maples—have been cut, for the Lonely House's firewood and repairs, so that if you stand in the right place you can actually look down the entire southeastern end of the island and see the ocean: scumbled grey cliffs and beyond that nothing, an unbroken darkness that might be fog, or sea, or the end of the world.

The right place to see this is from an outcropping of granite that my mother named The Ledges. On a foggy day, if you stand there and look at the Lonely House, you have an illusion of gazing from one sea-island to another. If you turn, you see only darkness. The seas are too rough for recreational sailors; far from the major shipping lanes; too risky for commercial fishermen. The entire Grand Banks fishery has been depleted, so that you can stare out for hours or maybe even days and never see a single light, nothing but stars and maybe the blinking red eye of a distant plane flying the Great Circle Route to Gander or London.

It was a vista that terrified me, though I would dutifully point it out to first-time visitors, showing them where they could sit on The Ledges.

"On a clear day you can see Ireland," Katherine used to say, the joke being that on a Maine island you almost never had a clear day.

This had not been a clear day, of course, and, with evening, high grey clouds had come from the west. Only the easternmost horizon held a pale shimmer of blue-violet, lustrous as the inner curve of a mussel shell. Behind me the wind moved through the old pines, and I could hear the high rustling of the birch leaves. Not so far off a fox barked. The sound made my neck prickle.

But I'd left a single light on inside the Lonely House, and so I focused on that, walking slowly around the perimeter of Green Pond with the little beacon always at the edge of my vision, until I reached the far side, the eastern side. Ferns crackled underfoot; I smelled the sweet odor of dying bracken, and bladderwrack from the cliffs far below. The air had the bite of rain to it, and that smell you get sometimes, when a low pressure system carries the reek of places much farther south—a soupy thick smell, like rotting vegetation, mangroves or palmettos. I breathed it in and thought of Julia, and realized that for the first time in years, an hour had gone by and I had not thought about her at all. From the trees on the other side of Green Pond the fox barked again, even closer this time.

For one last moment I stood, gazing at The Ledges. Then I turned and walked back to where my dory waited, clambered in and rowed myself home.

——

The tattoo took me till dawn to finish. Once inside the Lonely House I opened the bottle of Toquai, poured myself a glassful and drank it. Then I went to retrieve the card, stuck inside that decrepit New Directions paperback in my bag. The book was the only thing of Julia's I had retained. She'd made a point of going through every single box of clothes and books I'd packed, through every sagging carton of dishware, and removed anything that had been hers. Anything we'd purchased together, anything that it had been her idea to buy. So that by the time she was done, it wasn't just like I'd never happened. It was like she'd never happened, either.

Except for this book. I found it a few months after the breakup. It had gotten stuck under the driver's seat of my old Volvo, wedged between a broken spring and the floor. In all the years I'd been with Julia, I'd never read it, or seen her reading it. But just a few weeks earlier I started flipping through the pages, casually, more to get the poet's smell than to actually understand him. Now I opened the book to the page where the card was stuck, and noticed several lines that had been highlighted with yellow marker.

> *The* duende, *then, is a power and not a construct, is a struggle and not a concept. That is to say, it is not a question of aptitude, but of a true and viable style—of blood, in other words; of creation made act.*

A struggle not a concept. I smiled, and dropped the book on the couch; took the card and went into my studio to work.

I spent over an hour just getting a feel for the design, trying to copy it freehand onto paper before giving up. I'm a good draftsman, but one thing I've learned over the years is that the simpler a good drawing appears to be, the more difficult it is to copy. Try copying one of Picasso's late minotaur drawings and you'll see what I mean. Whoever did the design on this particular card probably wasn't Picasso; but the image still defeated me. There was a mystery to it, a sense of waiting that was charged with power; like that D. H. Lawrence poem, *those who have not exploded*. I finally traced it on my light board, the final stencil image exactly the same size as that on the card, outlined in black hectograph ink.

Then I prepped myself. My studio is as sterile as I can make it. There's no carpet on the bare wood floor, which I scrub every day. Beneath a blue plastic cover, the worktable is white Formica, so blood or dirt shows, or spilled ink. I don't bother with an apron or gloves when I'm doing myself, and between the lack of protection and a couple of glasses of Toquai, I always get a slightly illicit-feeling buzz. I feel like I'm pulling something over, even though there's never anyone around but myself. I swabbed the top of my thigh with 70 percent alcohol, used a new, disposable razor to shave it, swabbed it again, dried it with sterile gauze soaked in more alcohol. Then I coated the shaved skin with betadine, tossing the used gauze into a small metal biohazard bin.

I'd already set up my inks in their plastic presterilized caps— black; yellow and red to get the effect of gold leaf; white. I got ready to apply the stencil, rubbing a little bit of stick deodorant onto my skin, so that the ink would adhere, then pressing the square of stenciled paper and rubbing it for thirty seconds. Then I pulled the paper off. Sometimes I have to do this more than once, if the customer's skin is rough, or the ink too thick. This time, though, the design transferred perfectly.

I sat for a while, admiring it. From my angle, the figure was upside down—I'd thought about that, whether I should just say the hell with it and do it so I'd be the only one who'd ever see it properly. But I decided to go with convention, so that now I'd be drawing a reverse of what everyone else would see. I'm a bleeder, so I had a good supply of vaseline and paper towels at hand. I went into the living room and knocked back one last glass of Toquai, returned to the studio, switched on my machine, and went at it.

I did the outlines first. There's always this *frisson* when the needles first touch my own skin, sterilized metal skimming along the surface so that it burns, as though I'm running a flame-tipped spike along my flesh. Before Julia did my first tattoo I'd always imagined the process would be like pricking myself with a needle, a series of fine precise jabs of pain.

It's not like that at all. It's more like carving your own skin with the slanted nib of a razor-sharp calligraphy pen, or writing on flesh with a soldering iron. The pain is excruciating, but contained: I look down at the vibrating tattoo gun, its tip like a wasp's sting, and see beneath the needle a flowing line of black ink, red weeping from the black: my own blood. My left hand holds the skin taut—this also hurts like hell—while my right fingers manipulate the machine and the wad of paper towel that soaks up blood as the needle moves on, its tip moving in tiny circles, being careful not to press too hard, so it won't scab. I trace a man's shoulders, a crescent that becomes a neck, a skull's crown above a single thick line that signals a cascade of hair. Then down and up to outline his knees, his arms.

When the pain becomes too much I stop for a bit, breathing deeply. Then I smooth vaseline over the image on my thigh, take a bit of gauze and clean the needle tip of blood and ink. After twenty minutes or so of being scarred with a vibrating needle your endorphins kick in, but they don't block the pain; they merely blur it, so that it diffuses over your entire body, not just a few square inches of stretched skin burning like a fresh brand. It's perversely like the aftermath of a great massage, or great sex: exhausting, unbearable, exhilarating. I finished the outline and took a break, turning on the radio to see if WERU had gone off the air. Two or three nights a week they sign off at midnight, but Saturdays sometimes the DJ stays on.

This was my lucky night. I turned the music up and settled back into my chair. My entire leg felt sore, but the outline looked good. I changed the needle tip and began to do the shading, the process that would give the figure depth and color. The tip of the needle tube is flush against my skin, but only for an instant; then I flick it up and away. This way the ink is dispersed beneath the epidermis, deepest black feathering up to create grey.

It takes days and days of practice before you get this technique down, but I had it. When I was done edging the figure's hair, I cleaned and changed the needle tube again, mixing gamboge yellow and crimson until I got just the hue I wanted, a brilliant tigerlily orange. I sprayed the tattoo with disinfectant, gave it another swipe of vaseline, then went to work with the orange. I did some shading around the man's figure, until it looked even better than the original, with a numinous glow that made it stand out from the other designs around it.

It was almost two more hours before I was done. At the very last I put in a bit of white, a few lines here and there, ambient color, really, the eye didn't register it as white but it charged the image with a strange, almost eerie brilliance. White ink pigment is paler than human skin; it changes color the way skin does, darkening when exposed to the sun until it's almost indistinguishable from ordinary flesh tone.

But I don't spend a lot of time outside: inks don't fade much on my skin. When I finally put down the machine, my hand and entire right arm ached. Outside, rain spattered the pond. The wind rose, and moments later I heard droplets lashing the side of the house. A barred owl called its four querulous notes. From my radio came a low steady hum of static. I hadn't even noticed when the station went off the air. Soon it would be five A.M., and the morning DJ would be in. I cleaned my machine and work area quickly, automatically; washed my tattoo, dried it and covered the raw skin with antibacterial ointment, and finally taped on a Telfa bandage. In a few hours, after I woke, I'd shower and let the warm water soften the bandage until it slid off. Now I went into the kitchen, stumbling with fatigue and the post-orgasmic glow I get from working on myself.

I'd remembered to leave out a small porterhouse steak to defrost. I heated a cast-iron skillet, tossed the steak in and seared it, two minutes on one side, one on the other. I ate it standing over the sink, tearing off meat still cool and bloody in the center. There's some good things about living alone. I knocked back a quart of skim milk, took a couple of ibuprofen and a high-iron formula vitamin, went to bed, and passed out.

The central conceit of *Five Windows One Door* is that the same story is told and retold, with constantly shifting points of view, abrupt changes of narrator, of setting, of a character's moral or political beliefs. Even the city itself changed, so that the bistro frequented by Nola's elderly lover Hans Liep was sometimes at the end of Tufnell Street; other times it could be glimpsed in a cul-de-sac near the Boulevard El-Baz. There were madcap scenes in which Shakespearean plot reversals were enacted— the violent reconciliation between Mabel and her father; Nola Flynn's decision to enter a Carmelite convent after her discovery of the blind child Kelson; Roberto Metropole's return from the dead; even the reformation of the incomparably wicked Elwell, who, according to the notes discovered after Fox's death, was to have married Mabel and fathered her six children, the eldest of whom grew up to become Amantine, Popess of Tuckahoe and the first saint to be canonized in the Reformed Catholic Church.

Volume five, *Ardor ex Cathedra*, was unfinished at the time of Fox's death. He had completed the first two chapters, and in his study was a box full of hand-drawn genealogical charts and plot outlines, character notes, a map of the city, even names for new characters—Billy Tyler, Gordon MacKenzie-Hart, Paulette Houdek, Ruben Kirstein. Fox's editor at Griffin/Sage compiled these remnants into an unsatisfactory final volume that was published a year after Fox died. I bought a copy, but it was a sad relic, like the blackened lump of glass that is all that remains of a stained-glass window destroyed by fire. Still, I kept it with its brethren on a bookshelf in my bedroom, the five volumes in their uniform dust jackets, scarlet letters on a brilliant indigo field with the author's name beneath in gold.

—•—

I dreamed I heard the fox barking, or maybe it really was the fox barking. I turned, groaning as my leg brushed against the bedsheet. The bandage had fallen off while I slept. I groped under the covers till I found it, a clump of sticky brown gauze and I tossed it on the floor, sat up and rubbed my eyes. It was morning. My bedroom window was blistered with silvery light, the glass flecked with rain. I looked down at my thigh. The tattoo had scabbed over, but not much. The figure of the kneeling man was stark and precise, its orange nimbus glazed with clear fluid. I got up and limped into the bathroom, sat on the edge of the tub and laved my thigh tenderly, warm water washing away dead skin and dried blood. I patted it dry and applied another thin layer of antibiotic ointment, and headed for the kitchen to make coffee.

The noise came again—not barking at all but something tapping against a window. It took me a minute to figure out what it was: the basket the Lonely House used as a message system. Blakie had devised it forty years ago, a pulley and old-fashioned clothesline, strung between the Lonely House and a birch tree on the far shore. A small wicker basket hung from the line, with a plastic zip lock bag inside it, and inside the bag magic markers and a notepad. Someone could write a note on shore then send the basket over; it would bump against the front window, alerting us to a visitor. A bit more elegant than standing onshore and shouting, it also gave the Lonely House's inhabitants the chance to hide, if we weren't expecting anyone.

I couldn't remember the last time someone had used it. I had a cell phone now, and customers made appointments months in advance. I'd almost forgotten the clothesline was there.

I went to the front window and peered out. Fog had settled in during the night; on the northern side of the island the foghorn moaned. No one would be leaving Aranbega today. I could barely discern the other shore, thick grey mist striated with white birch trees. I couldn't see anyone.

But sure enough, there was the basket dangling between the window and the front door. I opened the window and stuck my hand out, brushing aside a mass of cobwebs strung with dead crane flies and mosquitoes to get at the basket. Inside was the zip lock bag and the notebook, the latter pleached with dark green threads. I grimaced as I pulled it out, the pages damp and molded into a block of viridian pulp.

But stuck to the back of the notebook was a folded square of yellow legal paper. I unfolded it and read the message written in strong square letters.

Ivy—

Christopher Sa'adah here, I'm staying in Aran. Harbor, stopped by to say hi. You there? Call me @ 462-1117. Hope you're okay.

C

I stared at the note for a full minute. Thinking, this is a mistake, this is a sick joke, someone trying to torment me about Julia. Christopher was dead. Nausea washed over me, that icy chill like a shroud, my skin clammy and the breath freezing in my lungs.

"Ivy? You there?"

I rested my hand atop the open window and inhaled deeply. "Christopher." I shook my head, gave a gasping laugh. "Jesus—"

I leaned out the open window. "Christopher?" I shouted. "Is that really you?"

"It's really me," a booming voice yelled back.

"Hold on! I'll get the dory and come right over—"

I ran into the bedroom and pulled on a pair of loose cutoffs and faded T-shirt, then hurried outside. The dory was where I'd left it, pulled up on shore just beyond the fringe of cattails and bayberries. I pushed it into the lake, a skein of dragonflies rising from the dark water to disappear in the mist. There was water in the boat, dead leaves that nudged at my bare feet; I grabbed the oars and rowed, twenty strong strokes that brought me to the other shore.

"Ivy?"

That was when I saw him, a tall figure like a shadow breaking from the fog thick beneath the birches. He was so big that I had to blink to make sure that this, too, wasn't some trick of the mist: a black-haired, bearded man, strong enough to yank one of the birch saplings up by the roots if he'd wanted to. He wore dark-brown corduroys, a flannel shirt and brown Carhart jacket, heavy brown work boots. His hair was long and pushed back behind his ears; his hands were shoved in his jacket pockets. He was a bit stooped, his shoulders raised in a way that made him look surprised, or unsure of himself. It made him look young, younger than he really was; it made him look like Christopher, Julia's thirteen-year-old brother.

He wasn't thirteen any more. I did the math quickly, bringing the boat round and grabbing the wet line to toss on shore. Christopher was Narouz Sa'adah's son by his third wife. He was eighteen years younger than Julia; that would make him eleven years younger than me, which would make him—

"Little Christopher!" I looked up at him from the dory, grinning. "How the hell old are you?"

He shrugged, leaned down to grab the end of the line and loop it around the granite post at the shoreline. He took out a cigarette and lit it, inhaled rapidly—nervously, I see now—and let his arm dangle so that the smoke coiled up around his wrist.

"I'm thirty-four." He had an almost comically basso voice that echoed across Green Pond like the foghorn. An instant later I heard a loon give its warning cry. Christopher dropped his cigarette and stubbed it out, cocking his head towards the dory. "Is that the same boat you used to have?"

"Sure is." I hopped into the water, wincing at the cold, then waded to shore. "Jesus. Little Christopher. I can't believe it's you. You—Christ! I—well, I thought you were dead."

"I got better." He stared down at me and for the first time smiled, his teeth still a little crooked and nicotine-stained, not Julia's teeth at all: his face completely guileless, close-trimmed black beard, long hair falling across tawny eyes. "After the bombing? I was in hospital for a long time, outside Cairo. It wasn't just you—everyone thought I was dead. My father finally tracked me down and brought me back to Washington. I think you and Julia had broken up by then."

I just stared at him. I felt dizzy: even though it was a small piece of the world, of history, it meant everything was different. Everything was changed. I blinked and looked away from him, saw the birch leaves spinning in the breeze, pale gold and green, goldenrod past its prime, tall stalks of valerian with their flower-heads blown to brown vein. I looked back at Christopher: everything was the same.

He said, "I can't believe it's you either, Ivy."

I threw my arms around him. He hugged me awkwardly—he was so much bigger than I was!—and started laughing in delight. "Ivy! I walked all the way over here! From the village, I'm staying at the Inn. That lady at the General Store?"

"Mary?"

"Right, Mary—she remembered me, she said you still lived here—"

"Why didn't you call?"

He looked startled. "You have a phone?"

"Of course I have a phone! Actually, it's a cell phone, and I only got it a year ago, after they put up a tower over on Blue Hill." I drew away from him, balancing on my heels to make myself taller. "Jeez, you're all growed up, Christopher. I'm trying to think, when was the last time I saw you—"

"Twelve years ago. I was just starting grad school in Cairo. I came to see you and Julia in Rockland before I left. Remember?"

I tried, but couldn't; not really. I'd never known him well. He'd been a big ungainly teenager, extremely quiet and sitting at the edges of the room, where he always seemed to be listening carefully to everything his older sister or her friends said. He'd grown up in D.C. and Cairo, but he spent his summers in the States. I first met him when he was twelve or thirteen, a gangly kid into Dungeons & Dragons and Star Wars, who'd recently read Tolkien and had just started on Terry Brooks.

"Jesus, don't read *that*," I'd said, snatching away *The Sword of Shannara* and shoving my own copy of *Love Plucking Rowan Berries* into his big hands. For a moment he looked hurt. Then, "Thanks," he said, and gave me that sweet slow smile. He spent the rest of that summer in our apartment overlooking Rockland Harbor, hunched into a wicker chair on the decrepit back deck as he worked his way through *Sybylla and the Summer Sky*, *Mellors' Plasma Bistro*, *Love Regained in Idleness*, and finally the tattered remnants of *Ardor ex Cathedra*.

"Of course I remember," I said. I swiped at a mosquito, looked up and grinned. "Gosh. You were still a kid then. How're you doing? *What* are you doing? Are you married?"

"Divorced." He raised his arms, yawning, and stretched. His silhouette blotted out the grey sky, the blurred shapes of trees and boulders. "No kids, though. I'm at the Center for Remote Sensing at B.U., coordinating a project near the Chephren Quarries, in the Western Desert. Upper Egypt."

He dropped his arms and looked down at me again. "So Ivy— would you—how'd you feel about company? I could use a cup of coffee. We can walk back to town if you want. Have a late lunch. Or early dinner."

"Christ, no." I glanced at my raw tattoo. "I should clean that again, before I do anything. And I haven't even had breakfast yet."

"Really? What were you doing? I mean, are you with a customer or something?"

I shook my head. "I was up all night, doing this—" I splayed my fingers above the figure on my thigh. "What time is it, anyway?"

He looked at his watch. "Almost four."

"Almost *four?*" I grabbed his hand and twisted it to see his wristwatch. "I don't believe it! How could I, I—" I shivered. "I slept through the whole day."

Christopher stared at me curiously. I was still holding his wrist, and he turned his hand, gently, his fingers brushing mine. "You okay, Ivy? Did I get you in the middle of something? I can come back—"

"I don't know." I shook my head and withdrew my hand from his; but slowly, so I wouldn't hurt his feelings. "I mean no, I'm fine, just—"

I looked at my thigh. A thread of blood ran down my leg, and as I stared a damselfly landed beneath the tattoo, its thorax a metallic blue needle, wings invisible against my skin. "I was up all night, doing that—"

I pointed at the kneeling man; only from my angle he wasn't kneeling but hanging suspended above my knee, like a bat. "I—I don't think I finished until five o'clock this morning. I had no idea it was so late—"

I could hear the panic in my own voice. I took a deep breath, trying to keep my tone even; but Christopher just put one hand lightly on my shoulder and said, "Hey, it's okay. I really can come back. I just wanted to say hi."

"No. Wait." I counted ten heartbeats, twelve. "I'm okay. I'll be okay. Just, can you row us back?"

"Sure." He stooped to grab a leather knapsack leaning against a tree. "Let's go."

With Christopher in it, the dory sat a good six inches lower in the water, and it took a little longer with him rowing. Halfway across the brief stretch of pond I finally asked him.

"How is Julia?"

My voice was shaky, but he didn't seem to notice. "I don't know. One of my sisters talked to her about five years ago. She was in Toronto, I think. No one's heard from her." He strained at the oars, then glanced at me measuringly. "I never really knew her, you know. She was so much older. I always thought she was kind of a bitch, to tell you the truth. The way she treated you—it made me uncomfortable."

I was silent. My leg ached from the tattoo, searing pain like a bad sunburn. I focused on that, and after a few minutes I could bear to talk.

"Sorry," I said. The dory ground against the shore of the islet. The panic was receding; I could breathe again. "I get these sometimes. Panic attacks. Usually it's not at home, though, only when I go off island."

"That's no fun." Christopher gave me an odd look. Then he clambered out and helped me pull the dory into the reeds. He followed me through the overgrown stands of phlox and aster, up the steps and into the Lonely House. The floor shuddered at his footsteps. I closed the door, looked up at him, and laughed.

"Boy, you sure fill this place up—watch your head, no, wait—"

Too late. As he turned he cracked into a beam. He clutched his head, grimacing. "Shit—I forgot how small this place is—"

I led him to the couch. "Here, sit—I'll get some ice."

I hurried into the kitchen and pulled a tray from the freezer. I was still feeling a little wonky. For about twenty-four hours after you get tattooed, it's like you're coming down with the flu. Your body's been pretty badly treated; your entire immune system fires up, trying to heal itself. I should have just crawled back into bed. Instead I called, "You want something to drink?"

I walked back in with a bowl of ice and a linen towel. Christopher was on the sofa, yanking something from his knapsack.

"I brought this." He held up a bottle of tequila. "And these—"

He reached into the knapsack again and pulled out three limes. They looked like oversized marbles in his huge hand. "I remember you liked tequila."

I smiled vaguely. "Did I?" It had been Julia who liked tequila, going through a quart every few days in the summer months. I sat beside him on the couch, wrapped the ice in the towel, and held it out. He lowered his head, childlike; and after a moment I very gently touched it. His hair was thick and coarse, darker than his sister's; when I extended my fingers I felt his scalp, warm as though he'd been sitting in the sun all day. "You're hot," I said softly, and felt myself flush. "I mean your head—your skin feels hot. Like heatstroke."

He kept his head lowered, saying nothing. His long hair grazed the top of my thigh. He reached to take my hand, and his was so much bigger, it was as though my own hand was swallowed in a heated glove, his palm calloused, fingertips smooth and hard, soft hairs on the back of his wrist. I said nothing. I could smell him, an acrid smell, not unpleasant but strange; he smelled of limes and sweat, and raw earth, stones washed by the sea. My mouth was dry, and as I moved to place the ice-filled towel on his brow I felt his hand slip from mine, to rest upon the couch between us.

"There." I could feel my heart racing, the frantic thought *It's just a symptom, there's nothing to be scared of, it's just a symptom, it's just—*

"Christopher," I said thickly. "Just—sit. For a minute."

We sat. My entire body felt hot, and damp; I was sweating now myself, not cold anymore, my heartbeat slow and even. From outside came the melancholy sound of the foghorn, the ripple of rain across the lake. The room around us was full of that strange, translucent green light you get here sometimes: being on an island on an island suspended in fog, droplets of mist and sea and rain mingling to form a shimmering glaucous veil. Outside the window the world seemed to tremble and break apart into countless motes of silver, steel-grey, emerald, then cohere again into a strangely solid-looking mass. As though someone had tossed a stone into a viscous pool, or probed a limb with a needle: that sense of skin breaking, parting then closing once more around the wound, the world, untold unseen things flickering and diving, ganglia, axons, otters, loons. A bomb goes off, and it takes twelve years to hear its explosion. I lifted my head and saw Christopher watching me. His mouth was parted, his amber eyes sad, almost anguished.

"Ivy," he said. When his mouth touched mine I flinched, not in fear but in shock at how much bigger it was than my own, than Julia's, any woman's. I had not touched a man since I was in high school; and that was a boy, boys. I had never kissed a man. His face was rough; his mouth tasted bitter, of nicotine and salt. And blood, too—he'd bitten his lip from nervousness, my tongue found the broken seam just beneath the hollow of his upper lip, the hollow hidden beneath soft hair, not rough as I had thought it would be, and smelling of some floral shampoo.

It was like nothing I had imagined—and I *had* imagined it, of course. I'd imagined everything, before I fell in love with Julia Sa'adah. I'd fallen in love with *her*—her soul, her *duende*, she would have called it—but in a way it had almost nothing to do with her being another woman. I'd seen movies, porn films even, lots of them, watching with Julia and some of her wilder friends, the ones who were bisexual, or beyond bisexual, whatever that might be; read magazines, novels, pornography, glanced at sites online; masturbated to dim images of what it was like, what I thought it might be like. Even watched once as a couple we knew went at it in our big untidy bed, slightly revved-up antics for our benefit I suspect, a lot of whimpering and operatic sound effects.

This was nothing like that. This was slow, almost fumbling; even formal. He seemed afraid, or maybe it was just that he couldn't believe it, that it wasn't real to him, yet.

"I was always in love with you." He was lying beside me on the couch; not a lot of room left for me, but his broad arm kept me from rolling off. Our shirts were stuffed behind our heads for pillows, I still wore my cut-offs, and he still had his corduroy jeans on. We hadn't gotten further than this. On the floor beside us was the half-empty bottle of tequila, Christopher's pocketknife, and the limes, cloven in two so that they looked like enormous green eyes. He was tracing the designs on my body: the full sleeve on my left arm, Chinese water-dragons, stylized waves, all in shades of turquoise and indigo and green. Green is the hardest ink to work with—you mix it with white, the white blends into your skin tone, you don't realize the green pigment is there and you overdo, going over and over until you scar. I'd spent a lot of time with green when I started out; yellow too, another difficult pigment.

"You are so beautiful. All this—" His finger touched coils of vines, ivy that thrust from the crook of my elbow and extended up to my shoulder. His own body was unblemished, as far as I could see. Skin darker than Julia's, shading more to olive than bronze; an almost hairless chest, dappled line of dark hair beneath his navel. He tapped the inside of my elbow, tender soil overgrown with leaves. "That must have hurt."

I shrugged. "I guess. You forget. All you remember afterwards is how intense it was. And then you have these—"

I ran my hand down my arm, turned to sit up. "This is what I did last night." I flexed my leg, pulled up the edge of my shorts to better expose the new tattoo. "See?"

He sat up, ran a hand through his black hair, then leaned forward to examine it. His hair spilled down from his forehead; he had one hand on my upper thigh, the other on his own knee. His broad back was to me, olive skin, a paler crescent just above his shoulders where his neck was bent: a scar. There were others, jagged smooth lines, some deep enough to hide a fingertip. Shrapnel, or glass thrown off by the explosion. His long hair grazed my leg, hanging down like a dark waterfall.

I swallowed, my gaze flicking from his back to what I could glimpse of my tattoo, a small square of flesh framed between his arms, his hair, the ragged blue line of my cut-offs. A tall man, leaning forward so that his hair fell to cover his face. A waterfall. A curtain. Christopher lifted his head to stare at me.

A veil, torn away.

"Shit," I whispered. "Shit, shit—"

I pushed away from him and scrambled to my feet. "What? What is it?" He looked around as though expecting to see someone else in the room with us. "Ivy—"

He tried to grasp me but I pulled away, grabbing my T-shirt from the couch and pulling it on. "Ivy! What happened?" His voice rose, desperate; I shook my head, then pointed at the tattoo.

"This—" He looked at the tattoo, then at me, not comprehending. "That image? I just found it yesterday. On a card. This sort of tarot card, this deck. I got it at a rummage sale—"

I turned and ran into my studio. Christopher followed.

"Here!" I darted to my work table and yanked off the protective blue covering. The table was empty. "It was here—"

I whirled, went to my light table. Acetates and sheets of rag paper were still strewn across it, my pencils and inks were where I'd left them. A dozen pages with failed versions of the card were scattered across the desk, and on the floor. I grabbed them, holding up each sheet and shaking it as though it were an envelope, as though something might fall out. I picked up the pages from the floor, emptied the stainless steel wastebasket and sifted through torn papers and empty ink capsules. Nothing.

The card was gone.

"Ivy?"

I ignored him and ran back into the living room. "Here!" I yanked the paisley-wrapped deck from my purse. "It was like this, it was one of these—"

I tore the scarf open. The deck was still there. I let the scarf fall and fanned the cards out, face-down, a rainbow arc of labyrinthine wheels; then twisted my hand to show the other side.

"They're blank," said Christopher.

I nodded. "That's right. They're all blank. Only there was one— last night—"

I pointed at the tattoo. "That design. There was one card with that design. I copied it. It was with me in the studio, I had it on my drafting table. I ended up tracing it for the stencil."

"And now you can't find it."

I shook my head. "No. It's gone." I let my breath out in a long low whoosh. I felt sick at my stomach, but it was more like sea-sickness than panic, a nausea I could override if I wanted to. "It's— I won't find it. It's just gone."

My eyes teared. Christopher stood beside me, his face dark with concern. After a minute he said, "May I?"

He held out his hand, and I nodded and gave him the cards. He riffled through them, frowning. "Are they all like this?"

"All except two. There's another one—" I gestured at my purse. "I put it aside. I got them at the rummage sale at St. Bruno's yesterday. They were—"

I stopped. Christopher was still examining the cards, holding them up to the light as though that might reveal some hidden pattern. I said, "You read Walter Burden Fox, right?"

He glanced up at me. "Sure. *Five Windows One Door*? You gave it to me, remember? That first summer I stayed with you down at that place you had by the water. I loved those books." His tone softened; he smiled, a sweet, sad half-smile, and held the cards up as though to show a winning hand. "That really changed my life, you know. After I read them; when I met you. That's when I decided to become an archaeologist. Because they were—well, I don't know how to explain it—"

He tapped the cards thoughtfully against his chin. "I loved those books so much. I couldn't believe it, when I got to the end? That he never finished them. I used to think, if I had only one wish, it would be that somehow he finished that last book. Like maybe if his son hadn't died, or something. Those books just amazed me!"

He shook his head, still marveling. "They made me think how the world might be different than what it is; what we think it is.

That there might be things we still don't know, even though we think we've discovered everything. Like the work I do? We scan all these satellite images of the desert, and we can see where ancient sites were, under the sand; under the hills. Places so changed by wind erosion you would never think anything else was ever there—but there were temples and villages, entire cities! Empires! Like in the third book, when you read it and find out there's this whole other history to everything that happened in the first two. The entire world is changed."

The entire world is changed. I stared at him, then nodded. "Christopher—these cards are from his books. The last one. 'The least trumps.' When I got them, there was a little piece of paper—"

My gaze dropped to the floor. The scrap was there, by Christopher's bare foot. I picked up the scrap and handed it to him. "'The least trumps.' It's in the very first chapter of the last book, the one he never finished. Mabel's in bed with Tarquin and he takes out this deck of cards. He holds them in front of her, and when she breathes on them it somehow makes them come alive. There's an implication that everything that happened before has to maybe do with the cards. But he died before he ever got to that part."

Christopher stared at the fragment of paper. "I don't remember," he said at last. He looked at me. "You said there's one other card. Can I see it?"

I hesitated, then went to get my bag. "It's in here."

I took out my wallet. Everything around me froze; my hand was so numb I couldn't feel it when I slid my finger behind my license. I couldn't feel it, it wasn't there at all—

But it was. The wallet fell to the floor. I stood and held the card in both hands. The last one: the least trump. The room around me was grey, the air motionless. In my hands a lozenge of spectral color glimmered and seemed to move. There were airships and flaming birds, two old women dancing on a beach, an exploding star above a high-rise building. The tiny figure of a man wasn't being carried in a litter, I saw now, but lying in a bed borne by red-clad women. Above them all a lash-fringed eye stared down.

I blinked and rubbed my eye; then gave the card to Christopher. When I spoke my voice was thick. "I—I forgot it was so beautiful. That's it. The last one."

He walked over to the window, leaned against the wall and angled the card to catch the light. "Wow. This is amazing. Was the other one like it? All this detail—"

"No. It was much simpler. But it was still beautiful. It makes you realize how hard it is, drawing something that simple."

I looked down at my leg and smiled wryly. "But you know, I think I got it right."

For some minutes he remained by the window, silent. Suddenly he looked up. "Could you do this, Ivy? On me?"

I stared at him. "You mean a tattoo?" He nodded, but I shook my head. "No. It's far too intricate. It would take days, something like that. Days, just to make a decent stencil. The tattoo would proba-bly take a week, if you were going to do it right."

"This, then." He strode over to me, pointing to the sun that was an eye. "Just that part, there—could you do just that? Like maybe on my arm?"

He flexed his arm, a dark sheen where the bicep rose, like a wave. "Right there—"

I ran my hand across the skin appraisingly. There was a scar, a small one; I could work around it, make it part of the design. "You should think about it. But yeah, I could do it."

"I have thought about it. I want you to do it. Now."

"Now?" I looked at the window. It was getting late; light was leaking from the sky, everything was fading to lavender-grey, twilight. The fog was coming in again, pennons of mist trailing above Green Pond. I could no longer see the far shore. "It's kind of late . . . "

"Please." He stood above me; I could feel the heat radiating from him, see the card glinting in his hand like a shard of glass. "Ivy—"

His deep voice dropped, a whisper I felt more than heard. "I'm not my sister. I'm not Julia. Please."

He touched the outer corner of my eye, where it was still damp. "Your eyes are so blue," he said. "I forgot how blue they are."

We went into the studio. I set the card on the light table, with the deck beside it, used a loupe to get a better look at the image he wanted. It would not be so hard to do, really, just that one thing. I sketched it a few times on paper, finally turned to where Christopher sat waiting in the chair beside my work table.

"I'm going to do it freehand. I usually don't, but this is pretty straightforward, and I think I can do it. You sure about this?"

He nodded. He looked a little pale, there beneath the bright lights I work under, but when I walked over to him he smiled. "I'm sure."

I prepped him, swabbing the skin then shaving his upper arm twice, to make sure it was smooth enough. I made sure my machine was thoroughly cleaned, and set up my inks. Black; cerulean and cobalt; Spaulding and Rogers Bright Yellow.

"Ready?"

He nodded, and I set to.

It took about four hours, though I pretty much lost track of the time. I did the outline first, a circle. I wanted it to look very slightly uneven, like this drawing by Odilon Redon I liked—you can see how the paper absorbed his ink, it made the lines look powerful, like black lightning. After the circle was done I did the eye inside it, a half-circle of white, because in the card the eye is looking down, at the world beneath it. Then I did the flattened ovoid of the pupil. Then the flickering lashes all around it. Christopher didn't talk. Sweat ran in long lines from beneath his arms; he swallowed a lot, and sometimes closed his eyes. There was so much muscle beneath his skin that it was difficult to keep it taut—no fat, and the skin wasn't loose enough—so I had to keep pulling it tight. I knew it hurt.

"That's it, take a deep breath. I can stop, if you need to take a break. I need to take a break, anyway."

But I didn't. My hand didn't cramp up; there was none of that fuzzy feeling that comes after holding a vibrating machine for hours at a stretch. Now and then Christopher would shift in his chair, never very much. Once I moved to get a better purchase on his arm, sliding my knee between his legs: I could feel his cock, rigid beneath his corduroys, and hear his breath catch.

He didn't bleed much. His olive skin made the inks seem to glow, the blue-and-gold eye within its rayed penumbra, wriggling lines like cilia. At the center of the pupil was the scar. You could hardly see it now, it looked like a shadow, the eye's dark heart.

"There." I drew back, shut the machine off and nestled it in my lap. "It's finished. What do you think?"

He pulled his arm towards him, craning his head to look. "Wow. It's gorgeous." He looked at me and grinned ecstatically. "It's fucking gorgeous."

"All right then." I stood and put the machine over by the sink, turned to get some bandages. "I'll just clean it up, and then—"

"Not yet. Wait, just a minute. Ivy."

He towered above me, his long hair lank and skin sticky with sweat, pink fluid weeping from beneath the radiant eye. When he kissed me I could feel his cock against me, heat arcing above my groin. His leg moved, it rubbed against my tattoo and I moaned but it didn't hurt, I couldn't feel it, anything at all, just heat everywhere now, his hands tugging my shirt off then drawing me into the bedroom.

Not like Julia. His mouth was bigger, his hand; when I put my arms around him my fingers scarcely met, his back was so broad. The scars felt smooth and glossy; I thought they would hurt if I touched them but he said no, he liked my fingernails against them, he liked to press my mouth against his chest, hard, as I took his nipple between my lips, tongued it then held it gently between my teeth, the aureole with its small hairs radiating beneath my mouth. He went down on me and that was different too, his beard against the inside of my thighs, his tongue probing deeper; my fingers tangled in his hair and I felt his breath on me, his tongue still inside me when I came. He kissed me and I tasted myself, held his head between my hands, his beard wet. He was laughing. When he came inside me he laughed again, almost shouted; then collapsed alongside me.

"Ivy. Ivy—"

"Shhh." I lay my palm against his face and kissed him. The sheet between us bore the image of a blurred red sun. "Christopher."

"Don't go." His warm hand covered my breast. "Don't go anywhere."

I laughed softly. "Me? I never go anywhere."

We slept. He breathed heavily, but I was so exhausted I passed out before I could shift towards my own side of the bed. If I dreamed, I don't remember; only knew when I woke that everything was different, because there was a man in bed beside me.

"Huh." I stared at him, his face pressed heavily into the pillow. Then I got up, as quietly as I could. I tiptoed into the bathroom, peed, washed my face and cleaned my teeth. I thought of making coffee, and peered into the living room. Outside all was still fog, dark-grey, shredded with white to mark the wind's passing. The clock read six thirty. I turned and crept back to the bedroom.

Christopher was still asleep. I sat on the edge of the bed, languidly, and let my hand rest upon my tattoo. Already it hurt less; it was healing. I looked up at the head of the bed, where my mother's books were, and Walter Burden Fox's. The five identical dust jackets, deep blue, with their titles and Fox's name in gold letters.

Something was different. The last volume, the one completed posthumously by Fox's editor, with the spine that read *Ardor ex Cathedra* ★ *Walter Burden Fox.*

I yanked it from the shelf, holding it so the light fell on the spine.

Ardor ex Cathedra ★ *Walter Burden Fox & W. F. Fox*

My heart stopped. Around me the room was black. Christopher moved on the bed behind me, yawning. I swallowed, leaning forward until my hands rested on my knees as I opened the book.

ARDOR EX CATHEDRA

By Walter Burden Fox
Completed by Walter F. Fox

"No," I whispered. Frantically I turned to the end, the final twenty pages that had been nothing but appendices and transcriptions of notes.

Chapter Seventeen: The Least Trumps.

I flipped through the pages in disbelief, and yes, there they were, new chapter headings, every one of them—

Pavell Saved From Drowning. One Leaf Left. Hermalchio and Lachrymatory. Villainous Saltpetre. The Scars. The Radiant Eye. I gasped, so terrified my hands shook and I almost dropped it, turning back to the frontispiece.

Completed by Walter F. Fox.

I went to the next page—the dedication.

To the memory of my father

I cried out. Christopher sat up, gasping. "What is it? Ivy, what happened—"

"The book! It's different!" I shook it at him, almost screaming. "He didn't die! The son—he finished it, it's all different! *It's changed.*"

He took the book from me, blinking as he tried to wake up. When he opened it I stabbed the frontispiece with my finger.

"There! See—it's all changed. *Everything has changed.*"

I slapped his arm, the raw image that I'd never cleaned, never bandaged. "Hey! Stop—Ivy, stop—"

I started crying, sat on the edge of the bed with my head in my hands. Behind me I could hear him turning pages. Finally he sighed, put a hand on my shoulder and said, "Well, you're right. But—well, couldn't it be a different edition? Or something?"

I shook my head. Grief filled me, and horror: something deeper than panic, deeper even than fear. "No," I said at last. My voice was hoarse. "It's the book. It's everything. We changed it, somehow—the card—"

I stood and walked into my studio, slowly, as though I were drunk. I put the light on and looked at my work table.

"There," I said dully. In the middle of the table, separate from the rest of the deck, was the last card. It was blank. "The last one. The last trump. Everything is different."

I turned to stare at Christopher. He looked puzzled, concerned but not frightened. "So?" He shook his head, ventured a small smile. "Is that bad? Maybe it's a good book."

"That's not what I mean." I could barely speak. "I mean, everything will be different. Somehow. Even if it's just in little ways—it won't be what it was—"

Christopher walked into the living room. He looked out the window, then went to the door and opened it. A bar of pale gold light slanted into the room and across the floor, to end at my feet. "Sun's coming up." He stared at the sky, shading his hands. "The fog is lifting. It'll be nice, I think. Hot though."

He turned and looked at me. I shook my head. "No. No. I'm not going out there."

Christopher laughed, then gave me that sad half-smile. "Ivy—"

He walked over to me and tried to put his arms around me, but I pushed him away and walked into the bedroom. I began pulling on the clothes I'd worn last night. "No. No. Christopher—I can't. I won't."

"Ivy." He watched me, then shrugged and came into the room and got dressed, too. When he was done, he took my hand.

"Ivy, listen." He pulled me to his side, with his free hand pointed at the book lying on the bed. "Even if it *is* different—even if *everything* is different—why does that have to be so terrible? Maybe it's not. Maybe it's better."

I began to shake my head, crying again. "No no no . . . "

"Look—"

Gently he pulled me into the living room. Full sun was streaming through the windows now; outside, on the other side of Green Pond, a deep-blue sky glowed above the green treetops. There was still mist close to the ground but it was lifting. The pines moved in the wind, and the birches; I heard a fox barking, no not a fox: a dog. "Look," Christopher said, and pointed at the open front door. "Why don't we do this, you come with me, I'll stay right by you— shit, I'll *carry* you if you want—we'll just go look, okay?"

I shook my head, No; but when he eased slowly through the door I followed, his hand tight around mine but not too tight: I could slip free if I wanted. He wouldn't keep me. He wouldn't make me go.

"Okay," I whispered. I shut my eyes then opened them. "Okay, okay."

Everything looked the same. A few more of the asters had opened, deep mauve in the misty air. One tall yellow coneflower was still in bloom. We walked through them, to the shore, to the dory. There were dragonflies and damselflies inside it, and something else. A butterfly, brilliant orange edged with cobalt blue, its wings fringed, like an eye. We stepped into the boat and the butterfly lifted into the air, hanging between us then fluttering across the water, towards the western shore. My gaze followed it, watching as it rose above The Ledges then continued down the hillside.

"I've never been over there," said Christopher. He raised one oar to indicate where the butterfly had gone. "What's there?"

"You can see." It hurt to speak, to breathe; but I did it. I didn't die. You can't die, from this. "Katherine—she always says you can see Ireland from there, on a clear day."

"Really? Let's go that way, then."

He rowed to the farther shore. Everything looked different, coming up to the bank; tall blue flowers like irises, a yellow sedge that had a faint fragrance like lemons. A turtle slid into the water, its smooth black carapace spotted with yellow and blue. As I stepped onto the shore I saw something like a tiny orange crab scuttling into the reeds.

"You all right?" Christopher cocked his head and smiled. "Brave little ant. Brave Ivy."

I nodded. He took my hand, and we walked down the hillside. Past The Ledges, past some boulders I had never even known were there, through a stand of trees like birches only taller, thinner, their leaves round and shimmering, silver-green. There was still a bit of fog here but it was lifting, I felt it on my legs as we walked, a damp cool kiss upon my left thigh. I looked over at Christopher, saw a golden rayed eye gazing back at me, a few flecks of dried blood beneath. Overhead, the trees moved and made a high rustling sound in the wind. The ground beneath us grew steeper, the clefts between rocks overgrown with thick masses of small purple flowers. I had never known anything to bloom so lushly, this late in the year. Below us I could hear the sound of waves, not the crash and violent roar of the open Atlantic but a softer sound; and laughter, a distant voice that sounded like my mother's. The fog was almost gone but I still could not glimpse the sea; only through the moving scrim of leaves and mist a sense of vast space, still dark because the sun had not struck it yet in full, pale grey-blue, not empty at all, not anymore. There were lights everywhere, gold and green and red and silver, stationary lights and lights that wove slowly across the lifting veil, as through wide streets and boulevards, haloes of blue and gold hanging from ropes across a wide sandy shore.

"There," said Christopher, and stopped. "There, do you see?"

He turned and smiled at me, reached to touch the corner of my eye, blue and gold; then pointed. "Can you see it now?"

I nodded. "Yeah. Yeah, I do."

The laughter came again, louder this time. Someone calling a name. The trees and grass shivered as a sudden brilliance overtook them, the sun breaking at last from the mist behind me.

"Come on!" said Christopher, and turning he sprinted down the hill. I took a deep breath, looked back at what was behind us. I could just see the grey bulk of The Ledges, and beyond them the thicket of green and white and grey that was the Lonely House. It looked like a picture from one of my mother's books, a crosshatch hiding a hive, a honeycomb; another world. "Ivy!"

Christopher's voice echoed from not very far below me. "Ivy, you have to see this!"

"Okay," I said, and followed him.

WONDERWALL

A long time ago, nearly thirty years now, I had a friend who was waiting to be discovered. His name was David Baldanders; we lived with two other friends in one of the most disgusting places I've ever seen, and certainly the worst that involved me signing a lease.

Our apartment was a two-bedroom third-floor walkup in Queenstown, a grim brick enclave just over the District line in Hyattsville, Maryland. Queenstown Apartments were inhabited mostly by drug dealers and bikers who met their two-hundred-dollars a-month leases by processing speed and bad acid in their basement rooms; the upper floors were given over to wasted welfare mothers from P.G. County and students from the University of Maryland, Howard, and the University of the Archangels and Saint John the Divine.

The Divine, as students called it, was where I'd come three years earlier to study acting. I wasn't actually expelled until the end of my junior year, but midway through that term my roommate, Marcella, and I were kicked out of our campus dormitory, precipitating the move to Queenstown. Even for the mid-1970s our behavior was excessive; I was only surprised the university officials waited so long before getting rid of us. Our parents were assessed for damages to our dorm room, which were extensive; among other things, I'd painted one wall floor-to-ceiling with the image from the cover of Transformer, surmounted by *Je suis damne par l'arc-en-ciel* scrawled in foot-high letters. Decades later, someone who'd lived in the room after I left told me that, year after year, Rimbaud's words would bleed through each successive layer of new paint. No one ever understood what they meant.

Our new apartment was at first an improvement on the dorm room, and Queenstown itself was an efficient example of a closed ecosystem. The bikers manufactured Black Beauties, which they sold to the students and welfare mothers upstairs, who would zigzag a few hundred feet across a wasteland of shattered glass and broken concrete to the Queenstown Restaurant, where I worked making pizzas that they would then cart back to their apartments. The pizza boxes piled up in the halls, drawing armies of roaches. My friend Oscar lived in the next building; whenever he visited our flat he'd push open the door, pause, then look over his shoulder dramatically.

"Listen—!" he'd whisper.

He'd stamp his foot, just once, and hold up his hand to command silence. Immediately we heard what sounded like surf washing over a gravel beach. In fact it was the susurrus of hundreds of cockroaches clittering across the warped parquet floors in retreat.

There were better places to await discovery.

David Baldanders was my age, nineteen. He wasn't much taller than me, with long thick black hair and a soft-featured face: round cheeks, full red lips between a downy black beard and mustache, slightly crooked teeth much yellowed from nicotine, small well-shaped hands. He wore an earring and a bandana that he tied, pirate-style, over his head; filthy jeans, flannel shirts, filthy black Converse high-tops that flapped when he walked. His eyes were beautiful—indigo, black-lashed, soulful. When he laughed, people stopped in their tracks—he sounded like Herman Munster, that deep, goofy, foghorn voice at odds with his fey appearance.

We met in the Divine's Drama Department, and immediately recognized each other as kindred spirits. Neither attractive nor talented enough to be in the center of the golden circle of aspiring actors that included most of our friends, we made ourselves indispensable by virtue of being flamboyant, unapologetic fuckups. People laughed when they saw us coming. They laughed even louder when we left. But David and I always made a point of laughing loudest of all.

"Can you fucking believe that?" A morning, it could have been any morning: I stood in the hall and stared in disbelief at the Department's sitting area. White walls, a few plastic chairs and tables overseen by the glass windows of the secretarial office. This was where the other students chainsmoked and waited, day after day, for news: casting announcements for Department plays; cattle calls for commercials, trade shows, summer reps. Above all else, the Department prided itself on graduating Working Actors—a really successful student might get called back for a walk-on in *Days of Our Lives*. My voice rose loud enough that heads turned. "It looks like a fucking dentist's office."

"Yeah, well, Roddy just got cast in a Trident commercial," David said, and we both fell against the wall, howling.

Rejection fed our disdain, but it was more than that. Within weeks of arriving at the the Divine, I felt betrayed. I wanted—hungered for, thirsted for, craved like drink or drugs—High Art. So did David. We'd come to the Divine expecting Paris in the 1920s, Swinging London, Summer of Love in the Haight.

We were misinformed.

What we got was elocution taught by the Department Head's wife; tryouts where tone-deaf students warbled numbers from *The Magic Show*; Advanced Speech classes where, week after week, the beefy Department Head would declaim Macduff's speech—All my pretty ones? Did you say all?—never failing to move himself to tears.

And there was that sitting area. Just looking at it made me want to take a sledgehammer to the walls: all those smug faces above issues of *Variety* and *Theater Arts*, all those sheets of white paper neatly taped to white cinderblock with lists of names beneath: callbacks, cast lists, passing exam results. My name was never there. Nor was David's.

We never had a chance. We had no choice.

We took the sledgehammer to our heads.

Weekends my suitemate visited her parents, and while she was gone David and I would break into her dorm room. We drank her vodka and listened to her copy of *David Live!*, playing "Diamond Dogs" over and over as we clung to each other, smoking, dancing cheek to cheek. After midnight we'd cadge a ride down to Southwest, where abandoned warehouses had been turned into gay discos—the Lost and Found, Grand Central Station, Washington Square, Half Street. A solitary neon pentacle glowed atop the old Washington Star printing plant; we heard gunshots, sirens, the faint bass throb from funk bands at the Washington Coliseum, the ceaseless boom and echo of trains uncoupling in the railyards that extended from Union Station.

I wasn't a looker. My scalp was covered with henna-stiffened orange stubble that had been cut over three successive nights by a dozen friends. Marcella had pierced my ear with a cork and a needle and a bottle of Gordon's Gin. David usually favored one long drop earring, and sometimes I'd wear its mate. Other times I'd shove a safety pin through my ear, then run a dog leash from the safety pin around my neck. I had two-inch-long black-varnished fingernails that caught fire when I lit my cigarettes from a Bic lighter. I kohled my eyes and lips, used Marcella's Chloe perfume, shoved myself into Marcella's expensive jeans even though they were too small for me.

But mostly I wore a white poet's blouse or frayed striped boatneck shirt, droopy black wool trousers, red sneakers, a red velvet beret my mother had given me for Christmas when I was seventeen. I chainsmoked Marlboros, three packs a day when I could afford them. For a while I smoked clay pipes and Borkum Riff tobacco. The pipes cost a dollar apiece at the tobacconist's in Georgetown. They broke easily, and club owners invariably hassled me, thinking I was getting high right under their noses. I was, but not from Borkum Riff. Occasionally I'd forgo makeup and wear Army khakis and a boiled wool Navy shirt I'd fished from a dumpster. I used a mascara wand on my upper lip and wore my bashed-up old cowboy boots to make me look taller.

This fooled no one, but that didn't matter. In Southeast I was invisible, or nearly so. I was a girl, white, not pretty enough to be either desirable or threatening. The burly leather-clad guys who stood guard over the entrances to the L&F were always nice to me, though there was a scary dyke bouncer whom I had to bribe, sometimes with cash, sometimes with rough foreplay behind the door.

Once inside all that fell away. David and I stumbled to the bar and traded our drink tickets for vodka and orange juice. We drank fast, pushing upstairs through the crowd until we reached a vantage point above the dance floor. David would look around for someone he knew, someone he fancied, someone who might discover him. He'd give me a wet kiss, then stagger off; and I would stand, and drink, and watch.

The first time it happened David and I were tripping. We were at the L&F, or maybe Washington Square. He'd gone into the men's room. I sat slumped just outside the door, trying to bore a hole through my hand with my eyes. A few people stepped on me; no one apologized, but no one swore at me, either. After a while I stumbled to my feet, lurched a few feet down the hallway, and turned.

The door to the men's room was painted gold. A shining film covered it, glistening with smeared rainbows like oil-scummed tarmac. The door opened with difficulty because of the number of people crammed inside. I had to keep moving so they could pass in and out. I leaned against the wall and stared at the floor for a few more minutes, then looked up again

Across from me, the wall was gone. I could see men, pissing, talking, kneeling, crowding stalls, humping over urinals, cupping brown glass vials beneath their faces. I could see David in a crowd of men by the sinks. He stood with his back to me, in front of a long mirror framed with small round light bulbs. His head was bowed. He was scooping water from the faucet and drinking it, so that his beard glittered red and silver. As I watched, he slowly lifted his face, until he was staring into the mirror. His reflected image stared back at me. I could see his pupils expand like drops of black ink in a glass of water, and his mouth fall open in pure panic.

"David," I murmured.

Beside him a lanky boy with dirty-blond hair turned. He too was staring at me, but not with fear. His mouth split into a grin. He raised his hand and pointed at me, laughing.

"Poseur!"

"Shit—shit . . . " I looked up and David stood there in the hall. He fumbled for a cigarette, his hand shaking, then sank onto the floor beside me. "Shit, you, you saw—you—"

I started to laugh. In a moment David did too. We fell into each other's arms, shrieking, our faces slick with tears and dirt. I didn't even notice that his cigarette scorched a hole in my favorite shirt till later, or feel where it burned into my right palm, a penny-sized wound that got infected and took weeks to heal. I bear the scar even now, the shape of an eye, shiny white tissue with a crimson pupil that seems to wink when I crease my hand.

⚫

It was about a month after this happened that we moved to Queenstown. Me, David, Marcy, a sweet spacy girl named Bunny Flitchins, all signed the lease. Two hundred bucks a month gave us a small living room, a bathroom, two small bedrooms, a kitchen squeezed into a corner overlooking a parking lot filled with busted Buicks and shockshot Impalas. The place smelled of new paint and dry-cleaning fluid. The first time we opened the freezer, we found several plastic ziplock bags filled with sheets of white paper. When we removed the paper and held it up to the light, we saw where rows of droplets had dried to faint grey smudges.

"Blotter acid," I said.

We discussed taking a hit. Marcy demurred. Bunny giggled, shaking her head. She didn't do drugs, and I would never have allowed her to: it would be like giving acid to your puppy.

"Give it to me," said David. He sat on the windowsill, smoking and dropping his ashes to the dirt three floors below. "I'll try it. Then we can cut them into tabs and sell them."

"That would be a lot of money," said Bunny delightedly. A tab of blotter went for a dollar back then, but you could sell them for a lot more at concerts, up to ten bucks a hit. She fanned out the sheets from one of the plastic bags. "We could make thousands and thousands of dollars!"

"Millions," said Marcy.

I shook my head. "It could be poison. Strychnine. I wouldn't do it."

"Why not?" David scowled. "You do all kinds of shit."

"I wouldn't do it 'cause it's from here."

"Good point," said Bunny.

I grabbed the rest of the sheets from her, lit one of the gas jets on the stove and held the paper above it. David cursed and yanked the bandana from his head.

"What are you doing?"

But he quickly moved aside as I lunged to the window and tossed out the flaming pages. We watched them fall, delicate spirals of red and orange like tigerlilies corroding into black ash then grey then smoke.

"All gone," cried Bunny, and clapped.

We had hardly any furniture. Marcy had a bed and a desk in her room, nice Danish Modern stuff. I had a mattress on the other bedroom floor that I shared with David. Bunny slept in the living room. Every few days she'd drag a broken boxspring up from the curb. After the fifth one appeared, the living room began to look like the interior of one of those pawnshops down on F Street that sold you an entire roomful of aluminum-tube furniture for fifty bucks, and we yelled at her to stop. Bunny slept on the boxsprings, a different one every night, but after a while she didn't stay over much. Her family lived in Northwest, but her father, a professor at the Divine, also had an apartment in Turkey Thicket, and Bunny started staying with him.

Marcy's family lived nearby as well, in Alexandria. She was a slender, Slavic beauty with a waterfall of ice-blond hair and eyes like aqua headlamps, and the only one of us with a glamorous job—she worked as a model and receptionist at the most expensive beauty salon in Georgetown. But by early spring, she had pretty much moved back in with her parents, too.

This left me and David. He was still taking classes at the Divine, getting a ride with one of the other students who lived at Queenstown, or else catching a bus in front of Giant Food on Queens Chapel Road. Early in the semester he had switched his coursework: instead of theater, he now immersed himself in French language and literature.

I gave up all pretense of studying or attending classes. I worked a few shifts behind the counter at the Queenstown Restaurant, making pizzas and ringing up beer. I got most of my meals there, and when my friends came in to buy cases of Heineken I never charged them. I made about sixty dollars a week, barely enough to pay the rent and keep me in cigarettes, but I got by. Bus fare was eighty cents to cross the District line; the newly opened subway was another fifty cents. I didn't eat much. I lived on popcorn and Reuben sandwiches from the restaurant, and there was a sympathetic waiter at the American Cafe in Georgetown who fed me ice cream sundaes when I was bumming around in the city. I saved enough for my cover at the discos and for the Atlantis, a club in the basement of a fleabag hotel at 930 F Street that had just started booking punk bands. The rest I spent on booze and Marlboros. Even if I was broke, someone would always spring me a drink and a smoke; if I had a full pack of cigarettes, I was ahead of the game. I stayed out all night, finally staggering out into some of the District's worst neighborhoods with a couple of bucks in my sneaker, if I was lucky. Usually I was broke.

Yet I really was lucky. Somehow I always managed to find my way home. At two or three or four A.M. I'd crash into my apartment, alone except for the cockroaches—David would have gone home with a pickup from the bars, and Marcy and Bunny had decamped to the suburbs. I'd be so drunk I stuck to the mattress like a fly mashed against a window. Sometimes I'd sit cross-legged with the typewriter in front of me and write, naked because of the appalling heat, my damp skin grey with cigarette ash. I read *Tropic of Cancer*, reread *Dhalgren* and *A Fan's Notes* and a copy of *Illuminations* held together by a rubber band. I played Pere Ubu and Wire at the wrong speed, because I was too wasted to notice, and would finally pass out only to be ripped awake by the apocalyptic scream of the firehouse siren next door—I'd be standing in the middle of the room, screaming at the top of my lungs, before I realized I was no longer asleep. I saw people in my room, a lanky boy with dark-blond hair and clogs who pointed his finger at me and shouted *Poseur!* I heard voices. My dreams were of flames, of the walls around me exploding outward so that I could see the ruined city like a freshly tilled garden extending for miles and miles, burning cranes and skeletal buildings rising from the smoke to bloom, black and gold and red, against a topaz sky. I wanted to burn too, tear through the wall that separated me from that other world, the real world, the one I glimpsed in books and music, the world I wanted to claim for myself.

But I didn't burn. I was just a fucked-up college student, and pretty soon I wasn't even that. That spring I flunked out of the Divine. All of my other friends were still in school, getting boyfriends and girlfriends, getting cast in university productions of *An Inspector Calls* and *Ubu Roi*. Even David Baldanders managed to get good grades for his paper on Verlaine. Meanwhile, I leaned out my third-floor window and smoked and watched the speedfreaks stagger across the parking lot below. If I jumped I could be with them: that was all it would take.

It was too beautiful for words, too terrifying to think this was what my life had shrunk to. In the mornings I made instant coffee and tried to read what I'd written the night before. Nice words but they made absolutely no sense. I cranked up Marcy's expensive stereo and played my records, compulsively transcribing song lyrics as though they might somehow bleed into something else, breed with my words and create a coherent storyline. I scrawled more words on the bedroom wall:

I HAVE BEEN DAMNED BY THE RAINBOW
I AM AN AMERICAN ARTIST,
AND I HAVE NO CHAIRS

It had all started as an experiment. I held the blunt, unarticulated belief that meaning and transcendence could be shaken from the world, like unripe fruit from a tree; then consumed.

So I'd thrown my brain into the Waring blender along with vials of cheap acid and hashish, tobacco and speed and whatever alcohol was at hand. Now I wondered: did I have the stomach to toss down the end result?

Whenever David showed up it was a huge relief.

"Come on," he said one afternoon. "Let's go to the movies."

We saw a double bill at the Biograph, *The Story of Adele H* and *Jules Et Jim*. Torturously uncomfortable chairs, but only four bucks for four hours of air-conditioned bliss. David had seen *Adele H* six times already; he sat beside me, rapt, whispering the words to himself. I struggled with the French and mostly read the subtitles. Afterwards we stumbled blinking into the long ultraviolet D.C. twilight, the smell of honeysuckle and diesel, coke and lactic acid, our clothes crackling with heat like lightning and our skin electrified as the sugared air seeped into it like poison. We ran arm-in-arm up to the Cafe de Paris, sharing one of David's Gitanes. We had enough money for a bottle of red wine and a baguette. After a few hours the waiter kicked us out, but we gave him a dollar anyway. That left us just enough for the Metro and the bus home.

It took us hours to get back. By the time we ran up the steps to our apartment we'd sobered up again. It was not quite nine o'clock on a Friday night.

"Fuck!" said David. "What are we going to do now?"

No one was around. We got on the phone but there were no parties, no one with a car to take us somewhere else. We rifled the apartment for a forgotten stash of beer or dope or money, turned our pockets inside-out looking for stray seeds, Black Beauties, fragments of green dust.

Nada.

In Marcy's room we found about three dollars in change in one of her jean pockets. Not enough to get drunk, not enough to get us back into the city.

"Damn," I said. "Not enough for shit."

From the parking lot came the low thunder of motorcycles, a baby crying, someone shouting.

"You fucking motherfucking fucker."

"That's a lot of fuckers," said David.

Then we heard a gunshot.

"Jesus!" yelled David, and yanked me to the floor. From the neighboring apartment echoed the crack of glass shattering. "They shot out a window!"

"I said, not enough money for anything." I pushed him away and sat up. "I'm not staying here all night."

"Okay, okay, wait . . ."

He crawled to the kitchen window, pulled himself onto the sill to peer out. "They did shoot out a window," he said admiringly. "Wow."

"Did they leave us any beer?"

David looked over his shoulder at me. "No. But I have an idea."

He crept back into the living room and emptied out his pockets beside me. "I think we have enough," he said after he counted his change for the third time. "Yeah. But we have to get there now—they close at nine."

"Who does?"

I followed him back downstairs and outside.

"Peoples Drug," said David. "Come on."

We crossed Queens Chapel Road, dodging Mustangs and blasted pickups. I watched wistfully as the 80 bus passed, heading back into the city. It was almost nine o'clock. Overhead, the sky had that dusty gold-violet bloom it got in late spring. Cars raced by, music blaring; I could smell charcoal burning somewhere, hamburgers on a grill and the sweet far-off scent of apple blossom.

"Wait," I said.

I stopped in the middle of the road, arms spread, staring straight up into the sky and feeling what I imagined David must have felt when he leaned against the walls of Mr. P's and Grand Central Station: I was waiting, waiting, waiting for the world to fall on me like a hunting hawk.

"What the fuck are you doing?" shouted David as a car bore down and he dragged me to the far curb. "Come on."

"What are we getting?" I yelled as he dragged me into the drugstore.

"Triaminic."

I had thought there might be a law against selling four bottles of cough syrup to two messed-up looking kids. Apparently there wasn't, though I was embarrassed enough to stand back as David shamelessly counted pennies and nickels and quarters out onto the counter.

We went back to Queenstown. I had never done cough syrup before; not unless I had a cough. I thought we would dole it out a spoonful at a time, over the course of the evening. Instead David unscrewed the first bottle and knocked it back in one long swallow. I watched in amazed disgust, then shrugged and did the same.

"Aw, fuck."

I gagged and almost threw up, somehow kept it down. When I looked up David was finishing off a second bottle, and I could see him eyeing the remaining one in front of me. I grabbed it and drank it as well, then sprawled against the boxspring. Someone lit a candle. David? Me? Someone put on a record, one of those Eno albums, *Another Green World*. Someone stared at me, a boy with long black hair unbound and eyes that blinked from blue to black then shut down for the night.

"Wait," I said, trying to remember the words. "I. Want. You. To—"

Too late: David was out. My hand scrabbled across the floor, searching for the book I'd left there, a used New Directions paperback of Rimbaud's work. Even pages were in French; odd pages held their English translations.

I wanted David to read me *Le lettre du voyant*, Rimbaud's letter to his friend Paul Demeny; the letter of the seer. I knew it by heart in English and on the page but spoken French eluded me and always would. I opened the book, struggling to see through the scrim of cheap narcotic and nausea until at last I found it.

> *Je dis qu'il faut être voyant, se faire voyant.*

> *Le Poète se fait voyant par un long, immense et raisonné*
> *dérèglement de tous les sens.*
> *Toutes les formes d'amour, de souffrance,*
> *de folie; il cherche lui-même . . .*

> I say one must be a visionary,
> one must become a seer.

> The poet becomes a seer through a long, boundless
> and systematic derangement of all the senses.
> All forms of love, of suffering, of madness;
> he seeks them within himself . . .

As I read I began to laugh, then suddenly doubled over. My mouth tasted sick, a second sweet skin sheathing my tongue. I retched, and a bright-red clot exploded onto the floor in front of me; I dipped my finger into it then wrote across the warped parquet.

DEAR DAV

I looked up. There was no light save the wavering flame of a candle in a jar. Many candles, I saw now; many flames. I blinked and ran my hand across my forehead. It felt damp. When I brought my finger to my lips I tasted sugar and blood. On the floor David sprawled, snoring softly, his bandanna clenched in one hand. Behind him the walls reflected candles, endless candles; though as I stared I saw they were not reflected light after all but a line of flames, upright, swaying like figures dancing. I rubbed my eyes, a wave cresting inside my head then breaking even as I felt something splinter in my eye. I started to cry out but could not: I was frozen, freezing. Someone had left the door open.

"Who's there?" I said thickly, and crawled across the room. My foot nudged the candle; the jar toppled and the flame went out.

But it wasn't dark. In the corridor outside our apartment door a hundred-watt bulb dangled from a wire. Beneath it, on the top step, sat the boy I'd seen in the urinal beside David. His hair was the color of dirty straw, his face sullen. He had muddy green-blue eyes, bad teeth, fingernails bitten down to the skin; skeins of dried blood covered his fingertips like webbing. A filthy bandanna was knotted tightly around his throat

"Hey," I said. I couldn't stand very well so slumped against the wall, slid until I was sitting almost beside him. I fumbled in my pocket and found one of David's crumpled Gitanes, fumbled some more until I found a book of matches. I tried to light one but it was damp; tried a second time and failed again.

Beside me the blond boy swore. He grabbed the matches from me and lit one, turned to hold it cupped before my face. I brought the cigarette close and breathed in, watched the fingertip flare of crimson then blue as the match went out.

But the cigarette was lit. I took a drag, passed it to the boy. He smoked in silence, after a minute handed it back to me. The acrid smoke couldn't mask his oily smell, sweat and shit and urine; but also a faint odor of green hay and sunlight. When he turned his face to me I saw that he was older than I had first thought, his skin dark-seamed by sun and exposure.

"Here," he said. His voice was harsh and difficult to understand. He held his hand out. I opened mine expectantly, but as he spread his fingers only a stream of sand fell onto my palm, gritty and stinking of piss. I drew back, cursing. As I did he leaned forward and spat in my face.

"Poseur."

"You fuck," I yelled. I tried to get up but he was already on his feet. His hand was tearing at his neck; an instant later something lashed across my face, slicing upwards from cheek to brow. I shouted in pain and fell back, clutching my cheek. There was a red veil between me and the world; I blinked and for an instant saw through it. I glimpsed the young man running down the steps, his hoarse laughter echoing through the stairwell; heard the clang of the fire door swinging open then crashing shut; then silence.

"Shit," I groaned, and sank back to the floor. I tried to staunch the blood with my hand. My other hand rested on the floor. Something warm brushed against my fingers: I grabbed it and held it before me: a filthy bandana, twisted tight as a noose, one whip-end black and wet with blood.

—◆—

I saw him one more time. It was high summer by then, the school year over. Marcy and Bunny were gone till the fall, Marcy to Europe with her parents, Bunny to a private hospital in Kentucky. David would be leaving soon, to return to his family in Philadelphia. I had found another job in the city, a real job, a GS-1 position with the

Smithsonian; the lowest-level job one could have in the government but it was a paycheck. I worked three twelve-hour shifts in a row, three days a week, and wore a mustard-yellow polyester uniform with a photo ID that opened doors to all the museums on the Mall. Nights I sweated away with David at the bars or the Atlantis; days I spent at the newly opened East Wing of the National Gallery of Art, its vast open white-marble space an air-conditioned vivarium where I wandered stoned, struck senseless by huge moving shapes like sharks spun of metal and canvas: Calder's great mobile, Miro's tapestry, a line of somber Rothkos darkly shimmering waterfalls in an upstairs gallery. Breakfast was a Black Beauty and a Snickers bar, dinner whatever I could find to drink.

We were at the Lost and Found, late night early August. David as usual had gone off on his own. I was, for once, relatively sober: I was in the middle of my three-day work week, normally I wouldn't have gone out but David was leaving the next morning. I was on the club's upper level, an area like the deck of an ocean liner where you could lean on the rails and look down onto the dancefloor below. The club was crowded, the music deafening. I was watching the men dance with each other, hundreds of them, maybe thousands, strobelit beneath mirrorballs and shifting layers of blue and grey smoke that would ignite suddenly with white blades of laser-light, strafing the writhing forms below so they let out a sudden single-voiced shriek, punching the air with their fists and blasting at whistles. I rested my arms on the rounded metal rail and smoked, thinking how beautiful it all was, how strange, how alive. It was like watching the sea.

And as I gazed slowly it changed, slowly something changed. One song bled into another, arms waved like tendrils; a shadow moved through the air above them. I looked up, startled, glanced aside, and saw the blond young man standing there a few feet from me. His fingers grasped the railing; he stared at the dancefloor with an expression at once hungry and disdainful and disbelieving. After a moment he slowly lifted his head, turned, and stared at me.

I said nothing. I touched my hand to my throat, where his bandanna was knotted there, loosely. It was stiff as rope beneath my fingers: I hadn't washed it. I stared back at him, his green-blue eyes hard and somehow dull; not stupid, but with the obdurate matte gleam of unpolished agate. I wanted to say something but I was afraid of him; and before I could speak he turned his head to stare back down at the floor below us.

"*Cela s'est passé,*" he said, and shook his head.

I looked to where he was gazing. I saw that the dancefloor was endless, eternal: the cinderblock warehouse walls had disappeared. Instead the moving waves of bodies extended for miles and miles until they melted into the horizon. They were no longer bodies but flames, countless flickering lights like the candles I had seen in my apartment, flames like men dancing; and then they were not even flames but bodies consumed by flame, flesh and cloth burned away until only the bones remained and then not even bone but only the memory of motion, a shimmer of wind on the water then the water gone and only a vast and empty room, littered with refuse: glass vials, broken plastic whistles, plastic cups, dog collars, ash.

I blinked. A siren wailed. I began to scream, standing in the middle of my room, alone, clutching at a bandanna tied loosely around my neck. On the mattress on the floor David turned, groaning, and stared up at me with one bright blue eye.

"It's just the firehouse," he said, and reached to pull me back beside him. It was five A.M. He was still wearing the clothes he'd worn to the Lost and Found. So was I: I touched the bandanna at my throat and thought of the young man at the railing beside me. "C'mon, you've hardly slept yet," urged David. "You have to get a little sleep."

He left the next day. I never saw him again.

◄►

A few weeks later my mother came, ostensibly to visit her cousin in Chevy Chase but really to check on me. She found me spreadeagled on my bare mattress, screenless windows open to let the summer's furnace heat pour like molten iron into the room. Around me were the posters I'd shredded and torn from the walls; on the walls were meaningless phrases, crushed remains of cockroaches and waterbugs, countless rust-colored handprints, bullet-shaped gouges where I'd dug my fingernails into the drywall.

"I think you should come home," my mother said gently. She stared at my hands, fingertips netted with dried blood, my knuckles raw and seeping red. "I don't think you really want to stay here. Do you? I think you should come home."

I was too exhausted to argue. I threw what remained of my belongings into a few cardboard boxes, gave notice at the Smithsonian, and went home.

▸◂

It's thought that Rimbaud completed his entire body of work before his nineteenth birthday; the last prose poems, *Illuminations*, indicate he may have been profoundly affected by the time he spent in London in 1874. After that came journey and exile, years spent as an arms trader in Abyssinia until he came home to France to die, slowly and painfully, losing his right leg to syphilis, electrodes fastened to his nerveless arm in an attempt to regenerate life and motion. He died on the morning of November 10, 1891, at ten o'clock. In his delirium he believed that he was back in Abyssinia, readying himself to depart upon a ship called "Aphinar." He was thirty-seven years old.

▸◂

I didn't live at home for long—about ten months. I got a job at a bookstore; my mother drove me there each day on her way to work and picked me up on her way home. Evenings I ate dinner with her and my two younger sisters. Weekends I went out with friends I'd gone to high school with. I picked up the threads of a few relationships begun and abandoned years earlier. I drank too much but not as much as before. I quit smoking.

I was nineteen. When Rimbaud was my age, he had already finished his life work. I hadn't even started yet. He had changed the world; I could barely change my socks. He had walked through the wall, but I had only smashed my head against it, fruitlessly, in anguish and despair. It had defeated me, and I hadn't even left a mark.

Eventually I returned to D.C. I got my old job back at the Smithsonian, squatted for a while with friends in Northeast, got an apartment, a boyfriend, a promotion. By the time I returned to the city David had graduated from the Divine. We spoke on the phone a few times: he had a steady boyfriend now, an older man, a businessman from France. David was going to Paris with him to live. Marcy married well and moved to Aspen. Bunny got out of the hospital and was doing much better; over the next few decades, she would be my only real contact with that other life, the only one of us who kept in touch with everyone.

Slowly, slowly, I began to see things differently. Slowly I began to see that there were other ways to bring down a wall: that you could dismantle it, brick by brick, stone by stone, over years and years and years. The wall would always be there—at least for me it is—but sometimes I can see where I've made a mark in it, a chink where I can put my eye and look through to the other side. Only for a moment; but I know better now than to expect more than that.

I talked to David only a few times over the years, and finally not at all. When we last spoke, maybe fifteen years ago, he told me that he was HIV positive. A few years after that Bunny told me that the virus had gone into full-blown AIDS, and that he had gone home to live with his father in Pennsylvania. Then a few years after that she told me no, he was living in France again, she had heard from him and he seemed to be better.

Cela s'est passé, the young man had told me as we watched the men dancing in the L&F twenty-six years ago. That is over.

+-+

Yesterday I was at Waterloo Station, hurrying to catch the train to Basingstoke. I walked past the Eurostar terminal, the sleek Paris-bound bullet trains like marine animals waiting to churn their way back through the Chunnel to the sea. Curved glass walls separated me from them; armed security patrols and British soldiers strode along the platform, checking passenger IDs and waving people towards the trains.

I was just turning towards the old station when I saw them. They were standing in front of a glass wall like an aquarium's: a middle-aged man in an expensive-looking dark blue overcoat, his black hair still thick though greying at the temples, his hand resting on the shoulder of his companion. A slightly younger man, very thin, his face gaunt and ravaged, burned the color of new brick by the sun, his fair hair gone to grey. He was leaning on a cane; when the older man gestured he turned and began to walk, slowly, pains-takingly down the platform. I stopped and watched: I wanted to call out, to see if they would turn and answer, but the blue-washed glass barrier would have muted any sound I made.

I turned, blinking in the light of midday, touched the bandanna at my throat and the notebook in my pocket; and hurried on. They would not have seen me anyway. They were already boarding the train. They were on their way to Paris.

THE LOST DOMAIN:

four story variations

FOR DAVID STREITFELD

Meum et teum

For you beautiful ones my thought is not changeable

Sappho, fragment 41
Translated by Anne Carson

KRONIA

"Nothing sorts out memories from ordinary moments. It is only later that they claim remembrance, when they show their scars."

Chris Marker, *La Jetée*

We never meet. Not never, fleetingly: five times in the last eighteen years. The first time I don't recall; you say it was late spring, a hotel bar. But I see you entering a restaurant five years later, stooping beneath the lintel behind our friend Andrew. You don't remember that.

We grew up a mile apart. The road began in Connecticut and ended in New York. A dirt road when we moved in, we both remember that; it wasn't paved till much later. We rode our bikes back and forth. We passed each other fifty-seven times. We never noticed. I fell once, rounding that curve by the golf course, a long scar on my leg now from ankle to knee, a crescent colored like a peony. Grit and sand got beneath my skin, there was blood on the bicycle chain. A boy with glasses stopped his bike and asked was I okay. I said yes, even though I wasn't. You rode off. I walked home, most of the mile, my leg black, sticky with dirt, pollen, deerflies. I never saw the boy on the bike again.

We went to different schools. But in high school we were at the same party. Your end, Connecticut. How did I get there? I have no clue. I knew no one. A sad fat girl's house, a girl with red kneesocks, beanbag chairs. She had one album: *The Shaggs*. More sad girls, a song called "Foot Foot." You stood by a table and ate pretzels and drank so much Hi-C you threw up. I left with my friends. We got stoned in the car and drove off. A tall boy was puking in the azaleas out front.

Wonder what he had? I said.

Another day. The New Canaan Bookstore, your end again. I was looking at a paperback book.

That's a good book, said a guy behind me. My age, sixteen or seventeen. Very tall, springy black hair, wire-rimmed glasses. You like his stuff?

I shook my head. No, I said. I haven't read it. I put the book back. He took it off the shelf again. As I walked off I heard him say Time Out of Joint.

We went to college in the same city. The Metro hadn't opened yet. I was in Northeast, you were in Northwest. Twice we were on the same bus going into Georgetown. Once we were at a party where a guy threw a drink in my face.

Hey! yelled my boyfriend. He dumped his beer on the guy's head.

You were by the table again, watching. I looked over and saw you laugh. I started laughing too, but you immediately looked down then turned then walked away.

Around that time I first had this dream. I lived in the future. My job was to travel through time, hunting down evildoers. I kept running into the same man, my age, darkhaired, tall. Each time I saw him my heart lurched. We kissed furtively, beneath a table while bullets zipped overhead, beside a waterfall in Hungary. For two weeks we hid in a shack in the Northwest Territory, our radio dying, waiting to hear that the first wave of fallout had subsided. A thousand years, back and forth, the world reshuffled. Our child was born, died, grew old, walked for the first time. Sometimes your hair was grey, sometimes black. Once your glasses shattered when a rock struck them. You still have the scar on your cheek. Once I had an abortion. Once the baby died. Once you did. That was just a dream.

You graduated and went to the Sorbonne for a year to study economics. I have never been to France. I got a job at NASA collating photographs of spacecraft. You came back and started working for the newspaper. Those years, I went to the movies almost every night. Flee the sweltering heat, sit in the Biograph's crippling seats for six hours, Pasolini, Fellini, Truffaut, Herzog, Weir. "La Jetée," a lightning bolt: an illuminated moment when a woman's black-and-white face moves in the darkness. A tall man sat in front of me and I moved to another seat so I could see better; he turned and I glimpsed your face. Unrecognized: I never knew you. Later in the theater's long corridor you hurried past me, my head bent over an elfin spoonful of coke.

Other theaters. We didn't meet again when we sat through "Berlin Alexanderplatz," though I did read your review. "Our Hitler" was nine hours long; you stayed awake, I fell asleep halfway through the last reel, curled on the floor, but after twenty minutes my boyfriend shook me so I wouldn't miss the end.

How could I have missed you then? The theater was practically empty.

I moved far away. You stayed. Before I left the city I met your colleague Andrew: we corresponded. I wrote occasionally for your paper. You answered the phone sometimes when I called there.

You say you never did.

But I remember your voice: you sounded younger than you were, ironic, world-weary. A few times you assigned me stories. We spoke on the phone. I knew your name.

At some point we met. I don't remember. Lunch, maybe, with Andrew when I visited the city? A conference?

You married and moved three thousand miles away. E-mail was invented. We began to write. You sent me books.

We met at a conference: we both remember that. You stood in a hallway filled with light, midday sun fogging the windows. You shaded your eyes with your hand, your head slightly downturned, your eyes glancing upward, your glasses black against white skin. Dark eyes, dark hair, tall and thin and slightly stooped. You were smiling; not at me, at someone talking about about the mutability of time. Abruptly the sky darkened, the long rows of windows turned to mirrors. I stood in the hallway and you were everywhere, everywhere.

You never married. I sent you books.

I had children. I never wrote you back.

You traveled everywhere: Paris, Beirut, London, Cairo, Tangier, Cornwall, Fiji. You sent me postcards. I never left this country.

I was living in London with my husband and children when the towers fell. I e-mailed you. You wrote back:

Oh sure, it takes a terrorist attack to hear from you!

I was here alone on the mountain when I found out. A brilliant cloudless day, the loons calling outside my window. I have no TV; I was online when a friend e-mailed me:

Terrorism. An airplane flew into the
World Trade Center. Bombs. Disaster.

I tried to call my partner but the phone lines went down. I drove past the farmstand where I buy tomatoes and basil and stopped to see if anyone knew what had happened. A van was there with DC plates: the woman inside was talking on a cell phone and weeping. Her brother worked in one of the towers: he had rung her to say he was safe. The second tower fell. He had just rung back to say he was still alive.

When the phone lines were restored that night I wrote you. You didn't write back. I never heard from you again.

I was in New York. I had gone to Battery Park. I had never been there before. The sun was shining. You never heard from me again.

I had no children. At the National Zoo, I saw a tall man walking hand in hand with a little girl. She turned to stare at me: grey eyes, glasses, wispy dark hair. She looked like me.

Two years ago you came to see me here on the lake. We drank two bottles of champagne. We stayed up all night talking. You slept on the couch. When I said goodnight, I touched your forehead. I had never touched you before. You flinched.

Once in 1985 we sat beside each other on the Number 80 bus from North Capitol Street. Neither of us remembers that.

I was fifteen years old, riding my bike on that long slow curve by the golf course. The Petro Oil truck went by, too fast, and I lost my balance and went careening into the stone wall. I fell and blacked out. When I opened my eyes a tall boy with glasses knelt beside me, so still he was like a black and white photograph. A sudden flicker: for the first time he moved. He blinked, dark eyes, dark hair. It took a moment for me to understand he was talking to me.

"Are you okay?" He pointed to my leg. "You're bleeding. I live just down there—"

He pointed to the Connecticut end of the road.

I tried to move but it hurt so much I threw up. Then started to cry.

He hid my ruined bike in the ferns. "Come on."

You put your arm around me and we walked very slowly to your house. A plane flew by overhead. This is how we met.

Yesterday morning, he left. I had known he would only be here for those seven days. Now, just like that, they were gone.

It had stormed all night, but by the time I came downstairs to feed the woodstove the gale had blown out to sea. It was still dark, chill October air sifting through cracks in the walls. Red and yellow leaves were flung everywhere outside. I stepped into the yard to gather a handful and pressed my face against them, cold and wet.

From the other side of the island a coyote yelped. I could hear the Pendleton's rooster and a dog barking. Finally I went back inside, sat and watched the flames through the stove's isinglass window. When Philip finally came down, he took one look at me, shook his head and said "No! I still have to go, stop it!"

I laughed and turned to touch his hand. He backed away quickly and said, "None of that."

I saw how he recoiled. I have never kept him here against his will.

When Odysseus left, he was suspicious, accusatory. They say he wept for his wife and son, but he slept beside me each night for seven years and I saw no tears. We had two sons. His face was imprinted upon mine, just as Philip's was centuries later: unshaven, warm, my cheeks scraped and my mouth swollen. In the morning I would wake to see Philip watching me, his hand moving slowly down the curve of my waist.

"No hips, no ass," he said once. "You're built like a boy."

He liked to hold my wrists in one hand and straddle me. I wondered sometimes about their wives: were they taller than me? Big hips, big tits? Built like a woman?

Calypso. The name means the concealer. "She of the lovely braids," that's how Homer describes her. One morning Philip walked about my cottage, taking photos off the bookshelves and looking at them.

"Your hair," he said, holding up a picture. "It was so long back then."

I shrugged. "I cut it all off a year ago. It's grown back—see?" Shoulder-length now, still blonde, no grey.

He glanced at me then put the picture back. "It looked good that way," he said.

⋅⋅

This is what happens to nymphs: they are pursued or they are left. Sometimes, like Echo, they are fled. We turn to trees, seabirds, sea-foam, running water, the sound of wind in the leaves. Men come to stay with us, they lie beside us in the night, they hold us so hard we can't breathe. They walk in the woods and glimpse us: a diving kingfisher, an owl caught in the headlights, a cold spring on the hillside. Alcyone, Nyctimene, Peirene, Echo, Calypso: these are some of our names. We like to live alone, or think we do. When men find us, they say we are lovelier than anything they have ever seen; wilder, stranger, more passionate; elemental. They say they will stay forever. They always leave.

⋅⋅

We met when Philip missed a flight out of Logan. I had business at the gallery that represents me in Cambridge and offered him a place to stay for the night: my hotel room.

"I don't know too many painters," he said. "Free spirits, right?"

He was intrigued by what I told him of the island. The sex was good. I told him my name was Lyssa. After that we'd see each other whenever he was on the East Coast. He was usually leaving for work overseas, but would add a few days to either end of his trip, a week even, so we could be together. I had been on the island for— how long? I can't remember now.

I began sketching him the second time he came here. He would never let me do it while he was awake. He was too restless, jumping up to pull a book off the shelf, make coffee, pour more wine.

So I began to draw him while he slept. After we fucked he'd fall heavily asleep; I might doze for a few minutes, but sex energizes me, it makes me want to work.

He was perfect for me. Not conventionally handsome, though. His dark eyes were small and deepset, his mouth wide and uneven. Dark thick hair, grey-flecked. His skin unlined. It was uncanny—he was in his early fifties but seemed as ageless as I was, as though he'd been untouched by anything, his time in the Middle East, his children, his wife, his ex-wife, me. I see now that this is what obsessed me— that someone human could be, not merely beautiful, but untouched. There wasn't a crack in him; no way to get inside. He slept with his hands crossed behind his head, long body tipped across the bed. Long arms, long legs; torso almost hairless; a dark bloom on his cheeks when he hadn't shaved. His cock long, slightly curved, moisture on his thigh.

I sketched and painted him obsessively, for seven years. Over the centuries there have been others. Other lovers, always; but only a few whom I've drawn or painted on walls, pottery, tapestry, paper, canvas, skin. After a few years I'd grow tired of them—Odysseus was an exception—and gently send them on their way. As they grew older they interested me less, because of course I did not grow old. Some didn't leave willingly. I made grasshoppers of them, or mayflies, and tossed them into the webs of the golden orbweaver spiders that follow me everywhere I live.

But I never grew tired of Philip.

And I never grew tired of painting him. No one could see the paintings, of course, which killed me. He was so paranoid that he would be recognized, by his wife, his ex, one of his grown children. Co-workers.

I was afraid of losing him, so I kept the canvases in a tiny room off the studio. The sketchbooks alone filled an entire shelf. He still worried that someone would look at them, but no one ever came to visit me, except for him. My work was shown in the gallery just outside Boston. Winter landscapes of the bleak New England countryside I loved; skeletons of birds, seals. Temperas, most of them; some pen-and-ink drawings. I lived under Andrew Wyeth's long shadow, as did everyone else in my part of the country. I thought that the paintings I'd done of Philip might change that perception. Philip was afraid that they would.

"Those could be your Helga paintings," he said once. It was an accusation, not encouragement.

"They would be Calypso's paintings," I said. He didn't understand what I meant.

⚓

Odysseus's wife was a weaver. I was, too. It's right there in Homer. When Hermes came to give me Zeus's command to free Odysseus, I was in my little house on the island, weaving scenes into tunics for Odysseus and the boys. They were little then, three and five. We stood on the shore and watched him go. The boys ran screaming after the boat into the water. I had to grab them and hold them back, I thought the three of us would drown, they were fighting so to follow him.

It was horrible. Nothing was as bad as that, ever; not even when Philip left.

Penelope. Yes, she had a son, and like me she was a weaver. But we had more in common than that. I was thinking about her unraveling her loom each night and it suddenly struck me: this was what I did with my paintings of Philip. Each night I would draw him for hours as he slept. Each day I would look at my work and it was beautiful. They were by far my best paintings. They might even have been great.

And who knows what the critics or the public might have thought? My reputation isn't huge, but it's respectable. Those paintings could have changed all that.

But I knew that would be it: if I showed them, I would never see him again, never hear from him, never smell him, never taste him.

Yet even that I could live with. What terrified me was the thought that I would never paint him again. If he was gone, my magic would die. I would never paint again.

And that would destroy me: to think of eternity without the power to create. Better to draw and paint all night, better to undo my work each dawn by hiding it in the back room.

I thought I could live like that. For seven years I did.

And then he left. The storm blew out to sea, the leaves were scattered across the lake. The house smelled of him still, my breath smelled of him, my hair. I stood alone at the sink, scrubbing at the pigments caked under my fingernails; then suddenly doubled over, vomiting on the dishes I hadn't done yet from last night's dinner.

I waited until I stopped shaking. Then I cleaned the sink, cleaned the dishes, squeezed lemons down the drain until the stink was gone. I put everything away. I went into the back room, stood for a long time and stared at the paintings there.

Seven years is a long time. There were a lot of canvases; a lot of sheets of heavy paper covered with his body, a lot of black books filled with his eyes, his cock, his hands, his mouth. I looked up at the corner of the room by the window, saw the web woven by the big yellow spider, grey strands dusted with moth-wings, fly husks, legs. I pursed my lips and whistled silently, watched as the web trembled and the spider raced to its center, her body glistening like an amber bead. Then I went to my computer and booked a flight to Berlin.

It was a city that Philip loved, a city he had been to once, decades ago, when he was studying in Florence. He spent a month there—this was long before the Wall fell—never went back but we had spoken, often, of going there together.

I had a passport—I'm a nymph, not an agoraphobe—and so I e-mailed my sister Arethusa, in Sicily. We are spirits of place; we live where the world exhales in silence. As these places disappear, so do we.

But not all of us. Arethusa and I kept in touch intermittently. Years ago she had lived on the Rhine. She said she thought she might still know someone in Germany. She'd see what she could do.

It turned out the friend knew someone who had a sublet available. It was in an interesting part of town, said Arethusa, she'd been there once. I was a little anxious about living in a city—I'm attached to islands, to northern lakes and trees, and I worried that I wouldn't thrive there, that I might in fact sicken.

But I went. I paid in advance for the flat, then packed my paintings and sketchbooks and had them shipped over. I carried some supplies and one small sketchbook, half-filled with drawings of Philip, in my carry-on luggage. I brought my laptop. I closed up the cottage for the winter, told the Pendletons I was leaving and asked them to watch the place for me. I left them my car as well.

Then I caught the early morning ferry to the mainland, the bus to Boston. There was light fog as the plane lifted out of Logan, quickly dispersing into an arctic-blue sky. I looked down and watched a long serpentine cloud writhing above the Cape and thought of Nephele, a cloud nymph whom Zeus had molded to resemble Hera.

Why do they always have to change us into something else? I wondered, and sat back to watch the movie.

Berlin was a shock. We are by nature solitary and obsessive, which has its own dangers—like Narcissus, we can drown in silence, gazing at a reflection in a still pool.

But in a city, we can become disoriented and exhausted. We can sicken and die. We are long-lived, but not immortal.

So Arethusa had chosen my flat carefully. It was in Schoneberg, a quiet residential part of the city. There were no highrises. Chestnut trees littered the sidewalks with armored fruit. There were broad streets where vendors sold sunflowers and baskets of hazelnuts; old bookstores, a little shop that stocked only socks, several high-end art galleries; green spaces and much open sky.

"Poets lived there," Arethusa told me, her voice breaking up over my cellphone. "Before the war."

My flat was in a street of century-old apartment buildings. The foyer was high and dim and smelled of pipe tobacco and pastry dough. The flat itself had been carved from a much larger suite of rooms. There was a pocket-sized kitchenette, two small rooms facing each other across a wide hallway, a tiny ultramodern bath.

But the rooms all had high ceilings and polished wooden floors glossy as bronze. And the room facing a courtyard had wonderful northern light.

I set this up as my studio. I purchased paints and sketchpads, a small easel. I set up my laptop, put a bowl of apples on the window-sill where the cool fall air moved in and out. Then I went to work.

◂▸

I couldn't paint.

Philip said that would happen. He used to joke about it—you're nothing without me, you only use me, what will you do if ever I'm gone, hmmmm?

Now he was gone, and it was true. I couldn't work. Hours passed, days; a week.

Nothing.

I flung open the casement windows, stared down at the enclosed courtyard and across to the rows of windows in other flats just like mine. There were chestnut trees in the yard below, neat rows of bicycles lined up beneath them. Clouds moved across the sky as storms moved in from the far lands to the north. The wind tore the last yellow leaves from the trees and sent them whirling up towards where I stood, shivering in my motheaten sweater.

The wind brought with it a smell: the scent of pine trees and the sea, of rock and raw wool. It was the smell of the north, the scent of my island—my true island, the place that had been my home, once. It filled me not with nostalgia or longing but with something strange and terrible, the realization that I no longer had a home. I had only what I made on the page or canvas. I had bound myself to a vision.

Byblis fell hopelessly in love and became a fountain. Echo wasted into a sound in the night. Hamadryads die when their trees die.

What would become of me?

➻

I decided to go for a walk.

It is a green city. Philip had never told me that. He spoke of the wars, the Nazis, the bombs, the wall. I wandered along the Ebersstrasse to the S-Bahn station; then traveled to the eastern part of the city, to the university, and sat at a cafe beneath an elevated railway where I ate roasted anchovies and soft white cheese while trains racketed overhead. The wall behind me was riddled with bullet holes. If this building had been in the western part of the city, it would have been repaired or torn down. In the east there was never enough money for such things. When I placed my hand upon the bullet holes they felt hot, and gave off a faint smell of blood and scorched leather. I finished my lunch and picked up a bit of stone that had fallen from the wall, put it in my pocket with some chestnuts I had gathered, and walked on.

The sun came out after a bit. Or no, that may have been another day—almost certainly it was. The leaves were gone from the linden trees but it was still lovely. The people were quiet, speaking in low voices.

But they were seemingly as happy as people ever are. I began to take my sketchbooks with me when I walked, and I would sit in a cafe or a park and draw. I found that I could draw Philip from memory. I began to draw other things, too—the lindens, the ugly modern buildings elbowing aside the older terraces that had not been destroyed by the bombings. There were empty fountains everywhere, and again, in the eastern part of the city there had been no money to restore them or to keep the water flowing. Bronze Nereids and Neptunes decorated them, whitened with bird droppings thick. Lovers still sat beside the empty pools, gazing at drifts of dead leaves and old newspapers while pigeons pecked around their feet. I found this beautiful and strange, and also oddly heartening.

⊷

A few weeks after my arrival, Philip called. It was easy to find me—I hadn't replied to his e-mails, but when my cellphone rang I answered.

"You're in Berlin?" He sounded amused but not surprised. "Well, I wanted to let you know I'm going to be gone again, a long trip this time. Damascus. I'll come see you for a few days before I go."

He told me his flight time, then hung up.

What did I feel then? Exhilaration, desire, joy: but also fear. I had just begun to paint again; I was just starting to believe that I could, in fact, work without him.

But if he were here?

I went into the bedroom. On the bed, neatly folded, was another thing I had brought with me: Philip's sweater. It was an old, tweed-patterned wool sweater, in shades of umber and yellow and russet, with holes where the mice had nested in it back in the cottage. He had wanted to throw it out, years ago, but I kept it. It still smelled of him, and I slept wearing it, here in the flat in Schoneberg, the wool prickling against my bare skin. I picked it up and buried my face in it, smelling him, his hair, his skin, sweat.

Then I sat down on the bed. I adjusted the lamp so that the light fell upon the sweater in my lap, and began, slowly and painstakingly, to unravel it.

It took a while, maybe an hour. I was careful not to fray the worn yarn, careful to tie the broken ends together. When I was finished, I had several balls of wool, enough to make a new sweater. It was late by then, and the shops were closed. But first thing next morning I went to the little store that sold only socks and asked in my halting German where I might find a knitting shop. I had brought a ball of wool to show the woman behind the counter. She laughed and pointed outside, then wrote down the address. It wasn't far, just a few streets over. I thanked her, bought several pairs of thick argyle wool socks, and left.

I found the shop without any trouble. I know how to knit, though I haven't done so for a long time. I found a pattern I liked in a book of Icelandic designs. I bought the book, bought the special circular needles you use for sweaters, bought an extra skein of wool in a color I liked because it reminded me of woad, not quite as deep a blue as indigo. I would work this yarn into the background. Then I returned home.

I had nearly a week before Philip arrived. I was too wound up to paint. But I continued to walk each day, finding my way around the hidden parts of the city. Small forgotten parks scarcely larger than a backyard, where European foxes big as dogs peered from beneath patches of brambles; a Persian restaurant near my flat, where the smells of coriander and roasting garlic made me think of my island long ago. A narrow canal like a secret outlet of the Spree, where I watched a kingfisher dive from an overhanging willow. I carried my leather satchel with me, the one that held my sketchbooks and charcoal pencils and watercolors. I wanted to try using watercolors.

But now the satchel held my knitting too, the balls of wool and the pattern book and the half-knit sweater. When I found I couldn't paint or draw, I'd take the sweater out and work on it. It was repetitive work, dreamlike, soothing. And one night, back in the flat, I dug around in the bureau drawer until I found something else I'd brought with me, an envelope I'd stuck into one of my notebooks.

Inside the envelope was a curl of hair I'd cut from Philip's head one night while he slept. I set the envelope in a safe place and, one by one, carefully teased out the hairs. Over the next few days I wove them into the sweater. Now and then I would pluck one of my own hairs, much longer, finer, ash-gold, and knit that into the pattern as well.

They were utterly concealed, of course, his dark curls, my fair straight hair: all invisible. I finished the sweater the morning Philip arrived.

‒‒

It was wonderful seeing him. He took a taxi from the airport. I had coffee waiting. We fell into bed. Afterwards I gave him the sweater.

"Here," I said. "I made you something."

He sat naked on the bed and stared at it, puzzled. "Is this mine?"

"It was. Try it on. I want to see if it fits."

He shrugged, then pulled it on over his bare chest.

"Does it fit?" I asked. "I had to guess the measurements."

"It seems to." He smoothed the thick wool, October gold and russet flecked with woad; then tugged at a loose bit of yarn on the hem.

"Oops," I said, frowning. "Don't worry, I'll fix that."

"It's beautiful. Thank you. I didn't know you knew how to knit."

I adjusted it, tugging to see if it hung properly over his broad shoulders.

"It does," I said, and laughed in relief. "It fits! Does it feel right?"

"Yeah. It's great." He pulled it off then got dressed again, white T-shirt, blue flannel shirt, the sweater last of all. "Didn't I used to have a sweater like this, once?"

"You did," I said. "Come on, I'm hungry."

We walked arm-in-arm to the Persian restaurant, where we ate chicken simmered in pomegranates and crushed walnuts, and drank wine the color of oxblood. Later, on the way back to the flat, we ambled past closed shops, pausing to look at a display of icons, a gallery showing the work of a young German artist I had read about.

"Are you thinking of showing here?" Philip asked. "I don't mean this gallery, but here, in Berlin?"

"I don't know. I hadn't really thought about it much." In truth I hadn't thought about it at all, until that very moment. "But yes, I guess I might. If Anna could arrange it."

Anna owned the gallery back in Cambridge. Philip said nothing more, and we turned and walked home.

But back in the flat, he started looking around. He went into my studio and glanced at the canvas on the easel, already primed, with a few blocked-in shapes—a barren tree, scaffolding, an abandoned fountain.

"These are different," he said. He glanced around the rest of the studio and I could tell, he was relieved not to see anything else. The other paintings, the ones I'd done of him, hadn't arrived yet. He didn't ask after them, and I didn't tell him I'd had them shipped from the island.

We went back to bed. Afterwards, he slept heavily. I switched on the small bedside lamp, turning it so it wouldn't awaken him, and watched him sleep. I didn't sketch him. I watched the slow rise of his chest, the beard coming in where he hadn't shaved, grayer now than it had been; the thick black lashes that skirted his closed eyes. His mouth.

If he had wakened then and seen me, would anything have changed? If he had ever seen me watching him like this . . . would he have changed? Would I?

I watched him for a long time, thinking. At last I curled up beside him and fell asleep.

⟶⟵

Next morning, we had breakfast, then wandered around the city like tourists. Philip hadn't been back in some years, and it all amazed him. The bleak emptiness of the Alexanderplatz where a dozen teenagers sat around the empty fountain, each with a neon-shaded Mohawk and a ratty mongrel at the end of a leash; the construction cranes everywhere, the crowds of Japanese and Americans at the Brandenburg Gate; the disconcertingly elegant graffiti on bridges spanning the Spree, as though the city, half-awake, had scrawled its dreams upon the brickwork.

"You seem happy here," he said. He reached to stroke my hair, and smiled.

"I am happy here," I said. "It's not ideal, but . . ."

"It's a good place for you, maybe. I'll come back." He was quiet for a minute. "I'm going to be gone for a while. Damascus—I'll be there for two months. Then Deborah's going to meet me, and we're going to travel for a while. She found a place for us to stay, a villa in Montevarchi. It's something we've talked about for a while."

We were scuffing through the leaves along a path near the Grunewald, the vast and ancient forest to the city's west. I went there often, alone. There were wild animals, boar and foxes; there were lakes, and hollow caves beneath the earth that no one was aware of. So many of Berlin's old trees had been destroyed in the bombings, and more died when the wall fell and waves of new construction and congestion followed.

Yet new trees had grown, and some old ones flourished. These woods seemed an irruption of a deep, rampant disorder: the trees were black, the fallen leaves deep, the tangled thorns and hedges often impenetrable. I had found half-devoured carcasses here, cats or small dogs, those pretty red squirrels with tufted ears, as well as empty beer bottles and the ashy remnants of campfires in stone circles. You could hear traffic, and the drone of construction cranes; but only walk a little further into the trees and these sounds disappeared. It was a place I wanted to paint, but I hadn't yet figured out where, or how.

"I'm tired." Philip yawned. Sun filtered through the leafless branches. It was cool, but not cold. He wore the sweater I'd knitted, beneath a tweed jacket. "Jet lag. Can we stop a minute?"

There were no benches, not even any large rocks. Just the leaf-covered ground, a few larches, many old beeches. I dropped the satchel holding my watercolors and sketchpad and looked around. A declivity spread beneath one very large old beech, a hollow large enough for us to lie in, side by side. Leaves had drifted to fill the space like water in a cupped hand; tender yellow leaves, soft as tissue and thin enough that when I held one to the sun I could see shapes behind the fretwork of veins. Trees. Philip's face.

The ground was dry. We lay side by side. After a few minutes he turned and pulled me to him. I could smell the sweet mast beneath us, beechnuts buried in the leaves. I pulled his jacket off and slid my hands beneath his sweater, kissed him as he pulled my jeans down, then tugged the sweater free from his arms, until it hung loose like a cowl around his neck. The air was chill despite the sun, there were leaves in his hair. A fallen branch raked my bare back, hard enough to make me gasp. His eyes were closed, but mine were open; there was grit on his cheek and a fleck of green moss, a tiny greenfly with gold-faceted eyes that lit upon his eyelid then rubbed its front legs together then spun into the sunlight. All the things men never see. When he came he was all but silent, gasping against my chest. I lay my hand upon his face, before he turned aside and fell asleep.

For a moment I sat, silent, and looked for the greenfly. Then I pulled my jeans back up and zipped them, shook the leaves from my hair and plucked a beechnut husk from my shirt. I picked up Philip's jacket and tossed it into the underbrush, then knelt beside him. His flannel shirt had ridden up, exposing his stomach; I bent my head and kissed the soft skin beneath his navel. He was warm and tasted of semen and salt, bracken. For a moment I lingered; then sat up.

A faint buzzing sounded, but otherwise the woods were still. The sweater hung limp round his neck. I ran my fingers along the hem until I found the stray bit of yarn there. I tugged it free, the loose knot easily coming undone; then slowly and with great care, bit by bit by bit while he slept, I unraveled it. Only at the very end did Philip stir, when just a ring of blue and brown and gold hung about his neck, but I whispered his name and, though his eyelids trembled, they did not open.

I got to my feet, holding the loose armful of warm wool, drew it to my face and inhaled deeply.

It smelled more of him than his own body did. I teased out one end of the skein and stood above him, then let the yarn drop until it touched his chest. Little by little, I played the yarn out, like a fisherman with his line, until it covered him. More greenflies came and buzzed about my face.

Finally I was done. A gust sent yellow leaves blowing across the heap of wool and hair as I turned to retrieve my satchel. The greenflies followed me. I waved my hand impatiently and they darted off, to hover above the shallow pool that now spread beneath the beech tree. I had not consciously thought of water, but water is what came to me; perhaps the memory of the sea outside the window where I had painted Philip all those nights, perhaps just the memory of green water and blue sky and gray rock, an island long ago.

The small still pool behind me wasn't green but dark brown, with a few spare strokes of white and gray where it caught the sky, and a few yellow leaves. I got my bag and removed my pencils and watercolors and sketchpad, then folded Philip's jacket and put it at the bottom of the satchel, along with the rest of his clothes. Then I filled my metal painting cup with water from the pool. I settled myself against a tree, and began to paint.

It wasn't like my other work. A broad wash of gold and brown, the pencil lines black beneath the brushstrokes, spattered crimson at the edge of the thick paper. The leaves floating on the surface of the pool moved slightly in the wind, which was hard for me to capture—I was just learning to use watercolors. Only once was I worried, when a couple walking a dog came through the trees up from the canal bank.

"*Guten tag*," the woman said, smiling. I nodded and smiled politely, but kept my gaze fixed on my painting. I wasn't worried about the man or the woman; they wouldn't notice Philip. No one would. They walked towards the pool, pausing as their dog, a black dachshund, wriggled eagerly and sniffed at the water's edge, then began nosing through the leaves.

"Strubbel!" the man scolded.

Without looking back at him the dog waded into the pool and began lapping at the water. The man tugged at the leash and started walking on; the dog ran after him, shaking droplets from his muzzle.

I finished my painting. It wasn't great—I was still figuring it out, the way water mingles with the pigments and flows across the page—but it was very good. There was a disquieting quality to the picture; you couldn't quite tell if there was a face there beneath the water, a mouth, grasping hands; or if it was a trick of the light, the way the thin yellow leaves lay upon the surface. There were long shadows across the pool when at last I gathered my things and replaced them in my satchel, heavier now because of Philip's clothes.

I disposed of these on my way back to the flat. I took a long circuitous route on the U, getting off at one stop then another, leaving a shoe in the trash bin here, a sock there, dropping the flannel shirt into the Spree from the bridge at Oberbaumbrucke. The pockets of the tweed jacket were empty. At the Alexanderplatz I walked up to the five or six punks who were still sitting by the empty fountain and held up the jacket.

"Anyone want this?" I asked in English.

They ignored me, all save one boy, older than the rest, with blue-white skin and a shy indigo gaze.

"*Bitte*." He leaned down to pat his skinny mongrel, then reached for the jacket. I gave it to him and walked away. Halfway across the plaza I looked back. He was ripping the sleeves off; as I watched he walked over to a trash bin and tossed them inside, then pulled the sleeveless jacket over his T-shirt. I turned and hurried home, the chill wind blowing leaves like brown smoke into the sky.

⊷

For the first few months I read newspapers and checked online to see if there was any news of Philip's disappearance. There were a few brief articles, but his line of work had its perils, and it was assumed these had contributed to his fate. His children were grown. His wife would survive. No one knew about me, of course.

I painted him all winter long. Ice formed and cracked across his body; there was a constellation of bubbles around his mouth and open eyes. People began to recognize me where I set up my easel and stool in the Grunewald, but, respectful of my concentration, few interrupted me. When people did look at my work, they saw only an abstract painting, shapes that could be construed as trees or building cranes, perhaps, etched against the sky; a small pool where the reflection of clouds or shadows bore a fleeting, eerie similarity to a skeletal figure, leaves trapped within its arched ribs.

But nearly always I was alone. I'd crack the ice that skimmed the pool, dip my watercolor cup into the frigid water, then retreat a few feet away to paint. Sometimes I would slide my hand beneath the surface to feel a soft mass like a decomposing melon, then let my fingers slip down to measure the almost imperceptible pulse of a heart, cold and slippery as a carp. Then I would return to work.

As the winter wore on it grew too cold for me to work outdoors. There was little snow or rain, but it was bitterly cold. The pool froze solid. Ice formed where my watercolor brush touched the heavy paper, and the ink grew sluggish in my Rapidograph pen.

So I stayed at home in the studio where the orbweavers again hung beside the windows, and used the watercolor studies to begin work on other, larger, paintings—oils on canvas, urban landscapes where a small, frozen woodland pool hinted that a green heart still beat within the city. These paintings were extremely good. I took some digital photos of them and sent them to Anna, along with the name of two galleries in Schoneberg and one in Kreuzberg. Then I went to visit Arethusa in Sicily.

I had planned on staying only a few weeks, but the Mediterranean warmth, the smell of olive groves and sight of flying fish skimming across the blue sea seduced me. I stayed in Sicily until early spring, and then returned briefly to Ogygia, my true island. I could not recall the last time I had visited—a steamship brought me, I do remember that, and the trip then took many hours.

Now it was much faster, and the island itself noisier, dirtier, more crowded. I found myself homesick—not for any island, but for the flat in Schoneberg and the quiet place in the Grunewald where Philip was. I had thought that the time in Sicily might give me other distractions; that I might find myself wanting to paint the sea, the bone-white sand and stones of Ogygia.

Instead I found that my heart's needle turned towards Philip. I breathed in the salt air above the cliffs, but it was him I smelled, his breath, the scent of evergreen boughs beside shallow water, the leaves in his hair. I returned to Berlin.

I'd deliberately left my laptop behind, and asked Anna not to call while I was gone. Now I found a number of messages from her.

Two of the galleries were very interested in my paintings. Could I put together a portfolio for a possible show the following autumn?

I arranged for my most recent canvases to be framed. The sleeping nudes I had done of him back in Maine had arrived some months earlier; I chose the best of these and had them mounted as well. All of this took some time to arrange, and so it was mid-April before I finally took my satchel and my easel and returned to the pool in the Grunewald to paint again.

It was a soft warm morning, the day fragrant with young grass pushing its way through the soil. The flower vendors had baskets of freesia and violets on the sidewalk. On the Landwehrcanal, grey cygnets struggled in the wake of the tourist boat as the adult swans darted after crusts of sandwiches tossed overboard. The captain of the boat waved to me from his cockpit. I waved back, then continued on to an S-Bahn station and the train that would bear me to the Grunewald.

There was no one in the forest when I arrived. High above me the sky stretched, the pale blue-green of a frog's belly. Waxwings gave their low whistling cries and fluttered in the upper branches of the beeches, where tiny new leaves were just starting to unfurl. I stopped hurrying, the sun's warmth tugging at my skin, the sunlight saying slow, slow. A winter storm had brought down one of the larches near the pool; I had to push my way through a scrim of fallen branches, yellow hawthorn-shoots already covering the larch's trunk. I could smell the sweet green scent of new growth; and then I saw it.

The pool was gone: there had been no snow to replenish it. Instead, a cloud of blossoms moved above the earth, gold and azure, crimson and magenta and shining coral. Anemones, adonis, hyacinth, clematis: all the windflowers of my girlhood turned their yellow eyes towards me. I fell to my knees and buried my face in them so that they stained my cheeks with pollen, their narrow petals crushed beneath my fingertips.

I cried as though my heart would break, as the wind stirred the blossoms and a few early greenflies crawled along their stems.

I could see Philip there beneath them. His hair had grown, twining with the white roots of the anemones and pale beetle grubs. Beneath rose-veined lids his eyes twitched, and I could see each iris contract then swell like a seed. He was dreaming. He was beautiful.

I wiped my eyes. I picked up my satchel, careful not to step on the flowers, and got out my easel and brushes. I began to paint.

Anemones, adonis, hyacinth, clematis. I painted flowers, and a man sleeping, and the black scaffolding of a city rising from the ruins. I painted in white heat, day after day after day, then took the watercolors home and transferred what I had seen to canvases that took up an entire wall of my flat. I worked at home, through the spring and into the first weeks of summer, and now the early fall, thinking how any day I will have to return to the pool in the Grunewald, harvest what remains of the windflowers, and set him free.

But not yet.

Last week my show opened at the gallery in Akazienstrasse. Anna, as always, did her job in stellar fashion. The opening was well-attended by the press and wealthy buyers. The dark winterscapes were hung in the main room, along with the nudes I had painted for those seven years. I had thought the nudes would get more attention than they did—not that anyone would have recognized Philip. When I look at those drawings and paintings now, I see a naked man, and that's what everyone else sees, as well. Nothing is concealed, and these days there is nothing new in that.

But the other ones, the windflower paintings, the ones where only I know he is there—those are the paintings that people crowd around. I'm still not certain how I feel about exposing them to the world. I still feel a bit unsure of myself —the shift in subject matter, what feels to me like a tenuous, unsteady grasp of a medium that I will need to work much harder at, if I'm to be as good as I want to be. I'm not certain if I know yet how good these paintings really are, and maybe I never will be sure. But the critics—the critics say they are revelatory.

I've already found a new model.

This is not the first time this has happened. I've been here every time it has. Always I learn about it the same way, a message from someone five hundred miles away, a thousand, comes flickering across my screen. There's no TV here on the island, and the radio reception is spotty: the signal comes across Penobscot Bay from a tower atop Mars Hill, and any kind of weather—thunderstorms, high winds, blizzards—brings the tower down. Sometimes I'm listening to the radio when it happens, music playing, Nick Drake, a promo for the Common Ground Country Fair; then a sudden soft explosive hiss like damp hay falling onto a bonfire. Then silence.

Sometimes I hear about it from you. Or, well, I don't actually hear anything: I read your messages, imagine your voice, for a moment neither sardonic nor world-weary, just exhausted, too fraught to be expressive. Words like feathers falling from the sky, black specks on blue.

The Space Needle. Sears Tower. LaGuardia Airport. Golden Gate Bridge. The Millennium Eye. The Bahrain Hilton. Sydney, Singapore, Jerusalem.

Years apart at first; then months; now years again. How long has it been since the first tower fell? When did I last hear from you?

I can't remember.

This morning I took the dog for a walk across the island. We often go in search of birds, me for my work, the wolfhound to chase for joy. He ran across the ridge, rushing at a partridge that burst into the air in a roar of copper feathers and beech leaves. The dog dashed after her fruitlessly, long jaw sliced open to show red gums, white teeth, a panting unfurled tongue.

"Finn!" I called and he circled round the fern brake, snapping at bracken and crickets, black splinters that leapt wildly from his jaws. "Finn, get back here."

He came. Mine is the only voice he knows now.

—

There was a while when I worried about things like food and water, whether I might need to get to a doctor. But the dug well is good. I'd put up enough dried beans and canned goods to last for years, and the garden does well these days. The warming means longer summers here on the island, more sun; I can grow tomatoes now, and basil, scotch bonnet peppers, plants that I never could grow when I first arrived. The root cellar under the cottage is dry enough and cool enough that I keep all my medications there, things I stockpiled back when I could get over to Ellsworth and the mainland—albuterol inhalers, alprazolam, amoxicillin, Tylenol and codeine, ibuprofen, aspirin; cases of food for the wolfhound. When I first put the solar cells up, visitors shook their heads: not enough sunny days this far north, not enough light. But that changed too as the days got warmer.

Now it's the wireless signal that's difficult to capture, not sunlight. There will be months on end of silence and then it will flare up again, for days or even weeks, I never know when. If I'm lucky, I patch into it then sit there, waiting, holding my breath until the messages begin to scroll across the screen, looking for your name. I go downstairs to my office every day, like an angler going to shore, casting my line though I know the weather's wrong, the currents too strong, not enough wind or too much, the power grid like the Grand Banks scraped barren by decades of trawlers dragging the bottom. Sometimes my line would latch onto you: sometimes, in the middle of the night, it would be the middle of the night where you were, too, and we'd write back and forth. I used to joke about these letters going out like messages in bottles, not knowing if they would reach you, or where you'd be when they did.

London, Paris, Petra, Oahu, Moscow. You were always too far away. Now you're like everyone else, unimaginably distant. Who would ever have thought it could all be gone, just like that? The last time I saw you was in the hotel in Toronto, we looked out and saw the spire of the CN Tower like Cupid's arrow aimed at us. You stood by the window and the sun was behind you and you looked like a cornstalk I'd seen once, burning, your gray hair turned to gold and your face smoke.

I can't see you again, you said. Deirdre is sick and I need to be with her.

I didn't believe you. We made plans to meet in Montreal, in Halifax, Seattle. Grey places; after Deirdre's treatment ended. After she got better.

But that didn't happen. Nobody got better. Everything got worse.

In the first days I would climb to the highest point on the island, a granite dome ringed by tamaracks and hemlock, the grey stone covered with lichen, celadon, bone-white, brilliant orange: as though armfuls of dried flowers had been tossed from an airplane high overhead. When evening came the aurora borealis would streak the sky, crimson, emerald, amber, as though the sun were rising in the west, in the middle of the night, rising for hours on end. I lay on my back wrapped in an old Pendleton blanket and watched, the dog Finn stretched out alongside me. One night the spectral display continued into dawn, falling arrows of green and scarlet, silver threads like rain or sheet lightning racing through them. The air hummed, I pulled up the sleeve of my flannel shirt and watched as the hairs on my arm rose and remained erect; looked down at the dog, awake now, growling steadily as it stared at the trees edging the granite, its hair on end like a cat's. There was nothing in the woods, nothing in the sky above us. After perhaps thirty minutes I heard a muffled sound to the west, like a far-off sonic boom; nothing more.

After Toronto we spoke only once a year; you would make your annual pilgrimage to mutual friends in Paris and call me from there. It was a joke, that we could only speak like this.

I'm never closer to you than when I'm in the seventh arrondissement at the Bowlses', you said.

But even before then we'd seldom talked on the phone. You said it would destroy the purity of our correspondence, and refused to give me your number in Seattle. We had never seen that much of each other anyway, a handful of times over the decades. Glasgow once, San Francisco, a long weekend in Liverpool, another in New York. Everything was in the letters; only of course they weren't actual letters but bits of information, code, electrical sparks; like neurotransmitters leaping the chasm between synapses. When I dreamed of you, I dreamed of your name shining in the middle of a computer screen like a ripple in still water. Even in dreams I couldn't touch you: my fingers would hover above your face and you'd fragment into jots of grey and black and silver. When you were in Basra I didn't hear from you for months. Afterward you said you were glad; that my silence had been like a gift.

For a while, the first four or five years, I would go down to where I kept the dinghy moored on the shingle at Amonsic Cove. It had a little two-horsepower engine that I kept filled with gasoline, in case I ever needed to get to the mainland.

But the tides are tricky here, they race high and treacherously fast in the Reach; the *Ellsworth American* used to run stories every year about lobstermen who went out after a snagged line and never came up, or people from away who misjudged the time to come back from their picnic on Egg Island, and never made it back. Then one day I went down to check on the dinghy and found the engine gone. I walked the length of the beach two days running at low tide, searching for it, went out as far as I could on foot, hopping between rocks and tidal pools and startling the cormorants where they sat on high boulders, wings held out to dry like black angels in the thin sunlight. I never found the motor. A year after that the dinghy came loose in a storm and was lost as well, though for months I recognized bits of its weathered red planking when they washed up onshore.

⁃⁃

The book I was working on last time was a translation of Ovid's *Metamorphosis*. The manuscript remains on my desk beside my computer, with my notes on the nymph "whose tongue did not still when others spoke," the girl cursed by Hera to fall in love with beautiful, brutal Narkissos. He hears her pleading voice in the woods and calls to her, mistaking her for his friends.

But it is the nymph who emerges from the forest. And when he sees her Narkissos strikes her, repulsed; then flees. *Emoriar quam sit tibi copia nostri!* he cries; and with those words condemns himself.

Better to die than be possessed by you.

And see, here is Narkissos dead beside the woodland pool, his hand trailing in the water as he gazes at his own reflection. Of the nymph,

She is vanished, save for these:
her bones and a voice that
calls out amongst the trees.
Her bones are scattered in the rocks.
She moves now in the laurels and beeches,
she moves unseen across the mountaintops.
You will hear her in the mountains and wild places,
but nothing of her remains save her voice,
her voice alone, alone upon the mountaintop.

Several months ago, midsummer, I began to print out your letters. I was afraid something would happen to the computer and I would lose them forever. It took a week, working off and on. The printer uses a lot of power and the island had become locked in by fog; the rows of solar cells, for the first time, failed to give me enough light to read by during the endless grey days, let alone run the computer and printer for more than fifteen minutes at a stretch. Still, I managed, and at the end of a week held a sheaf of pages. Hundreds of them, maybe more; they made a larger stack than the piles of notes for Ovid.

I love the purity of our relationship, you wrote from Singapore. Trust me, it's better this way. You'll have me forever!

There were poems, quotes from Cavafy, Sappho, Robert Lowell, W. S. Merwin. It's hard for me to admit this, but the sad truth is that the more intimate we become here, the less likely it is we'll ever meet again in real life. Some of the letters had my responses copied at the beginning or end, —imploring, fractious—; lines from other poems, songs.

> *Swept with confused alarms of*
> *I long and seek after*
> *You can't put your arms around a memory.*

The first time, air traffic stopped. That was the eeriest thing, eerier than the absence of lights when I stood upon the granite dome and looked westward to the mainland. I was used to the slow constant flow overhead, planes taking the Great Circle Route between New York, Boston, London, Stockholm, passing above the islands, Labrador, Greenland, grey space, white. Now, day after day after day the sky was empty. The tower on Mars Hill fell silent. The dog and I would crisscross the island, me throwing sticks for him to chase across the rocky shingle, the wolfhound racing after them and returning tirelessly, over and over.

After a week the planes returned. The sound of the first one was like an explosion after that silence, but others followed, and soon enough I grew accustomed to them again. Until once more they stopped.

I wonder sometimes, How do I know this is all truly happening? Your letters come to me, blue sparks channeled through sunlight; you and your words are more real to me than anything else. Yet how real is that? How real is all of this? When I lie upon the granite I can feel stone pressing down against my skull, the trajectory of satellites across the sky above me a slow steady pulse in time with the firing of chemical signals in my head. It's the only thing I hear, now: it has been a year at least since the tower at Mars Hill went dead, seemingly for good.

One afternoon, a long time ago now, the wolfhound began barking frantically and I looked out to see a skiff making its way across the water. I went down to meet it: Rick Osgood, the part-time constable and volunteer fire chief from Mars Hill.

"We hadn't seen you for a while," he called. He drew the skiff up to the dock but didn't get out. "Wanted to make sure you were okay."

I told him I was, asked him up for coffee but he said no. "Just checking, that's all. Making a round of the islands to make sure everyone's okay."

He asked after the children. I told him they'd gone to stay with their father. I stood waving, as he turned the skiff around and it churned back out across the dark water, a spume of black smoke trailing it. I have seen no one since.

⊷

Three weeks ago I turned on the computer and, for the first time in months, was able to patch into a signal and search for you. The news from outside was scattered and all bad. Pictures, mostly; they seem to have lost the urge for language, or perhaps it is just easier this way, with so many people so far apart. Some things take us to a place where words have no meaning. I was readying myself for bed when suddenly there was a spurt of sound from the monitor. I turned and saw the screen filled with strings of words. Your name: they were all messages from you. I sat down elated and trembling, waiting as for a quarter-hour they cascaded from the sky and moved beneath my fingertips, silver and black and grey and blue. I thought that at last you had found me; that these were years of words and yearning, that you would be back. Then, as abruptly as it had begun, the stream ceased; and I began to read.

They were not new letters; they were all your old ones, decades-old, some of them. 2009, 2007, 2004, 2001, 1999, 1998, 1997, 1996. I scrolled backwards in time, a skein of years, words; your name popping up again and again like a bright bead upon a string. I read them all, I read them until my eyes ached and the floor was pooled with candle wax and broken light bulbs. When morning came I tried to tap into the signal again but it was gone. I go outside each night and stare at the sky, straining my eyes as I look for some sign that something moves up there, that there is something between myself and the stars. But the satellites too are gone now, and it has been years upon years since I have heard an airplane.

⊷

In fall and winter I watch those birds that do not migrate. Chicka-dees, nuthatches, ravens, kinglets. This last autumn I took Finn down to the deep place where in another century they quarried granite to build the Cathedral of Saint John the Divine. The quarry is filled with water, still and black and bone-cold. We saw a flock of wild turkeys, young ones; but the dog is so old now he can no lon-ger chase them, only watch as I set my snares. I walked to the water's edge and gazed into the dark pool, saw my face reflected there but there is no change upon it, nothing to show how many years have passed for me here, alone. I have burned all the empty crates and cartons from the root cellar, though it is not empty yet. I burn for kindling the leavings from my wood bench, the hoops that did not curve properly after soaking in willow-water, the broken dowels and circlets. Only the wolfhound's grizzled muzzle tells me how long it's been since I've seen a human face. When I dream of you now I see a smooth stretch of water with only a few red leaves upon its surface.

We returned from the cottage, and the old dog fell asleep in the late afternoon sun. I sat outside and watched as a downy woodpecker, *picus pubescens*, crept up one of the red oaks, poking beneath its soft bark for insects. They are friendly birds, easy to entice, sociable; unlike the solitary wrynecks they somewhat resemble. The wrynecks do not climb trees but scratch upon the ground for the ants they love to eat. "Its body is almost bent backward," Thomas Bewick wrote over two hundred years ago in his *History of British Birds*, "whilst it writhes its head and neck by a slow and almost involuntary motion, not unlike the waving wreaths of a serpent. It is a very solitary bird, never being seen with any other society but that of its female, and this is only transitory, for as soon as the domestic union is dissolved, which is in the month of September, they retire and migrate separately."

It was this strange involuntary motion, perhaps, that so fascinated the ancient Greeks. In Pindar's fourth Pythian Ode, Aphrodite gives the wryneck to Jason as the magical means to seduce Medea, and with it he binds the princess to him through her obsessive love. Aphrodite of many arrows: she bears the brown-and-white bird to him, "the bird of madness," its wings and legs nailed to a four-spoked wheel.

> And she shared with Jason
> the means by which a spell
> might blaze and burn Medea,
> burning away all love she had for her family
> a fire that would ignite her mind, already aflame
> so that all her passion turned to him alone.

The same bird was used by the nymph Simaitha, abandoned by her lover in Theokritos's Idyll: pinned to the wooden wheel, the feathered spokes spin above a fire as the nymph invokes Hecate. The isle is full of voices: they are all mine.

◆

Yesterday the wolfhound died, collapsing as he followed me to the top of the granite dome. He did not get up again, and I sat beside him, stroking his long grey muzzle as his dark eyes stared into mine and, at last, closed. I wept then as I didn't weep all those times when terrible news came, and held his great body until it grew cold and stiff between my arms. It was a struggle to lift and carry him, but I did, stumbling across the lichen-rough floor to the shadow of the thin birches and tamaracks overlooking the Reach. I buried him there with the others, and afterward lit a fire.

This is not the first time this has happened. There is an endless history of forgotten empires, men gifted by a goddess who bears arrows, things in flight that fall in flames. Always, somewhere, a woman waits alone for news. At night I climb alone to the highest point of the island. There I make a little fire and burn things that I find on the beach and in the woods. Leaves, bark, small bones, clumps of feathers, a book. Sometimes I think of you and stand upon the rock and shout as the wind comes at me, cold and smelling of snow. A name, over and over and over again.

Farewell, Narkissos said, and again Echo sighed and whispered Farewell.

THE SAFFRON
GATHERERS

He had almost been as much a place to her as a person; the lost domain, the land of heart's desire. Alone at night she would think of him as others might imagine an empty beach, blue water; for years she had done this, and fallen into sleep.

She flew to Seattle to attend a symposium on the Future. It was a welcome trip—on the East Coast, where she lived, it had rained without stopping for thirty-four days. A meteorological record, now a tired joke: only six more days to go! Even Seattle was drier than that.

She was part of a panel discussion on natural disasters and global warming. Her first three novels had presented near-future visions of apocalypse; she had stopped writing them when it became less like fiction and too much like reportage. Since then she had produced a series of time-travel books, wish-fulfillment fantasies about visiting the ancient world. Many of her friends and colleagues in the field had turned to similar themes, retro, nostalgic, historical. Her academic background was in classical archaeology; the research was joyous, if exhausting. She hated to fly, the constant round of threats and delay. The weather and concomitant poverty, starvation, drought, flooding, riots—it had all become so bad that it was like an extreme sport now, to visit places that had once unfolded from one's imagination in the brightly colored panoramas of 1920s postal cards. Still she went, armed with eyeshade, earplugs, music, and pills that put her to sleep. Behind her eyes, she saw Randall's arm flung above his head, his face half-turned from hers on the pillow. Fifteen minutes after the panel had ended she was in a cab on her way to SeaTac. Several hours later she was in San Francisco.

He met her at the airport. After the weeks of rain back East and Seattle's muted sheen, the sunlight felt like something alive, clawing at her eyes. They drove to her hotel, the same place she always stayed; like something from an old B-movie, the lobby with its ornate cast-iron stair-rail, the narrow front desk of polished walnut; clerks who all might have been played by the young Peter Lorre. The elevator with its illuminated dial like a clock that could never settle on the time; an espresso shop tucked into the back entrance, no bigger than a broom closet.

Randall always had to stoop to enter the elevator. He was very tall, not as thin as he had been when they first met, nearly twenty years earlier. His hair was still so straight and fine that it always felt wet, but the luster had faded from it: it was no longer dark-blond but grey, a strange dusky color, almost blue in some lights, like pale damp slate. He had grey-blue eyes; a habit of looking up through downturned black lashes that at first had seemed coquettish. She had since learned it was part of a deep reticence, a detachment from the world that sometimes seemed to border on the pathological. You might call him an agoraphobe, if he had stayed indoors.

But he didn't. They had grown up in neighboring towns in New York, though they only met years later, in D.C. When the time came to choose allegiance to a place, she fled to Maine, with all those other writers and artists seeking a retreat into the past; he chose Northern California. He was a journalist, a staff writer for a glossy magazine that only came out four times a year, each issue costing as much as a bottle of decent sémillon. He interviewed scientists engaged in paradigm-breaking research, Nobel Prize-winning writers; poets who wrote on their own skin and had expensive addictions to drugs that subtly altered their personalities, the tenor of their words, so that each new book or online publication seemed to have been written by another person. Multiple Poets' Disorder, Randall had tagged this, and the term stuck; he was the sort of writer who coined phrases. He had a curved mouth, beautiful long fingers. Each time he used a pen, she was surprised again to recall that he was left-handed. He collected incunabula—*Ars oratoria*, Jacobus Publicus's disquisition on the art of memory; the *Opera Philosophica of Seneca*, containing the first written account of an earthquake; Pico della Mirandola's *Hetaplus*—as well as manuscripts. His apartment was filled with quarter-sawn oaken barrister's bookcases, glass fronts bright as mirrors, holding manuscript binders, typescripts, wads of foolscap bound in leather. By the window overlooking the bay, a beautiful old mapchest of letters written by Neruda, Beckett, Asaré. There were signed broadsheets on the walls, and drawings, most of them inscribed to Randall. He was two years younger than she was. Like her, he had no children. In the years since his divorce, she had never heard him mention his former wife by name

The hotel room was small and stuffy. There was a wooden ceiling fan that turned slowly, barely stirring the white curtain that covered the single window. It overlooked an airshaft. Directly across was another old building, a window that showed a family sitting at a kitchen table, eating beneath a fluorescent bulb.

"Come here, Suzanne," said Randall. "I have something for you."

She turned. He was sitting on the bed—a nice bed, good mattress and expensive white linens and duvet—reaching for the leather mailbag he always carried to remove a flat parcel.

"Here," he said. "For you."

It was a book. With Randall it was always books. Or expensive tea: tiny, neon-colored foil packets that hissed when she opened them and exuded fragrances she could not describe, dried leaves that looked like mouse droppings, or flower petals, or fur; leaves that, once infused, tasted of old leather and made her dream of complicated sex.

"Thank you," she said, unfolding the mauve tissue the book was wrapped in. Then, as she saw what it was, "Oh! Thank you!"

"Since you're going back to Thera. Something to read on the plane."

It was an oversized book in a slipcase: the classic edition of *The Thera Frescoes*, by Nicholas Spirotiadis, a volume that had been expensive when first published, twenty years earlier. Now it must be worth a fortune, with its glossy thick photographic paper and fold-out pages depicting the larger murals. The slipcase art was a detail from the site's most famous image, the painting known as *The Saffron Gatherers*. It showed the profile of a beautiful young woman dressed in an elaborately patterned tiered skirt and blouse, her head shaven save for a serpentine coil of dark hair, her brow tattooed. She wore hoop earrings and bracelets, two on her right hand, one on her left. Bell-like tassels hung from her sleeves. She was plucking the stigma from a crocus blossom. Her fingernails were painted red.

Suzanne had seen the original painting a decade ago, when it was easier for American researchers to gain access to the restored ruins and the National Archaeological Museum in Athens. After two years of paperwork and bureaucratic wheedling, she had just received permission to return.

"It's beautiful," she said. It still took her breath away, how modern the girl looked, not just her clothes and jewelry and body art but her expression, lips parted, her gaze at once imploring and vacant: the fifteen-year-old who had inherited the earth,

"Well, don't drop it in the tub." Randall leaned over to kiss her head. "That was the only copy I could find on the Net. It's become a very scarce book."

"Of course," said Suzanne, and smiled.

"Claude is going to meet us for dinner. But not till seven. Come here—"

They lay in the dark room. His skin tasted of salt and bitter lemon; his hair against her thighs felt warm, liquid. She shut her eyes and imagined him beside her, his long limbs and rueful mouth; opened her eyes and there he was, now, sleeping. She held her hand above his chest and felt heat radiating from him, a scent like honey. She began to cry silently.

His hands. That big rumpled bed. In two days she would be gone, the room would be cleaned. There would be nothing to show she had ever been here at all.

——

They drove to an Afghan restaurant in North Beach. Randall's car was older, a second-generation hybrid; even with the grants and tax breaks, a far more expensive vehicle than she or anyone she knew back east could ever afford. She had never gotten used to how quiet it was.

Outside, the sidewalks were filled with people, the early evening light silvery-blue and gold, like a sun shower. Couples arm-in-arm, children, groups of students waving their hands as they spoke on their cell phones, a skateboarder hustling to keep up with a pack of parkour.

"Everyone just seems so much more absorbed here," she said. Even the panhandlers were antic.

"It's the light. It makes everyone happy. Also the drugs they put in our drinking water." She laughed, and he put his arm around her.

Claude was sitting in the restaurant when they arrived. He was a poet who had gained notoriety and then prominence in the late 1980s with the *Hyacinthus Elegies*, his response to the AIDS epidemic. Randall first interviewed him after Claude received his MacArthur Fellowship. They subsequently became good friends. On the wall of his flat, Randall had a hand-written copy of the second elegy, with one of the poet's signature drawings of a hyacinth at the bottom.

"Suzanne!" He jumped up to embrace her, shook hands with Randall then beckoned them both to sit. "I ordered some wine. A good cab I heard about from someone at the gym."

Suzanne adored Claude. The day before she left for Seattle, he'd sent flowers to her, a half-dozen delicate *narcissus serotinus*, with long white narrow petals and tiny yellow throats. Their sweet scent perfumed her entire small house. She'd e-mailed him profuse but also wistful thanks—they were such an extravagance, and so lovely; and she had to leave before she could enjoy them fully. He was a few years younger than she was, thin and muscular, his face and skull hairless save for a wispy black beard. He had lost his eyebrows during a round of chemo and had feathery lines, like antennae, tattooed in their place and threaded with gold beads. His chest and arms were heavily tattooed with stylized flowers, dolphins, octopi, the same iconography Suzanne had seen in Akrotiri and Crete; and also with the names of lovers and friends and colleagues who had died. Along the inside of his arms you could still see the stippled marks left by hypodermic needles—they looked like tiny black beads worked into the pattern of waves and swallows—and the faint white traces of an adolescent suicide attempt. His expression was gentle and melancholy, the face of a tired ascetic, or a benign Antonin Artaud.

"I should have brought the book!" Suzanne sat beside him, shaking her head in dismay. "This beautiful book that Randall gave me—Spirotiadis's Thera book?"

"No! I've heard of it, I could never find it. Is it wonderful?"

"It's gorgeous. You would love it, Claude."

They ate, and spoke of his collected poetry, forthcoming next winter; of Suzanne's trip to Akrotiri. Of Randall's next interview, with a woman on the House Committee on Bioethics who was rumored to be sympathetic to the pro-cloning lobby, but only in cases involving "only" children—no siblings, no twins or multiples—who died before age fourteen.

"Grim," said Claude. He shook his head and reached for the second bottle of wine. "I can't imagine it. Even pets . . . "

He shuddered, then turned to rest a hand on Suzanne's shoulder. "So: back to Santorini. Are you excited?"

"I am. Just seeing that book, it made me excited again. It's such an incredible place—you're there, and you think, What could this have been? If it had survived, if it all hadn't just gone *bam*, like that—"

"Well, then it would really have gone," said Randall. "I mean, it would have been lost. There would have been no volcanic ash to preserve it. All your paintings, we would never have known them. Just like we don't know anything else from back then."

"We know some things," said Suzanne. She tried not to sound annoyed—there was a lot of wine, and she was jet-lagged. "Plato. Homer . . . "

"Oh, them," said Claude, and they all laughed. "But he's right. It would all have turned to dust by now. All rotted away. All one with Baby Jesus, or Baby Zeus. Everything you love would be buried under a Tradewinds Resort. Or it would be like Athens, which would be even worse."

"Would it?" She sipped her wine. "We don't know that. We don't know what it would have become. This—"

She gestured at the room, the couple sitting beneath twinkling rose-colored lights, playing with a digital toy that left little chattering faces in the air as the woman switched it on and off. Outside, dusk and neon. "It might have become like this."

"This." Randall leaned back in his chair, staring at her. "Is this so wonderful?"

"Oh yes," she said, staring back at him, the two of them unsmiling. "This is all a miracle."

He excused himself. Claude refilled his glass and turned back to Suzanne. "So. How are things?"

"With Randall?" She sighed. "It's good. I dunno. Maybe it's great. Tomorrow—we're going to look at houses."

Claude raised a tattooed eyebrow. "Really?"

She nodded. Randall had been looking at houses for three years now, ever since the divorce.

"Who knows?" she said. "Maybe this will be the charm. How hard can it be to buy a house?"

"In San Francisco? Doll, it's easier to win the stem cell lottery. But yes, Randall is a very discerning buyer. He's the last of the true idealists. He's looking for the eidos of the house. Plato's eidos, not Socrates'," he added. "Is this the first time you've gone looking with him?"

"Yup."

"Well. Maybe that is great," he said. "Or not. Would you move out here?"

"I don't know. Maybe. If he had a house. Probably not."

"Why?"

"I don't know. I guess I'm looking for the eidos of something else. Out here, it's just too . . . "

She opened her hands as though catching rain. Claude looked at her quizzically.

"Too sunny?" he said. "Too warm? Too beautiful?"

"I suppose. The land of the lotus-eaters. I love knowing it's here, but." She drank more wine. "Maybe if I had more job security."

"You're a writer. It's against nature for you to have job security."

"Yeah, no kidding. What about you? You don't ever worry about that?"

He gave her his sweet sad smile and shook his head. "Never. The world will always need poets. We're like the lilies of the field."

"What about journalists?" Randall appeared behind them, slipping his cell phone back into his pocket. "What are we?"

"Quackgrass," said Claude.

"Cactus," said Suzanne.

"Oh, gee. I get it," said Randall. "Because we're all hard and spiny and no one loves us."

"Because you only bloom once a year," said Suzanne.

"When it rains," added Claude.

"That was my realtor." Randall sat and downed the rest of his wine. "Sunday's open house day. Two o'clock till four. Suzanne, we have a lot of ground to cover."

He gestured for the waiter. Suzanne leaned over to kiss Claude's cheek.

"When do you leave for Hydra?" she asked.

"Tomorrow."

"Tomorrow!" She looked crestfallen. "That's so soon!"

"'The beautiful life was brief,'" said Claude, and laughed. "You're only here till Monday. I have a reservation on the ferry from Piraeus, I couldn't change it."

"How long will you be there? I'll be in Athens Tuesday after next, then I go to Akrotiri."

Claude smiled. "That might work. Here—"

He copied out a phone number in his careful, calligraphic hand. "This is Zali's number on Hydra. A cell phone, I have no idea if it will even work. But I'll see you soon. Like you said—"

He lifted his thin hands and gestured at the room around them, his dark eyes wide. "This is a miracle."

Randall paid the check and they turned to go. At the door, Claude hugged Suzanne. "Don't miss your plane," he said.

"Don't wind her up!" said Randall.

"Don't miss yours," said Suzanne. Her eyes filled with tears as she pressed her face against Claude's. "It was so good to see you. If I miss you, have a wonderful time in Hydra."

"Oh, I will," said Claude. "I always do."

❦

Randall dropped her off at her hotel. She knew better than to ask him to stay; besides, she was tired, and the wine was starting to give her a headache.

"Tomorrow," he said. "Nine o'clock. A leisurely breakfast, and then . . . "

He leaned over to open her door, then kissed her. "The exciting new world of California real estate."

Outside, the evening had grown cool, but the hotel room still felt close: it smelled of sex, and the sweetish dusty scent of old books. She opened the window by the airshaft and went to take a shower. Afterwards she got into bed, but found herself unable to sleep.

The wine, she thought; always a mistake. She considered taking one of the anti-anxiety drugs she carried for flying, but decided against it. Instead she picked up the book Randall had given her.

She knew all the images, from other books and websites, and the island itself. Nearly four thousand years ago, now; much of it might have been built yesterday. Beneath fifteen feet of volcanic ash and pumice, homes with ocean views and indoor plumbing, pipes that might have channeled steam from underground vents fed by the volcano the city was built upon. Fragments of glass that might have been windows, or lenses. The great pithoi that still held food when they were opened millennia later. Great containers of honey for trade, for embalming the Egyptian dead. Yellow grains of pollen. Wine.

But no human remains. No bones, no grimacing tormented figures as were found beneath the sand at Herculaneum, where the fishermen had fled and died. Not even animal remains, save for the charred vertebrae of a single donkey. They had all known to leave. And when they did, their city was not abandoned in frantic haste or fear. All was orderly, the pithoi still sealed, no metal utensils or weapons strewn upon the floor, no bolts of silk or linen; no jewelry.

Only the paintings, and they were everywhere, so lovely and beautifully wrought that at first the excavators thought they had uncovered a temple complex.

But they weren't temples: they were homes. Someone had paid an artist, or teams of artists, to paint frescoes on the walls of room after room after room. Sea daffodils, swallows; dolphins and pleasure boats, the boats themselves decorated with more dolphins and flying seabirds, golden nautilus on their prows. Wreaths of flowers. A shipwreck. Always you saw the same colors, ochre-yellow and ferrous red; a pigment made by grinding glaucophane, a vitreous mineral that produced a grey-blue shimmer; a bright pure French blue. But of course it wasn't French blue but Egyptian blue—Pompeiian blue—one of the earliest pigments, used for thousands of years; you made it by combining a calcium compound with ground malachite and quartz, then heating it to extreme temperatures.

But no green. It was a blue and gold and red world. Not even the plants were green.

Otherwise, the paintings were so alive that, when she'd first seen them, she half-expected her finger would be wet if she touched them. The eyes of the boys who played at boxing were children's eyes. The antelopes had the mad topaz glare of wild goats. The monkeys had blue fur and looked like dancing cats. There were people walking in the streets. You could see what their houses looked like, red brick and yellow shutters.

She turned towards the back of the book, to the section on Xeste 3. It was the most famous building at the site. It contained the most famous paintings—the woman known as the "Mistress of Animals." "The Adorants," who appeared to be striding down a fashion runway. "The Lustral Basin."

The saffron gatherers.

She gazed at the image from the East Wall of Room Three, two women harvesting the stigma of the crocus blossoms. The flowers were like stylized yellow fireworks, growing from the rocks and also appearing in a repetitive motif on the wall above the figures, like the fleur-de-lis patterns on wallpaper. The fragments of painted plaster had been meticulously restored; there was no attempt to fill in what was missing, as had been done at Knossos under Sir Arthur Evans' supervision to sometimes cartoonish effect.

None of that had been necessary here. The fresco was nearly intact. You could see how the older woman's eyebrow was slightly raised, with annoyance or perhaps just impatience, and count the number of stigmata the younger acolyte held in her out-stretched palm.

How long would it have taken for them to fill those baskets? The crocuses bloomed only in autumn, and each small blossom contained just three tiny crimson threads, the female stigmata. It might take 100,000 flowers to produce a half-pound of the spice.

And what did they use the spice for? Cooking; painting; a pigment they traded to the Egyptians for dyeing mummy bandages.

She closed the book. She could hear distant sirens, and a soft hum from the ceiling fan. Tomorrow they would look at houses.

— — —

For breakfast they went to the Embarcadero, the huge indoor market inside the restored ferry building that had been damaged over a century before, in the 1906 earthquake. There was a shop with nothing but olive oil and infused vinegars; another that sold only mushrooms, great woven panniers and baskets filled with tree-ears, portobellos, fungus that looked like orange coral; black morels and matsutake and golden chanterelles.

They stuck with coffee and sweet rolls, and ate outside on a bench looking over the bay. A man threw sticks into the water for a pair of black labs; another man swam along the embankment. The sunlight was strong and clear as gin, and nearly as potent: it made Suzanne feel lightheaded and slightly drowsy, even though she had just gotten up.

"Now," said Randall. He took out the newspaper, opened it to the real estate section, and handed it to her. He had circled eight listings. "The first two are in Oakland; then we'll hit Berkeley and Kensington. You ready?"

They drove in heavy traffic across the Oakland-Bay bridge. To either side, bronze water that looked as though it would be too hot to swim in; before them the Oakland Hills, where the houses were ranged in undulating lines like waves. Once in the city they began to climb in and out of pocket neighborhoods poised between the arid and the tropic. Bungalows nearly hidden beneath overhanging trees suddenly yielded to bright white stucco houses flanked by aloes and agaves. It looked at once wildly fanciful and comfortable, as though all urban planning had been left to Dr. Seuss.

"They do something here called 'staging,' said Randall as they pulled behind a line of parked cars on a hillside. A phalanx of realtors' signs rose from a grassy mound beside them. "Homeowners pay thousands and thousands of dollars for a decorator to come in and tart up their houses with rented furniture and art and stuff. So, you know, it looks like it's worth three million dollars."

They walked to the first house, a Craftsman bungalow tucked behind trees like prehistoric ferns. There was a fountain outside, filled with koi that stared up with engorged silvery eyes. Inside, exposed beams and dark hardwood floors so glossy they looked covered with maple syrup. There was a grand piano, and large framed posters from Parisian cafés—Suzanne was to note a lot of these as the afternoon wore on—and much heavy dark Mediterranean-style furniture, as well as a few early Mission pieces that might have been genuine. The kitchen floors were tiled. In the master bath, there were mosaics in the sink and sunken tub.

Randall barely glanced at these. He made a beeline for the deck. After wandering around for a few minutes, Suzanne followed him.

"It's beautiful," she said. Below, terraced gardens gave way to stepped hillsides, and then the city proper, and then the gilded expanse of San Francisco Bay, with sailboats like swans moving slowly beneath the bridge.

"For four million dollars, it better be," said Randall.

She looked at him. His expression was avid, but it was also sad, his pale eyes melancholy in the brilliant sunlight. He drew her to him and gazed out above the treetops, then pointed across the blue water.

"That's where we were. Your hotel, it's right there, somewhere." His voice grew soft. "At night it all looks like a fairy city. The lights, and the bridges . . . You can't believe that anyone could have built it."

He blinked, shading his eyes with his hand, then looked away. When he turned back his cheeks were damp.

"Come on," he said. He bent to kiss her forehead. "Got to keep moving."

They drove to the next house, and the next, and the one after that. The light and heat made her dizzy, and the scents of all the unfamiliar flowers, the play of water in fountains and a swimming pool like a great turquoise lozenge. She found herself wandering through expansive bedrooms with people she did not know, walking in and out of closets, bathrooms, a sauna. Every room seemed lavish, the air charged as though anticipating a wonderful party, tables set with beeswax candles and bottles of wine and crystal stemware. Countertops of hand-thrown Italian tiles; globular cobalt vases filled with sunflowers, another recurring motif.

But there was no sign of anyone who might actually live in one of these houses, only a series of well-dressed women with expensively restrained jewelry who would greet them, usually in the kitchen, and make sure they had a flyer listing the home's attributes. There were plates of cookies, banana bread warm from the oven. Bottles of sparkling water and organic lemonade.

And, always, a view. They didn't look at houses without views. To Suzanne, some were spectacular; others, merely glorious. All were more beautiful than anything she saw from her own windows or deck, where she looked out onto evergreens and grey rocks and, much of the year, snow.

It was all so dreamlike that it was nearly impossible for her to imagine real people living here. For her, a house had always meant a refuge from the world; the place where you hid from whatever catastrophe was breaking that morning.

But now she saw that it could be different. She began to understand that, for Randall at least, a house wasn't a retreat. It was a way of engaging with the world; of opening himself to it. The view wasn't yours. You belonged to it, you were a tiny part of it, like the sailboats and the seagulls and the flowers in the garden; like the sunflowers on the highly polished tables.

You were part of what made it real. She had always thought it was the other way around.

"You ready?" Randall came up behind her and put his hand on her neck. "This is it. We're done. Let's go have a drink."

On the way out the door he stopped to talk to the agent.

"They'll be taking bids tomorrow," she said. "We'll let you know on Tuesday."

"Tuesday?" Suzanne said in amazement when they got back outside. "You can do all this in two days? Spend a million dollars on a house?"

"Four million," said Randall. "This is how it works out here. The race is to the quick."

She had assumed they would go to another restaurant for drinks and then dinner. Instead, to her surprise, he drove to his flat. He took a bottle of Pommery Louise from the refrigerator and opened it, and she wandered about examining his manuscripts as he made dinner. At the Embarcadero, without her knowing, he had bought chanterelles and morels, imported pasta colored like spring flowers, arugula and baby tatsoi. For dessert, orange-blossom custard. When they were finished, they remained out on the deck and looked at the bay, the rented view. Lights shimmered through the dusk. In a flowering quince in the garden, dozens of hummingbirds droned and darted like bees, attacking each other with needle beaks.

"So." Randall's face was slightly flushed. They had finished the champagne, and he had poured them each some cognac. "If this happens—if I get the house. Will you move out here?"

She stared down at the hummingbirds. Her heart was racing. The quince had no smell, none that she could detect, anyway; yet still they swarmed around it. Because it was so large, and its thousands of blossoms were so red. She hesitated, then said, "Yes."

He nodded and took a quick sip of cognac. "Why don't you just stay, then? Till we find out on Tuesday? I have to go down to San Jose early tomorrow to interview this guy, you could come and we could go to that place for lunch."

"I can't." She bit her lip, thinking. "No . . . I wish I could, but I have to finish that piece before I leave for Greece."

"You can't just leave from here?"

"No." That would be impossible, to change her whole itinerary. "And I don't have any of my things—I need to pack, and get my notes . . . I'm sorry."

He took her hand and kissed it. "That's okay. When you get back."

That night she lay in his bed as Randall slept beside her, staring at the manuscripts on their shelves, the framed lines of poetry. His breathing was low, and she pressed her hand against his chest, feeling his ribs beneath the skin, his heartbeat. She thought of canceling her flight; of postponing the entire trip.

But it was impossible. She moved the pillow beneath her head, so that she could see past him, to the wide picture window. Even with the curtains drawn you could see the lights of the city, faraway as stars.

Very early next morning he drove her to the hotel to get her things and then to the airport.

"My cell will be on," he said as he got her bag from the car. "Call me down in San Jose, once you get in."

"I will."

He kissed her and for a long moment they stood at curbside, arms around each other.

"Book your ticket back here," he said at last, and drew away. "I'll talk to you tonight."

She watched him go, the nearly silent car lost among the taxis and limousines, then hurried to catch her flight. Once she had boarded she switched off her cell, then got out her eyemask, earplugs, book, water bottle. She took one of her pills. It took twenty minutes for the drug to kick in, but she had the timing down pat: the plane lifted into the air and she looked out her window, already feeling not so much calm as detached, mildly stoned. It was a beautiful day, cloudless; later it would be hot. As the plane banked above the city she looked down at the skein of roads, cars sliding along them like beads or raindrops on a string. The traffic crept along 280, the road Randall would take to San José. She turned her head to keep it in view as the plane leveled out and began to head inland.

Behind her a man gasped, then another. Someone shouted. Everyone turned to look out the windows.

Below, without a sound that she could hear above the jet's roar, the city fell away. Where it met the sea the water turned brown then white then turgid green. A long line of smoke arose—no not smoke, Suzanne thought, starting to rise from her seat; dust. No flames, none that she could see; more like a burning fuse, though there was no fire, nothing but white and brown and black dust, a pall of dust that ran in a straight line from the city's tip north to south, roughly tracking along the interstate. The plane continued to pull away, she had to strain to see it now, a long green line in the water, the bridges trembling and shining like wires. One snapped then fell, another, miraculously, remained intact. She couldn't see the third bridge. Then everything was green crumpled hillsides, vineyards, distant mountains.

People began to scream. The pilot's voice came on, a blaze of static then silence. Then his voice again, not calm but ordering them to remain so. A few passengers tried to clamber into the aisles but flight attendants and other passengers pulled or pushed them back into their seats. She could hear someone getting sick in the front of the plane. A child crying. Weeping, the buzz and bleat of cell phones followed by repeated commands to put them all away.

Amazingly, everyone did. It wasn't a terrorist attack. The plane, apparently, would not plummet from the sky, but everyone was too afraid that it might to turn their phones back on.

She took another pill, frantic, fumbling at the bottle and barely getting the cap back on. She opened it again, put two, no three, pills into her palm and pocketed them. Then she flagged down one of the flight attendants as she rushed down the aisle.

"Here," said Suzanne. The attendant's mouth was wide, as though she were screaming; but she was silent. "You can give these to them—"

Suzanne gestured towards the back of the plane, where a man was repeating the same name over and over and a woman was keening. "You can take one if you want, the dosage is pretty low. Keep them. Keep them."

The flight attendant stared at her. Finally she nodded as Suzanne pressed the pill bottle into her hand.

"Thank you," she said in a low voice. "Thank you so much, I will."

Suzanne watched her gulp one pink tablet, then walk to the rear of the plane. She continued to watch from her seat as the attendant went down the aisle, furtively doling out pills to those who seemed to need them most. After about twenty minutes, Suzanne took another pill. As she drifted into unconsciousness she heard the pilot's voice over the intercom, informing the passengers of what he knew of the disaster. She slept.

The plane touched down in Boston, greatly delayed by the weather, the ripple effect on air traffic from the catastrophe. It had been raining for thirty-seven days. Outside, glass-green sky, the flooded runways and orange cones blown over by the wind. In the plane's cabin the air chimed with the sound of countless cell phones. She called Randall, over and over again; his phone rang but she received no answer, not even his voice mail.

Inside the terminal, a crowd of reporters and television people awaited, shouting questions and turning cameras on them as they stumbled down the corridor. No one ran; everyone found a place to stand, alone, with a cell phone. Suzanne staggered past the news crews, striking at a man who tried to stop her. Inside the terminal there were crowds of people around the TV screens, covering their mouths at the destruction. A lingering smell of vomit, of disinfectant. She hurried past them all, lurching slightly, feeling as though she struggled through wet sand. She retrieved her car, joined the endless line of traffic and began the long drive back to that cold green place, trees with leaves that had yet to open though it was already almost June, apple and lilac blossoms rotted brown on their drooping branches.

It was past midnight when she arrived home. The answering machine was blinking. She scrolled through her messages, hands shaking. She listened to just a few words of each, until she reached the last one.

A blast of static, satellite interference; then a voice. It was unmistakably Randall's.

She couldn't make out what he was saying. Everything was garbled, the connection cut out then picked up again. She couldn't tell when he'd called. She played it over again, once, twice, seven times, trying to discern a single word, something in his tone, background noise, other voices: anything to hint when he had called, from where.

It was hopeless. She tried his cell phone again. Nothing.

She stood, exhausted, and crossed the room, touching table, chairs, countertops, like someone on a listing ship. She turned on the kitchen faucet and splashed cold water onto her face. She would go online and begin the process of finding numbers for hospitals, the Red Cross. He could be alive.

She went to her desk to turn on her computer. Beside it, in a vase, were the flowers Claude had sent her, a half-dozen dead narcissus smelling of rank water and slime. Their white petals were wilted, and the color had drained from the pale yellow cups.

All save one. A stem with a furled bloom no bigger than her pinkie, it had not yet opened when she'd left. Now the petals had spread like feathers, revealing its tiny yellow throat, three long crimson threads. She extended her hand to stroke first one stigma, then the next, until she had touched all three; lifted her hand to gaze at her fingertips, golden with pollen, and then at the darkened window. The empty sky, starless. Beneath blue water, the lost world.

" THE LOST DOMAIN "

These stories are the result of an epistolary friendship that began sometime in the late 1980s, and which also produced two novels, *Mortal Love* and *Generation Loss*, as well as thousands of letters and e-mails. My correspondent and myself have met only a handful of times. We never, ever talk on the phone. We live thousands of miles apart, and never run into each other on the street.

But over the years, we learned that we had grown up within a few miles of each other, gone to college in the same city, knew some of the same people and had been at the same showings of the same movies when they first opened. Mostly, we found that we shared a passion for books. So we send each other novels, volumes of poetry, postcards; we endlessly discuss the writers we love—James Salter, John Fowles, Gene Wolfe, Anne Carson, W. H. Auden, among myriad others—and also the nature of writing itself, the mysteries of the creative process and, especially, the relationships between writers and their muses, that shifting border where the real life and the imagined one fleetingly touch and, sometimes, overlap. On those very few occasions when we do meet, our intense long-running conversation continues; but it's primarily a written conversation that has had few interruptions.

One of these interruptions occurred on 9/11, when for most of the day I was unable to contact my friend and feared that he'd died. An unreasonable fear, it turned out; he was fine. But in the weeks and months that followed, those few hours crystallized the grief I felt, and my sense of helplessness at living in a remote place so far removed from the tragedy. When, early in 2002, I finally began to write again, my friend had morphed into my muse, the embodiment of my own obsessions and anxieties—desire and loss; the threat of apocalypse; the power and vulnerability of the artist; my continuing failure to create something out of sorrow and despair.

"What is loved becomes *immediately* what can be lost," said G. K. Chesterton. I wrote "Echo," one of the four stories that comprise "The Lost Domain," when my friend was in Baghdad for a month in 2002. For the first (and so far, only) time in all those years, our conversation was suspended. Shortly afterwards I decided I'd make "Echo" part of a sequence of stories dealing with the nature of memory, loss, desire, grief; and also of muses. Lawrence Durrell's *Alexandria Quartet* had made a big impact on me as a teenager. I admired its shifting points of view and narrative voices; I wanted to use a similar technique, compressed into short stories. My own writing jumps from mimetic fiction to science fiction to fantasy to horror, and so I decided that each story would represent a different genre as well. The stories were published separately, but all were written with the intent that they be read as part of one sequence, which derives its title from Alain-Fournier's 1928 novel *Le Grand Meaulnes*, usually translated as *The Wanderer*. I'm not all that crazy about the novel, but I was fascinated by Alain-Fournier's depiction of *le domain perdu*, the lost domain—the land of heart's desire, a highly romanticized vision of youth and eros and daily life that is forever unattainable, irrevocably past.

These stories are exorcisms, exercises, love letters, entertainments, elegies, maps. They're also a small way of repaying an immense debt of gratitude to a friend who has showed me so many ways of seeing the world—our world, and the possible world; the lost domain.

—Tooley Cottage, Maine
September 11, 2006

ABOUT THE AUTHOR

ELIZABETH HAND is the author of the novels *Winterlong, Aestival Tide, Icarus Descending, Waking The Moon, Glimmering, Black Light,* and *Mortal Love,* as well as the short story collections *Last Summer at Mars Hill* and *Bibliomancy.* With Paul Witcover she created and wrote DC Comics' 1990s post-punk, post-feminist cult series *Anima.* Her fiction has received numerous awards including the Nebula Award and two World Fantasy Awards.

She is a longtime contributor to the *Washington Post Book World, Fantasy and Science Fiction,* and the *Village Voice Literary Supplement,* among others. She received a degree in playwriting and cultural anthropology from Catholic University in Washington, D.C., where she lived for many years, working at the Smithsonian's National Air and Space Museum until she quit to write full time in 1987. Her new novel, *Generation Loss,* will be published in 2007. She lives on the coast of Maine.